Calls from the Wild

ABOUT THE AUTHOR

Described by *Scottish Field* as 'Britain's foremost wildlife detective', Alan Stewart has almost fifty years of policing experience and is the author of seven books on wildlife and wildlife crime in the UK and Ireland. This is his first venture into crime fiction.

BY THE SAME AUTHOR:

Wildlife Detective (Argyll Publishing, 2007)
The Thin Green Line (Argyll Publishing, 2007)
A Lone Furrow (Argyll Publishing, 2007)
Wildlife and the Law (Argyll Publishing, 2012; Thirsty Books, 2019)
A Wealth of Wildlife (Thirsty Books, 2015)
Killing by Proxy (Thirsty Books, 2017)
Walking with Wildlife (Thirsty Books, 2019)

PRAISE FOR *CALLS FROM THE WILD*

Alan Stewart is a legend of wildlife crime enforcement. This thrilling tale and its cast of characters draws on his unparalleled experience and knowledge.

—Matt Cross, journalist and *Shooting Times* contributor

Well done to Alan Stewart using fiction to highlight the state of wildlife crime in Scotland. *Calls from the Wild* is both a good read, and very informative – a must for all of those interested in our wildlife.

—Eddie Palmer, Chair, Scottish Badgers

This powerful story pulls no punches, and although a work of fiction, is a stark illustration of the appalling impact these crimes can have on wildlife and people, and the efforts required to bring them to justice. Alan Stewart has transferred his many years of experience of rising to the challenges of investigating complex wildlife crime cases onto the pages of this book.

—Ian Thomson, Head of Investigations, RSPB Scotland

Calls from the Wild is an immensely enjoyable and informative read. Alan Stewart has dedicated his life to protecting Scotland's wildlife, and his knowledge and experience shines out from these pages.

—Tom Bowser, Argaty Red Kites

If you are interested in wildlife crime investigation you will enjoy *Calls from the Wild*. The challenges a wildlife crime officer faces in getting to the bottom of cases, particularly in the closed world of gamekeeping where whistle blowers are scarce, are very apparent. Spoiler alert – the amount of tea and biscuits consumed and the obsession with Scottish music are all true, just ask the author!

—Bob Elliot, Former RSPB Head of Investigations, Director OneKind

Alan Stewart draws on his long experience to provide a detailed insight into the wide range of wildlife crimes a busy Wildlife Crime Officer may have to deal with. In addition to the complexities of the legislation and the value of modern forensic methods, it also highlights the clear risks these cases can bring to people as well as wildlife. These crimes will be a real eye-opener to many readers.

—Guy Shorrock, Senior Investigations Officer, RSPB HQ

Alan has written many books and this one, possibly his most interesting, is fiction but based on fact. There are lots of good guys in *Calls from the Wild*, mainly farmers, and lots of baddies as well. Not all the gamekeepers are baddies, fortunately, but the same cannot be said about some of their fictional employers.

—Dr Colin Shedden, Director Scotland, British Association for Shooting and
Conservation

Calls from the Wild

ALAN STEWART

THIRSTY NOIR

First published 2021 by Thirsty Books, Edinburgh
thirstybooks.com

ISBN: 978-1-9161112-9-5

The paper used in this book is recyclable.
It is made from low chlorine pulps produced in a low energy,
low emission manner from renewable forests.

Printed and bound
by Bell & Bain Ltd., Glasgow

Typeset in Adobe Garamond
by Main Point Books, Edinburgh

Chapter 1

'Morning Bob.' It was PC Joan Lamond in the control room. 'That's hare coursing reported on the outskirts of Brechin, at Fingowan Farm.'

'You've made my day Joan,' was Bob's sarcastic reply. Hare coursing was one of the most frequently reported wildlife crimes in the Division and it made him mad.

'Glad to hear it Bob, always happy to help. The local officers are attending. The farmer reported two men and two dogs from an old blue Suzuki SJ16 VRM SL02MKK in one of his fields.'

Bob had been typing up an illegal snaring case to be sent to the procurator fiscal so he quickly switched channels on his radio to monitor what was going on in the Angus area. He continued typing and had another slurp of his tea to wash down a large slice of cake brought into the office by Shirley, one of the admin assistants. Bob knew from experience that hare coursers are often travellers who consider coursing hares a tradition and an entitlement. He had even heard a defence solicitor claim in court that the accused thought coursing hares was legal as long as only one hare was killed.

He could hear the officers attending the incident being updated on the registered keeper of the vehicle. It was little help as it was registered to a woman in Falkirk and had most likely been bought at a car market as part of a dodgy car deal. It would be kept for a few days, used in several coursing incidents, and sold on without ever being registered in the courser's name. Bob swore under his breath.

At the age of thirty five Bob had fifteen years police service, seven of those as the Division's Wildlife Crime Liaison Officer. As well as running his own investigations he provided support for other officers in the fight again wildlife crime. Half an hour after the initial call Bob heard the officers updating the control room. He recognised the voice as that of Constable Ronnie McKenzie.

'Hello control, we've attended at Fingowan Farm and spoken to the farmer. He had seen two dogs chasing a hare, right on its tail, though the dogs had disappeared from his view with the two men in close pursuit. Their car had been parked at the field gate. They were only in the field for a short time and had left five minutes before we arrived. We had a patrol in the area but there is no sign of the two men and dogs or their Suzuki.'

The vehicle had already been circulated to other police units but it had vanished into the ether. Bob was about to ask Ronnie McKenzie and his partner to make a search of the field to see if a hare had been caught but before he could do so the officers were diverted to another call in Forfar.

'Buggeration.' The admin staff looked up as Bob pushed his chair back, grabbed his jacket and rushed from the office. 'Great cake Shirley,' he shouted as he disappeared through the door.

It took about fifty minutes to drive to Fingowan Farm and Bob was racing against time. He knew that if a hare had been caught and not recovered quickly it would be predated by crows, gulls, buzzards – maybe all three, and it would be more difficult to prove that it had been taken by dogs. If this could not be shown, a defence solicitor would, quite rightly, argue that it might have been shot, injured on a road, or indeed died of natural causes. Even though no-one had been caught on this occasion Bob liked to have all available evidence collected just in case. It was simply basic policing.

Tom Burt, the farmer at Fingowan, was painting waste oil on a plough when Bob arrived at the farm steading. It looked like the spring ploughing had been completed and the plough would be put to rest in a shed free of rust until it was needed again.

'Hi Tom, I'm here to see what more we can find out about these guys that were after your hares'. Bob took his notebook from his pocket and began to record a description of the two men. 'Ah, a big bugger wearing a yellow fluorescent jacket, and a wee chap in a dark jacket. Have you any idea of their age Tom?'

'No, that's hard to say as they were a quarter of a mile away. They disappeared behind that wee roundel of larch trees in the centre of the field then they must have run down the dip in the field so I never saw them again.' Tom paused to carefully place his paint brush on the edge of the tray of oil. 'The dogs had chased a hare back and forward across the field before that and were close to catching it. The hare must have been knackered, jinking about to save its life, but with two dogs the odds were against it. I'd be surprised if they didn't catch it.'

'Can you describe the dogs for me Tom?'

'Aye, they were the usual lurchers, both big, both about the same size. One was white and the other was a tan colour.'

'Could we maybe have a look Tom and see if we can find the hare if it was killed?'

'Aye, give me just a couple o' minutes till I finish coating this plough.' He lifted the brush and set to work again and when he had finished, lifted some straw to rub the oil off his hands.

They set off down a field of permanent pasture to reach the field of winter barley where the coursing had taken place. 'It's great to hear peeweeps,' said Bob, as a pair of medium-sized black and white birds tumbled in the sky above them, voicing their *peeee weep, weep weep, peeee weep* call.

'They're displaying exceptionally early this year,' said Tom. 'It's only early March and I don't usually see them till early April. Everything in nature seems to be getting earlier now of course. We used to have loads of them all over the farm, now we're usually down to just one pair, and always nesting in this field.' He stopped and gazed off into the distance. 'They've little chance in fields that are regularly cultivated; the eggs or chicks just get crushed with the machinery. Even if they survive there's so much spraying done nowadays that insects are all but wiped out and the chicks have nothing at all to eat.'

They reached the winter barley field and clambered over the fence. 'If you take me to where you saw the men and dogs,' Bob said, 'we'll see what tracks there are in this damp ground and see what evidence I can get that might help a case. That's assuming we identify these guys of course.'

Fifty yards into the field Bob saw a fresh scuff mark in the earth and a few blades of barley, complete with roots, that had been knocked out of the ground. 'This is where one of the dogs has turned.' A bit further on there was a clear pawprint of a large dog on a slightly damper ground piece of ground. 'The claws are spread wide which tells us that the dog was going full pelt.'

Further over the field they found the footprints of the two hare coursers. The distance between the steps showed they had been running, no doubt trying to keep the dogs and the hare in sight as they went over the crest of the field. As they reached the crest a carrion crow rose from the field and flew off. 'I bet that's where the hare is,' said Bob. 'Hopefully the crow's not done too much damage.'

A short distance before they reached the hare there was an area of disturbed earth, including some shallow grooves and a scattering of white fur. 'This is where the dog has caught the hare,' said Bob. 'It has probably tumbled over a couple of times before the dog managed to get a grip and rag the poor beast. The dog's then run on a bit with the almost dead hare and dropped it there.' He pointed to the remains ten yards further on.

Luckily the crow had only pecked out one of the hare's eyes and had begun to peck a hole in the back leg, leaving small tufts of mostly white fur scattered round the field at the back end of the hare.

Bob took off his rucksack and reached in for his camera. 'I'm as well to gather evidence as if the men had been caught. It never does any harm.

I get really frustrated when there's a chance of finding a hare that's been killed and some of my colleagues don't even look for it. If someone is caught later, it weakens the case.' Bob filled out a production label, signed it and had Tom do the same. He placed the label beside the hare and took several photos before removing the label and taking several more, which he would use when giving talks.

Bob lifted the hare and felt its ribs. 'The ribs are broken, which is a sure sign of the hare being killed by a medium sized mammal such as a dog. It's typical too that there are very few external injuries, there's some blood coming from the mouth and a chunk of fur missing at its back end.' He put the hare in an evidence bag.

'Would you like to see where the car was parked Bob?' asked Tom.

'Yeh, that would be useful,' The two then set off for the gate that led to the quiet country road.

Bob signalled for them to stop before they crossed the gate. They studied the damp gateway and could clearly see the car tyre marks where it had been backed into the gateway. There were dog pawprints everywhere and footprints at the back and at either side of the car. 'Damn,' said Bob, 'none of the footprints show any worthwhile pattern.'

A minute later he shouted, 'Bingo'. There was a fresh cigarette end on the ground near the driver's door. 'This might give us a lead if it's one of our coursers that's ditched that.' He went through the same procedure with a production label again, before donning a pair of nitrile gloves, collecting the cigarette end and placing it in a poly bag.

'Which one was driving the car, Tom?'

'It was the bigger chap with the yellow jacket who got in the driver's side.'

Bob thanked the farmer for his help and watched him trudge back over the fields to the farm. He then fished out his phone. 'Hi Frank, I've picked up a hare on a farm near Brechin that I think has been taken by coursing dogs. Would you manage to have a look at it sometime for me please?' Frank McArthur was one of the two veterinary pathologists at the SRUC Veterinary Services in Perth, part of the Scottish Rural College. They carry out post-mortem examinations of fallen stock, mainly cattle and sheep, or birds found dead in winter, one of the purposes being surveillance for notifiable diseases. They are also paid a retainer by the Scottish Government to carry out post-mortem examinations of wildlife for the police. Frank had replied that he was not particularly busy that afternoon and for Bob to call in when he returned to Perth.

Before he left, Bob took photographs of the farm and fields to put the whole incident in context for the court. He also made a rough sketch which he would improve later. Bob found that sketches helped to show the court the sequence of events and are always appreciated by the procurator fiscal and sheriff, if not the defence solicitor.

An hour later Bob drew into Bertha Park View and parked in the Veterinary Services car park. He went to the office to register the hare, then returned to the car to collect it and take it round to the post-mortem examination bay, passing a block and tackle used to hoist heavy animals. Bob donned a pair of blue polythene overshoes at the door and entered the post-mortem room. Business was indeed quiet with only two dead sheep on the ground awaiting examination.

'So only one hare today Bob,' Frank commented. 'This shouldn't take long. Will you do the photography as usual?'

'Yeh, I'm happy to do that.

Frank knew that in Scotland all important aspects of an investigation must be corroborated. In some cases, two vets would be required to attend court but Frank was satisfied that Bob had attended enough post-mortem examinations of hares and rabbits over the years to corroborate his veterinary expertise and be able to explain the injuries to a court.

Frank placed the hare on a green plastic cutting board on the bench and signed and removed the label. He then skinned the hare to examine external injuries first. 'The ribs are bruised and crushed, and there is also bruising across the back, probably coinciding with where the dog has gripped the hare.' He stood back to allow Bob to take photographs. 'We'll see what it's like inside now.'

He cut the belly of the hare open with his scalpel. The most serious injuries of a hare or rabbit taken by a dog are always internal. Frank began to narrate the injuries in layman's terms. 'The liver is punctured, as is the heart and there is extreme internal haemorrhaging. You can also see puncture wounds on the lungs where the pressure of the dog's teeth has gone through the soft lungs without breaking the hare's skin. This combination of injuries would mean that the hare would be killed quickly through shock and blood loss, and these are similar to what we've seen in most of the hares you've brought.' Frank stood back again to allow Bob to photograph the injuries, which Bob knew would satisfy a court that the hare had been killed by a dog rather than having been shot or injured on the road.

Examination completed, Bob collected the label and Frank placed the hare in the freezer. 'No doubt I'll see you again soon with some other poor creature.'

'That would not surprise me Frank,' and Bob headed for the car.

As he was about to drive off his phone rang. It was a gamekeeper, Mike

Curtis. 'Bob, there's something that you need to know about Nigel Roberts. Are you able to look up and see me tomorrow?' Bob agreed, intrigued at the prospect of the meeting.

Bob knew a good deal about Nigel Roberts already. Roberts was a land agent who specialised in improving the numbers of grouse for grouse moor owners. He was known to have advised and assisted the owners of several driven grouse moors in both Scotland and England. He usually directed the work of the gamekeepers on these estates and while his methods seemed to be effective, he had the reputation of demanding the removal of any species that threatened red grouse, their eggs or their chicks. It was no coincidence that some of the worst incidents of wildlife crime occurred on estates where he was advising on grouse recovery.

Bob had also had a personal encounter with Roberts years earlier. During his second year as a police officer, he and a colleague were taking turns directing traffic on the Perth to Blairgowrie road, on the second day of the Game Fair at Scone Palace. Because of the volume of traffic trying to enter the showground in the morning there was a considerable tailback on to this A-road. Suddenly Bob saw a Range Rover coming speeding towards him on the wrong side of the road causing cars travelling in the opposite direction to take evasive action and a lorry to mount the grass verge to avoid a collision.

The Range Rover driver was indicating to turn left into the minor road that led to the showground and would have driven around Bob, completely disregarding him and his signal to stop had Bob not stepped further out onto the road in front of the vehicle. The driver, who turned out to be Nigel Roberts, was red-faced and furious. He shouted at Bob that he was a stallholder at the event, was late, and had to get in to the showground. Clearly he had no consideration for the other motorists in the queue of traffic who were also intent on getting to the Game Fair but knew they had to wait their turn.

Bob charged him with reckless or careless driving, getting his colleague to take over controlling the traffic while he did so. Being charged obviously infuriated Roberts even further and he was almost exploding with fury as he saw the waiting traffic gradually getting into the showground while he was stuck with an impertinent young constable.

The matter hadn't ended there. Roberts later made a complaint about Bob, which was dealt with by a chief superintendent who Bob knew was a keen shooting man. Bob was called before the senior officer and told in no uncertain terms that this should have been dealt with by a warning. The reckless or careless driving case never reached the procurator fiscal. Roberts had clearly used his power and influence to get his own way.

As he pulled away from the veterinary services Bob wondered what Mike had to tell him about Roberts that he didn't already know.

But that would have to wait – there was one more slice of Shirley's cake in the office with his name on it.

Chapter 2

It was a lovely sunny morning when Bob headed up the A9 to Highland Perthshire to visit Mike Curtis on Inversnood Estate. He loved this landscape, the forested and craggy slopes as he passed Dunkeld. It was here at Inver that one of Scotland's greatest fiddlers and composers, Niel Gow was born two-hundred years previously. Bob started to whistle the mournful tune *Niel Gow's Lament on the Death of his Second Wife* but after a few bars his thoughts turned to Dougie MacLean who lives in the village of Butterstone just east of Dunkeld. He was now tunefully whistling Dougie's well-known tune *Caledonia*, which he felt really should be Scotland's national anthem.

The forests opened up to hills dotted with birch trees as Bob approached Pitlochry. He was fascinated by trees and would love to have seen Scotland a few hundred years ago before human intervention 'improved' the landscape by removing vast areas of Scots pine and other native trees. The trees had yet to come into leaf, which would further alter the panorama as springtime made its welcome entrance. A buzzard was soaring lazily in the blue sky off to his left; before long it would be ospreys that could be seen by observant drivers and their passengers.

Bob drove into the track leading to the gamekeeper's cottage. Mike was hosing out his dog kennels and a mix of three black Labradors, two liver and white spaniels and a Jack Russell terrier barked at Bob's arrival but stopped immediately at a command from Mike.

Bob considered Mike to be an excellent keeper. Not only did he play by the rules, he also had a great knowledge of all aspects of nature, including being able to name most small birds that many people would simply refer to as 'wee brown birds.' He was furious at the extent of persecution of protected species by some of his colleagues and the fact that their illegal activities negatively affected everyone involved in shooting.

'Good morning Bob.' Mike greeted him with a wave and a smile. 'I thought you might like a tour of the hill and I could check some of my traps at the same time. But what about a cup of tea first?'

'That's perfect, thanks,' Bob replied. 'It's a lovely day to be out and about and I've no urgent jobs on this morning.'

They went into the kitchen, where Mike's wife, Margaret, had the kettle on the boil and some thin strips of venison ready to go into a frying pan.

'Would you like a roll with venison Bob?' Margaret asked. 'It's the best of roe deer venison.'

'That would be lovely, thanks. I've not had venison for ages. The last time I had anything from a roe deer it was fried liver and it was delicious.'

They ate with obvious appreciation of the flavour of meat, a second breakfast for all three of them. As Bob wiped crumbs from his chin Mike got up from the table and put on his deerstalker. 'Ready for the off then Bob?'

As the Land Rover bumped up the hill track Mike said, 'I wanted to tell you about my brother Albert's dilemma. He's an underkeeper on Loch Garr estate near to Amulree. He's been there for years and loves the area and the work on the estate. It's about five thousand acres and for most of that time there was only him and the headkeeper, Jock Scott. Shooting on the estate was walked-up grouse and deer stalking. Half of the estate is farmed in-hand and the other half is tenanted, with the tenant running about 800 blackfaced ewes.' Mike slowed the Land Rover and bumped through a hill burn that crossed the track.

'The estate owner has been quite happy with that but he's getting on in years and got a good offer for the estate from Nigel Roberts who wanted a grouse moor of his own and has given up his land agent role.

'Roberts took over the estate some months ago and wants big changes. Jock Scott has already left and been replaced by a new head keeper, Cyril Masterfield, from the north of England who's not much older than a school laddie. They've also brought in a young under keeper, Charles Brock, from another estate where Roberts formerly gave management advice and they're renovating one of the estate houses for him. They've also given Masterfield and Brock brand new Land Rovers and I'm damned sure they're getting a bigger wage than Albert.'

'Thankfully, I've only met Roberts once,' said Bob. 'He has the reputation of being able to produce big bags of grouse. I've heard one or two keepers and landowners singing his praises but others loath him, saying a lot of his methods are illegal and give grouse shooting a bad name.'

'That's exactly the point,' Mike replied, 'My brother is now being made to work all the hours under the sun. It's clear that they want him out and replaced by a younger man. Albert is nearing sixty, a few years older than me, and he's not up to working sixteen or eighteen hours a day. It's not right that he should be asked to do that anyway.' Bob could hear the anger rising in Mike's voice. 'His wife, Lizzie, doesn't keep too well and Albert can't afford to be out all night.'

Mike's face was reddening as his rage grew. 'The two new guys have been shooting red deer and roe deer at night in the spotlamp and just leaving them lying, not even putting the bloody things into the food chain.'

Mike knew that deer, mountain hares and sheep get the blame for carrying the ticks which can infect grouse and give them the disease louping ill so guessed why the deer were being slaughtered.

'Masterfield was even boasting that he shot a red deer stag last week, out of season of course, across the boundary fence on their neighbour's land. They're absolute bastards.'

The hill track Mike was driving on was now running parallel to the burn he crossed earlier. He stopped at a birch tree between the track and the burn and the two men got out. Mike pointed down to the burn where there was a log placed over the burn. In the middle of the log Bob could see a tunnel made of gridweld mesh with a trap in the centre of the tunnel. Bob recognised the trap as a Fenn Mk 4 trap and could see that both ends of the gridweld mesh were crimped in at either end to limit access to the tunnel to a mammal about the size of a rat.

'Nothing in the trap today Bob but that seems to be a really good trapping site. In the last month or so I've caught three stoats and two rats. Because of new legislation I can't use them where there are stoats from 1st April so I've a load of the new Tully traps to replace them.'

They drove on up the road for another hundred yards to where the remains of an old drystone dyke met the track. This time the trap was in a tunnel fashioned from the stones in the dyke.

Mike lifted the flat stone off the top of the tunnel to reveal a weasel with its body caught right in the centre of the two jaws of the trap.

'If they're set right these are great traps,' said Mike. 'I always set the trigger of the trap very lightly so that something even as light as a weasel would set it off. The trap would kill the weasel instantly. Hopefully the Tully traps will be as efficient.'

He removed the dead weasel from the trap and shoved it into a gap a bit further along the dyke. As Mike reset the trap Bob was wondering what harm a weasel would do to wildlife since it mostly catches and kills mice and voles, voles also being a serious vector for ticks and louping ill. He was a pragmatist; knowing what Mike was doing was legal, and part of his job, he said nothing.

When they got back into the Land Rover Mike took out a tin of tobacco and rolled a cigarette. He continued with the sorry tale of his brother's situation.

'The new headkeeper, Masterfield, came round to my brother yesterday and gave him a tub of Yaltox, telling him to get on and get rid of the vermin on the estate. It was clear to Albert he meant birds of prey as well as foxes and crows.'

Bob knew Yaltox as the trade name of the banned pesticide carbofuran. 'What the hell did your brother say about that?'

'He was dumbstruck. He'd heard this was happening on other estates where Roberts was involved. He'd read lots of stuff in the papers about crime on these estates, but he couldn't believe he was getting caught up in this illegal gamekeeping. He phoned me and I told him to bury the tub of Yaltox and to cut open and put out some shot rabbits as if he had put some of the pesticide on them. If the other keepers look closely at the rabbits, they'll see there's no poison on them as the dark blue granules would be visible. They'd also expect to see one or two dead insects on the carcasses, though there's not many bluebottles about yet, especially up at this height.'

Mike suddenly broke off, pointing. 'There's a female hen harrier over there hunting up that gully.'

Bob could see the brown raptor flying slowly close to the ground, stalling from time to time, turning and continuing into the wind. For a few minutes he watched the hunting technique of this magnificent bird, with the lovely white feathers on its rump and dark bars across the tail, and saw it suddenly drop into the white grass, probably for a field vole. It must have missed the vole and rose again and continued hunting for another fifty yards till it disappeared from view.

'They're fantastic birds, God knows how folk can kill them.'

'They cause no problem here,' said Mike. 'We're not high intensity but they're hated on most intensively managed driven grouse moors. We've usually got a nesting pair in that sloping bank of long heather at the far side of that burn.' He pointed to a slope about a quarter of a mile away. 'They reared chicks last year, four I think. The laird sometimes comes up and watches the food passes – the male passing food to the female – from just a wee bit further along the hill road. The female comes off the nest in the heather for the food pass then goes back with the prey to the chicks. We've never gone to the nest during the nesting time, but I've passed it after the chicks are away. We never tell any of the raptor folks about it as we don't want them disturbed.'

'Getting back to your brother Mike, would he talk to me about all of this?' Bob suspected the answer would be no as keepers are loath to give information or statements to the police that would put their job and tied house at risk. He hoped in this case, since Roberts obviously wanted rid of Albert to replace him with a young malleable keeper, that he might be one step nearer to charging someone committing criminal acts against protected wildlife.

'I think he would, though I doubt if he'd want to be involved in anything that finished up with him giving evidence in court. He'll have a hard enough job getting another job in gamekeeping at his age without being ostracised by his peers. I'll phone him and get back to you.' The short life of the cigarette long finished, Mike fired up the Land Rover and they set off to check a crow cage trap further out the hill.

They completed a circuit of the hill, checking the crow cage in which the decoy carrion crow still had no company in the trap. Bob was pleased to see that the mandatory sign in the trap was in order, showing the trap number issued by Scottish Natural Heritage. He also saw that the decoy crow had a fresh half-eaten rabbit and clean drinking water. The law was being complied with; he expected no less on this estate.

Before parting Mike said, 'I'll give you a call tomorrow morning Bob and tell you what my brother says. Hopefully things will work out for him and for you.' They shook hands.

On the journey back to his office in Perth Bob contemplated Albert's predicament. He hoped he could get evidence enough to get one of the three men he'd been told about to court.

Especially Nigel Roberts.

Chapter 3

As good as his word, Mike phoned the next morning. 'Bob, I spoke to my brother last night and he's okay about speaking to you. He's away all day today but said you could phone him in the evening.' He gave him Albert's phone number. 'There's a further development that he'll tell you about himself, and he said he'd rather meet you here so that the new keepers at Loch Garr don't get wind of him speaking to the police.'

Bob had barely replaced the phone in its cradle when it rang again. 'Bob McKay, wildlife crime liaison officer,' he advised the caller.

'Constable McKay this is Ron Southgate from Glenfarg. I was out walking in woodlands near my house yesterday when I found the skeleton of an animal in a snare. It's bothered me ever since because I think it's a badger, and badgers, as far as I am aware, are protected.'

'Indeed they are Mr Southgate, can you tell me exactly where the badger is?'

'I'll give you a ten-figure map reference that will land you right on top of it if that helps,' he chuckled, reading out the series of numbers. 'I do quite a bit of hillwalking and I had my Garmin GPS device with me.' He sounded more than a little pleased with himself. 'It never stops,' Bob muttered under his breath.

'That's great,' said Bob. 'Many thanks for that and I'll get back to you once I've had a look.'

He checked the list of police officers that were wildlife crime officers and of the nine only one, Constable Stuart Robertson, was on duty. Stuart was stationed at Pitlochry and said he would be free that afternoon to accompany Bob to the snared animal. Bob looked up the location of the suspected badger in an OS map. It was on the outskirts of Glenfarg but it didn't fit into any of the estates or farms that he knew. 'Ah well,' he said to himself, 'the mystery will just have to wait till we get there.'

Bob still had to send the cigarette end he had recovered at the hare coursing incident away for DNA testing. He completed the appropriate form, lodged it and the cigarette end for collection to go to Forensics, and hoped that might throw some light on at least one of the men involved.

Just after lunch Stuart Robertson and Bob arrived at their destination.

'This is the wood here Stuart. The badger, if that's what it is, is towards the far end of it.' The wood looked to be about twenty acres and the trees were predominantly oak with a sprinkling of ash and birch. Bob took his GPS device from his rucksack and set it to the ten-figure map reference. Studying the directional arrow on the device, Bob said, 'We should find the snared badger on this line quite easily.' They climbed the fence.

Ten minutes into their walk there was a clearing with a high-netted fence. Bob said quietly, 'Here's what looks like a pheasant release pen. It pretty run down but there are some signs it might have been used last season; look, there are still a couple of feed hoppers inside.' They began to walk round as they could see from the GPS they were almost at the spot indicated.

'Here it is. It's a badger right enough.' Bob could see a skeletal badger about ten yards ahead. 'It's in a snare and the snare's tied to the fence of the release pen. It's maybe been set for a fox looking for an easy meal and walking round the pen but it's certainly not a fox that it's caught.'

'How long do you think it's been in the snare Bob?' asked Stuart. He was looking at a pile of bones in the rough shape of a badger and some black and white hair still clinging to the bones in places.

'It's hard to say, but I think at least all winter. The snares would most likely have been set when pheasants were in the pen, which would be last summer. This snare has just been left and probably hasn't been checked in months.'

Bob was looking more closely at the snare. 'The poor beast has been caught round the waist. It would have had a lingering death. This is the result of laziness and total unprofessionalism on behalf of whichever bugger set the snare. I'll take some photos Stuart if you could look round the pen and see if there are any other snares.'

Bob started photographing the dead badger, homed in on where the snare had caught it, then photographed the release pen to put the badger in context. He removed the snare and put it in an evidence bag, noting that there was no identification tag attached to it as was required by law. He'd no intention of taking the skeletal badger as a production but collected some of the cleaner guard hairs and was putting them in a poly bag when Stuart returned. 'We'll just take some of these in case, if this ever gets to court, no smart defence solicitor can try to argue it wasn't a badger that was caught. How did you get on Stuart?'

'There are another two snares next the fence at the far side of the pen. One is still set and the other one has been knocked over. The snares, like this one, are standard snares, the AB type, and like this one, secured to the fence with the small pieces of rectangular metal with two holes that are bought with the snares. The interesting thing about the snares is they are both held off the ground not by the usual thin stick but by a pin made of thick wire with a loop at the top. I think they've been bits of an implement, maybe a hay turner or a baler. I've left them for you to photograph first before we lift them. I bet there's one of these wire pins lying around here somewhere.'

'Let's find it then Stuart, it could prove to be essential if we can catch this guy.'

The two officers painstakingly searched the ground around the snare. Luckily the grass was short after the winter frosts. 'Here it is.' Stuart had found it some five yards from the snare, having been thrown or kicked there by the badger during its struggles.

'I'll get a photo of it then we'll bag it and collect the other snares,' said Bob. 'That's the easy bit done. The hard bit is to trace and get evidence against whoever set these.'

They finished off with a search of as much of the rest of the wood as they could, then headed back towards the police station. 'Are you able to take this investigation on Stuart?'

'I'd love to,' said Stuart, 'but I go on night shift now and there's only two of us on at Pitlochry. Sorry.'

'That's a pity. I'll carry it on when I get a minute and try to trace whose pheasant pen it is. There's no great urgency and by that time you might be free again.'

'Good luck with this Bob,' shouted Stuart after he had changed vehicles and was driving off, 'I'll look forward to hearing of your progress.'

Like most wildlife crime officers, Bob already worked far more than his allocated hours, but he knew that, even with nine officers in the force who were part-time as wildlife crime officers, there were many times when none were free of their other duties.

Bob's erratic times returning home frequently annoyed his wife, Liz. He appreciated that he should give her advance warning of when he would arrive home but it wasn't always possible. He made a mental note to try to improve his communication, even if he could not improve his timekeeping. Liz would be pleased that on this occasion he would be home by 4.30pm but not as pleased as Toby, their newly acquired West Highland terrier.

Toby was a rescue dog that came to Bob and Liz under unusual circumstances. Bob had been driving along a quiet country road in west Perthshire one morning when he spotted the wee white Westie sitting alone on the grass verge. The dog was friendly and wagged his tail happily at Bob's approach. He could see he wasn't a young dog but looked in good enough condition. Thinking he may have wandered off, Bob took him into his car and drove to the nearest house he could see, a cottage half a mile along the road.

No-one in the cottage knew the dog and Bob began to wonder if the poor wee soul had been dumped out in the country. He radioed the control room but there had been no reports of a West Highland terrier being lost. He was sure that someone would claim the dog in due course and he put him in the car and drove to the kennels of PADS, the Perth Abandoned Dog Society, outside the village of Forteviot.

The dog sat quietly on the front seat, wagging his tail any time Bob looked at him. By the time he reached Forteviot the friendly dog had won Bob's heart and he could have happily taken him home. 'Let me know the outcome if he's claimed,' Bob said to Pam, the woman on duty at the kennels. 'I'd really like to know why the dog was on its own in the middle of the countryside. In fact, if he's not claimed I'd be delighted to give him a home.'

Bob was fairly sure that the Westie had been abandoned, and if so would like to trace whoever was responsible and get him or her before a court. He had photographed the dog before he left PADS and circulated a press release with the circumstances and photograph. After a week there was no response to the press release nor were there any enquiries either to the police or to PADS so Bob and Liz duly collected the dog, now called Toby. The PADS staff there though him a lovable wee dog and estimated him to be around eight years old.

Bob's early return from work meant a longer the usual walk for Toby in the woods bordering their cottage on the outskirts of Crieff.

Chapter 4

The next day Bob met Albert Curtis and his brother Mike on Inversnood estate as arranged. Mike made the introductions and left them to their discussion. Albert was a tall, thin, balding man with prominent ears and a bit of a stoop. He seemed tired and strained, looking much older than his fifty eight years. 'Let's have a seat in your Hilux, Albert,' said Bob. 'There's more room in it than in my car for me to take some notes.'

Bob sat in the passenger seat and began, 'Mike has told me in general terms what's going on at Loch Garr estate Albert. Could you go through it again so that I can get a bit more detail.'

Albert described the estate and his enjoyable years there working as underkeeper with Jock Scott. 'Everything's gone to hell since this new guy bought the estate. He says he intends to turn the estate around in five years from being a modest grouse shooting and deer stalking estate to being a driven grouse moor with decent bags of grouse, and within ten years producing really big bags of grouse. Thankfully he's an absentee landlord. He stays in a posh part of Edinburgh so he's only on the estate one day a week, or two at the most. As I'm sure Mike told you he's brought in these two new keepers who are little more than school laddies and know bugger all about grouse. Roberts is obviously telling them exactly what to do. Masterfield is the headkeeper in name only; it's really Roberts that's acting as the headkeeper.'

The more he spoke the more downhearted Albert became, 'Jock Scott saw the writing on the wall, especially since he was virtually demoted to deer controller, taking orders from Masterfield. He had no truck with shooting deer illegally at night and out of season. There was no written authority from Scottish Natural Heritage to do that. He was almost sick when he was told just to drop them and leave them. No decent stalker or gamekeeper would do that. He handed in his notice after the first night and refused to go out again. This was obviously part of Roberts' devious plan.'

Albert related the facts of the difficult situation he was in, being told to work much longer hours, the new keepers getting renovated houses, new vehicles and on a higher pay scale than him. He also repeated to Bob what Mike had told him the previous day about Masterfield shooting a deer on a neighbour's ground.

'What about the pesticide you got from Masterfield,' Bob queried, 'was it carbofuran; you maybe know it as as Yaltox?'

'As far as I know it was. The tub was full of blue granules.'

'Mike said he advised you to bury it and put out rabbits as if they had carbofuran on them. Did you do that?'

'I buried the tub, but I can get it again if you need it. I've shot three or four rabbits and put them in places where Masterfield and his sidekick Brock are not too likely to see them. Though they're just school laddies I've no doubt much of their schooling would be in the killing of predators, even protected ones, so they would realise that there was no carbofuran on the rabbits. If I had to show them where I'd put the rabbits I kind of hoped that the rabbits would be well eaten by crows and buzzards by that time, and it wouldn't be obvious that I'd never used the poison.' Albert thought it was a bit stupid of Masterfield telling someone who was never going to remain working on the estate to use an illegal substance.

'Then when I thought more about it, I wondered if I was going to be set up as the person responsible for poisoning wildlife if the police ever carried out a raid.' He gave a visible shiver and the continued angrily, 'I was intending to leave anyway but the crunch came a couple of days ago; the bastards left a rabbit bait not a hundred yards from my door. There was a freshly dead buzzard lying ten yards from it. These guys are evil, but of course the worst one is Roberts. He's sneaky, getting his minions to do the dirty work and keeping his distance. I bet he put Masterfield up to it.'

'What did you do with the bait and the bird?' asked Bob.

'They're buried as well. I can get them if you need them.'

'Any idea what's happening with the tenant farmer on the estate?'

'I haven't spoken to him for a couple of weeks but the last time we met he was telling me that on other estates where Roberts was involved, tenants got so much hassle that they gave up the tenancy. The farm is called Hilltop and Willie McLaren, the farmer, is still quite young with a wife and two kids at primary school. They've left him alone so far, but he's determined not to give into pressure. His tenancy still has seven years to run so they can't put him out.'

Bob had been noting a statement as Albert related his nightmare. 'If need be, would you be willing to give evidence in court?' Bob asked, knowing this was the crunch question.

'No. Much as I would like the bastards to get their just desserts I'd be treated like a leper by other gamekeepers. I enjoy gamekeeping but this would prevent me getting another job, which will be bloody difficult anyway at fifty eight.'

'That's a pity Albert, but I understand your problem. Gamekeepers can be a strange lot; a man like Roberts comes along and virtually destroys their reputation almost singlehandedly, yet they are likely to ostracize any of their peers who speak out. Could you and I manage to recover the stuff that you've buried?'

'I wouldn't want to be seen taking you on to the estate but next Sunday afternoon. Masterfield and Brock are having a meeting with Roberts and his solicitor in a hall somewhere between here and Edinburgh. There's no way I'm going to the meeting as my notice is in anyway. That could clear the way for you to come up, as long as you don't bring a marked police car.'

'That's no problem Albert. I use an unmarked car most of the time anyway and only wear my uniform when it suits the job I'm doing. I'll come to your house just after midday on Sunday.'

They shook hands and Bob returned to his office to submit intelligence to the Scottish Intelligence Database. He would also check with the UK National Wildlife Crime Unit to see if they held any intelligence on Masterfield and Brock, since they had formerly been working in the north of England.

The Scottish Intelligence Database, colloquially referred to as SID, threw up some interesting information: Roberts was just about to bid for a large run-down grouse moor in Inverness-shire. At Bob's level the database does not reveal who provides the intelligence, but he suspected it was Sam Bain, the wildlife crime liaison officer for the Highlands based at Inverness. Sam would be as keen as Bob to bring Roberts before a court, so he phoned him to try to find out more.

'Aye, that was me who submitted that intelligence log a couple of days ago,' said Sam. 'Roberts is the leading contender to take over Fank Estate. The current owner isn't much interested in shooting though did keep the deer under control. The local raptor study group tell me there's a golden eagle territory on the edge of the estate. The pair manage to rear a chick most years. There are two pairs of peregrines that also rear chicks most years. Because there's been little or no heather burning for years there are usually at least two successful nests of hen harriers fledge. In addition, there's the buzzards, merlin and occasional red kite that nest on or visit the estate.'

'So they might be getting blitzed as 'vermin' then Sam.'

'Exactly. If Roberts buys the estate there will be a trapping, shooting and poisoning regime just as soon as he replaces the present elderly keepers with his own murder squad.'

'We'll keep I touch then Sam, as I'm looking at a similar situation in my force area.'

Bob next phoned Donald Boag, the Senior Intelligence Manager at the UK National Wildlife Crime Unit and explained what he was looking for.

'Hi Bob, yes I've got Cyril Masterfield up on the screen, date of birth 6th November 1995, that makes him twenty four, which is pretty young for a head keeper. He was formerly a keeper on Heatherhills Estate in North Yorkshire. Three entries. Worked under the direction of Nigel Roberts, suspected of gassing a badger sett, also known to keep an eagle owl.'

'Thanks Donald, now Charles Brock?'

'His date of birth is 1st June 2000, which makes him just nineteen. Employed as a trainee keeper on Flatstones Estate in Lancashire. It doesn't say so here but I know that's another estate that Roberts has advised. Only one entry for Brock: shot a buzzard but for some reason only got a police warning. Lucky him.'

'You'll be able to link them into SID shortly then Donald, I put intelligence entries on about them earlier today.'

'Thanks Bob. I wish all police officers used the system as effectively as wildlife crime officers. Good luck with your investigation and if you need some help remember to call on PC Bruce Bannerman, our investigative support officer.

Chapter 5

Sunday mornings are favourites for the criminal activities of hare coursers and the Sunday Bob was due to meet Albert was no different. Normally off at the weekends, he'd decided to work when he saw on the divisional command and control system that there had been a hare coursing incident at Foggylea Farm near Burrelton. He phoned the control room immediately.

'Good morning, Bob McKay here. Can you update me please on the hare coursing incident at 7.45 this morning?'

Bob waited while the operator brought the incident up on the screen. 'Okay. Two men with two dogs were seen coursing by the farmer, who was the person that phoned in. The men were described as both probably in their forties, one quite short and stocky and the other one quite tall. The short one had on dark clothing and a beanie hat; the tall one was wearing a yellow fluorescent jacket. The farmer had driven round and met them getting into their car. It was a blue Suzuki SL02MKK, that comes up as a blue Suzuki SJ16 with no registered keeper. The farmer managed to get a photo of the driver, who was the taller man. The vehicle registration number was circulated but there's been no trace'.

'What about the dogs,' asked Bob, 'any description of them?'

'Yes, it says here one was a dark brown colour, possibly brindle. The other one was a light-coloured dog, probably white though it was covered in mud.'

'Any word whether or not the dogs caught a hare?'

'It seems they did, the farmer saw them throwing it under a hedge.'

'That's fine, where is the hare now?'

'There's nothing here about that, Constable Brewster never mentioned collecting it.'

Damn! Bob was angry that one of the most important pieces of evidence hadn't been mentioned. He knew Brian Brewster, stationed at Blairgowrie, as a lazy sod who couldn't wait to retire on his pension. It had been a wet morning and no doubt Brewster didn't want to get his boots dirtied. 'Give me the farmer's name and number and I'll call him.'

Bob also knew Matt Runciman who farmed Foggylea. He'd met him while investigating a hare coursing incident a year or so earlier. When his phone rang Matt was having his mid-morning cup of tea, having already fed the seventy or so Limousin heifers that were still inside in cattle courts, and checked two fields of Texel cross ewes that were shortly due to lamb.

'It's Bob McKay here, the wildlife crime officer. I was wondering if you could tell me a bit more about your hare coursers this morning?'

'Aye, this pair have been here before, I know the shorter one from his limp. He walks like a bloody puppet on a string, up and down and from side to side. Strangely the limp's not noticeable when he runs. The last time they were here the big guy also had on a fluorescent jacket, what a bloody stupid thing to wear if you don't want to be seen.' Matt related the detail already given to Bob by the control room.

'Can you tell me about the hare being caught?'

'Aye, the dogs raised the hare in a stubble field and chased it into the forty acre grass field next door. They hunted it back and forward across the field and eventually the light-coloured dog caught the hare and killed it up near the top of the field. The tall guy with the yellow jacket lifted the hare and tossed it under the hawthorn hedge.'

'What happened with the hare?'

'Bugger all. It's still there as far as I know.'

Bob cursed Brewster under his breath. 'And I believe you took a photo.'

'Aye, they were just getting into their car when I drove round to them. I stopped in the middle of the road. I didn't have time to get out, which was just as well as they drove at me, but I managed a photo as they passed me on my nearside. They had to drive up on the verge to get past. The big guy is reasonably clear in the photo. Constable Brewster looked at the photo on my phone but said he didn't know him. I didn't think he was much interested to be honest.'

'If I come out Matt, would you have a minute to show me where the hare is?'

'If you come right away that would be okay as my wife and I are going out for lunch.'

Bob was at the farm half an hour later. 'Let's see the photo on your phone first Matt, see if I recognise either of them.' Bob immediately responded to the photo that the farmer brought up. 'The driver, with the yellow jacket, is Archie Donaldson. He's always out coursing. He's often with his cousin, Cyril Donaldson, that's maybe who the second person is but the photo's not very clear. Cyril is from Aberdeen and Archie is from Dundee. Would you recognise him if you saw him again?'

'No, I never really got a close look at him. I was concentrating on the driver since he was driving straight at me. I'd certainly know him again. Bastard.'

'Can you email me the photo Matt. I should really get your SIM Card and get our technical folks to get a print but you'll need your phone.'

Matt then drove them across the grass field where the hare was lying under the hedge, luckily untouched by scavenging birds. Bob photographed the hare, then took photos from where the hare was lying back towards where Matt said he was standing while the coursing was ongoing. Next was a rough sketch in his notebook of the relevant fields. Bob was angry that a police officer with twenty five years on the job hadn't done all of this; it was elementary police work. With the time now 11.30am Bob had to make for Loch Garr estate at Amulree to keep his appointment with Albert Curtis.

Albert had seen Bob's car coming up the estate road and he and his wife Lizzie met him at the door of the house. 'We'll just walk Bob, we've only about half a mile to go.' They set off along a track through the heather till they reached a fence. 'The tub of carbofuran, if that's what it turns out to be, is buried beside this post.'

Bob studied the ground and could see no disturbance to the mossy grass at the base of the post. He was puzzled. 'How do you know it's this post Albert?'

'I took a wee nick out of the top corner of the fencepost with my knife. I took time to replace the turf I took out and made sure that there was no earth left on the surface when I filled in the hole. It's not deep, just six inches down.'

Bob saw the missing sliver of wood at the top of the post once Albert had pointed it out and stood back as Albert removed a small piece of turf and dug with his trowel. 'Here it is here,' Albert said as the lid of a small grey plastic tub was revealed by the work of the trowel. He removed the tub and handed it to Bob. A very careful peek inside revealed the dark blue granular contents.

'It certainly fits the bill for a carbamate-based pesticide, probably carbofuran right enough.' Bob said. 'I'll double-bag it just in case of any spillage, though the lid looks a good fit.' He bagged the tub and its deadly contents while Albert filled the hole and replaced the turf. When Bob looked down there was not a sign that the ground had been disturbed.

'Now the buzzard and rabbit are just along here bit,' explained Albert as they walked towards a single larch tree. Bob could see that rabbits had made use of the safety of the tree roots and made their burrow under them. Again, he could see no sign of interference.

'This was easier to camouflage,' said Albert. 'I enlarged a burrow entrance that came out between these two roots.' He pointed at the spot. 'Once I buried the rabbit and buzzard and filled in the hole, I covered it with larch needles so it blended exactly with the rest of the area round the tree.'

Within a few minutes Albert had unearthed the unfortunate buzzard and rabbit bait. Bob was more aware of the danger of pesticides than Albert and put on a pair of nitrile gloves then lifted out and examined the buzzard, shaking off some of the damp earth. 'It's in good condition and reasonably fresh Albert. What did you think when you found them?'

'I thought the same. Usually if something has been dead for a while the eyes are dull and sunken. This wasn't the case in either of them. They were hardly bright and shiny but certainly not sunk back into the head. When I picked them up, I don't think either had been dead for more than two or three days.'

Bob lifted out and examined the rabbit. It hadn't been gutted but had a slit at the top of one of the haunches. This appeared also to have been picked, probably by a buzzard as some of the fur was missing. 'If these had been left near your house to get you into bother – serious bother at that – that was wicked. I doubt if we'll prove it, but I can't see the perpetrator being other than one of the new keepers. Maybe both. Roberts and landowners like him are probably the worst thing that's happened to game shooting in the last decade. Hell knows why some keepers and landowners think they're the bees' knees.'

Before he put the three items in his rucksack he got Albert, somewhat reluctantly, to sign labels that he'd attach to the items. 'Remember I'm not going to give evidence in court Bob.'

'I'll respect that Albert, but could you keep me up to date with any development on the estate please? I'm sure we both want to see Roberts and his minions facing justice. I'll phone you and let you know the result of the tests on what's in my rucksack.'

It had been a full day. The testing process would start the following day with another visit to Frank McArthur. Before he left the office Bob asked the control room to have an officer on the night shift in Dundee drive past Archie Donaldson's house and see if the blue Suzuki was parked there. He would check with the control room for the answer in the morning.

Chapter 6

'You've got egg yolk all down your shirt,' Liz said to him as they both sat at the breakfast table. She was scowling and pointing at him. Bob looked down at his shirt, examining it carefully. He always hurried his food, a trait which sometimes annoyed Liz. 'Thankfully it's not an Indian takeaway you're having, it takes ages for me to get a turmeric stain out.' Toby had settled into the McKay household as if he'd been there all his life. Like many dogs, especially older ones, he had an insatiable appetite and was meantime benefiting from the crumbs falling to the floor; he really appreciated rushed and carelessly eaten human breakfasts.

Bob put his hands up in surrender, before pulling off his shirt, throwing it into the wash basket and retreating to the bedroom for a fresh one. Looking reasonably smart again, he kissed his wife and headed off for work.

A call to the control room was uppermost in Bob's mind and he was pleased that the night shift officers were able to confirm that the blue Suzuki was parked at Archie Donaldson's address. Bob considered the evidence against him so far. There was no identification of either man by Tom Burt at the first incident, though there was a cigarette butt still to be examined for DNA. There was one witness, Matt Runciman, at the second incident, who could identify him, plus there was the photograph of Archie in the car. Bob considered going to his house and bringing him in for interview but he would probably just make the usual 'no comment' response to the questions. He didn't want him arrested when he wasn't on duty as he had the best knowledge of the hare coursing incidents to interview him, plus there was no evidence yet against the second man. He'd sit on these cases a few days and await any further developments, though he suspected Archie wouldn't have the Suzuki much longer before changing it.

After he'd made himself a mug of tea and was back at his desk, Bob turned his attention to the snared badger case. There was no great urgency with this one though he wanted to make a start before Constable Stuart Robertson came back off night shift; he wanted to give him something to work from if he was in a position to pursue the investigation. One case that was urgent, though very much an ongoing investigation, was that relating to Nigel Roberts and his grouse moor. He phoned and made an appointment with the veterinary pathologist for mid-morning.

Frank McArthur was finishing off a post-mortem examination of a mute swan as Bob arrived. 'This is an interesting one Bob. We're always aware of bird flu when we examine wildfowl, in fact part of our role is surveillance for this disease. I'll send samples away but I don't think bird flu is the problem here. Look at this.' He prodded open the crop of the bird with his knife as it lay on the green chopping board. 'There are at least ten pieces of lead shot in here, and probably more in the gut. Despite the ban in Scotland on using lead shot over wetlands we're still seeing wildfowl being poisoned by ingesting lead. The simplest solution would just be to ban lead shot completely. Humans could even be at risk if they swallow lead shot when eating game. Anyway, rant over, what do you have today?'

Bob put the double-bagged rabbit and buzzard on the stainless-steel bench. 'It's likely the rabbit is a bait Frank and the buzzard is a victim.' He related to story of their recovery. 'If you're happy to take the usual samples I'll take photos. I'll get the samples along with the tub of suspected carbofuran to SASA when you're finished as I'd like a result from them as soon as possible.' SASA, Science and Advice for Scottish Agriculture, is a Division of the Scottish Government providing scientific services and advice to Scotland's agriculture. They also offer services in wildlife DNA, food safety, wildlife management and provide specialist advice to Scottish Ministers.

Frank started with the rabbit. 'This is interesting in that it's not been gutted with the pesticide scattered in the empty body cavity as is usually the case. I've only seen three examples with the pesticide put in a cut on the leg.'

'And they've all been from the same group of estates, linked to the same management practices.' Bob replied. 'They're as fly as hell, knowing that a rabbit with a cut on its back leg looks a lot less suspicious than one lying with its belly cut open. A scavenging bird is likely to start at the part of the carcass that's already opened so this is just as deadly.'

Frank cut open the leg a bit further to remove as much of the muscle as possible for examination. 'There's a wee bit of earth here with the rabbit having been buried but that won't interfere with the examination for pesticides at SASA.' He placed most of the remaining muscle into a sterile screw top pot and tightened the lid. 'Now for the buzzard.'

Frank started by opening the dead bird's beak and looking inside. 'I can see one or two blue granules and there is a bit of muscle just at the top of the gullet.'

'Would I get a photo of that Frank?'

'You should do, even without flash as the light's quite good in here.'

Bob took three photos and Frank removed the muscle tissue, along with the granules. 'That could well be from the rabbit leg.' Frank guessed as he placed the tiny samples in a smaller bijou. 'Some of the blue granules look very like a carbamate-based pesticide if that helps speed up your investigation, though they'll need to be tested at SASA for confirmation.'

'I've seen enough carbofuran to agree with you Frank,' replied Bob.

Frank cut down through the breastbone and into the body cavity, removing samples from the crop, the gizzard, kidneys and liver. When he was done, and all the white labels on the samples signed, Bob thanked him and set off for SASA, leaving the remains of the rabbit and buzzard with the vet for storage, the usual procedure.

Bob hated driving on boring motorways, much preferring country roads where there was normally much more to see. He slipped a CD into the player and listened to Fergie Macdonald's ceilidh band. The first tune was *Loch Maree Islands*. It started, almost frighteningly, with the loud roar of a rutting red deer stag. Fergie, the lead accordionist, sang about his desire for the peace and quiet of stalking a 'ten pointer or a royal' on an otherwise deserted hillside. A later scare for the first-time listener was the crack of a rifle shot at the end of the song.

The M90 was fairly quiet and he quickly reached the Queensferry Crossing pondering what little wildlife he had seen on his journey. Buzzards were most common; he had spotted four. Roe deer were next, with two does grazing in rough pasture on his left just past the Fife town of Kelty, and only a single hovering kestrel. Bob reflected that kestrels used to be the most commonly seen raptors on motorway journeys but their numbers had crashed. The only road casualty was a dead badger on the roadside near Glenfarg, near to where there was good population of badgers reminding him, of course, of the badger investigation he yet had to make.

Fergie's band was still in full flow as Bob drew into the SASA car park on the western edge of Edinburgh. After signing in at reception he was met by Dorothy Abernethy, head of the Chemistry Section. Dorothy, dressed in her white lab coat, was quite young at twenty six to be in charge of this unit. She had worked with the previous head for four years and succeeded him after he had to take early retirement a few months earlier. Having seen her at work and giving evidence in court, Bob knew that Dorothy would be competent and successful in her new role.

'Come through Bob and show me what surprises you have for us today.' She led him through a labyrinth of corridors to the part of her laboratory where she dealt with post-mortem examinations of either whole creatures or the various samples she received. Thankfully the smell of death was sucked away by an overhead extractor, making the atmosphere relatively pleasant.

Bob had already emailed completed forms to Dorothy explaining the background to the recovery of the suspected pesticide and the dead rabbit and buzzard. He took out the items from his rucksack and placed them on the table in the middle of the lab. 'I'll leave them with you Dorothy, but could you have a look at them before I go please?' He indicated the tub and its blue granular contents. 'What would you say that is?'

Dorothy careful opened the tub and studied the granules inside. 'It's almost certainly a carbamate pesticide, just the right shade of blue for carbofuran. The other commonly abused carbamate pesticides are aldicarb and bendiocarb, but they're not blue. They're all horrible to use to kill wildlife; you'll know as well as I do that the animals suffer from convulsions, difficulty breathing, vomiting, and are often found in death with the head and limbs arched back.'

'Could you have a look at the gullet content of the buzzard Dorothy and give me a comment on that? The vet and I saw dark blue granules on the muscle, which might have been part of the rabbit's leg.' Bob slid the bijou towards her.

Dorothy gently unscrewed the lid and studied the grisly contents. 'Yes, I see a couple of dark blue granules. They could well be carbofuran.'

'Do you recall when the use of carbofuran was banned Dorothy? Was it as long ago as 2001?'

'It was. All approvals for the use of carbofuran were revoked in December 2001, nearly nineteen years ago and it's still being used to kill wildlife.'

'Well, I look forward to your report in due course Dorothy. Could you phone me in advance of your written report please if and when you get positive results? I don't think there's any point in DNA analysis at this point to confirm that the muscle tissue taken from the buzzard's gullet is from the rabbit. I don't see that helping any prosecution case if we ever manage to submit one. It can always be done later if need be.'

'No problem Bob, I'll try to get it done next week. It doesn't take long with the LC/MS technology.' LC/MS trips much more easily off the tongue than liquid chromatography mass spectrometry

With the growing suspicion of carbofuran, Bob now had enough to apply for a search warrant if that became appropriate when he considered all of the evidence. He hoped for a quiet spell in the office the next day to look at the options.

Chapter 7

Bob and Toby were out of the house by 6 o'clock. Toby's walks the last few days had been quite short, and Bob was keen to spend a bit more time with his dog, so he decided to go into the office a bit later. He could see in the short time they'd had Toby that the Westie had little interest in walks on pavements but loved being off the lead in the countryside. They walked past the nearby pond, where three mallard drakes were pestering a single female. Ducks would be nesting so Bob kept Toby on the lead until they were clear of the water. They walked along the side of the forest, Toby now off the lead. A hare came through the fence ahead of them and hopped slowly out into the field for ten yards, then bolted back into the forest when it spotted man and dog. Toby hadn't seen the hare but picked up its scent when it came to where the hare had been. His tail wagged excitedly and he followed the scent to the fence, but thankfully was too portly to get through.

When he rounded a bend in the fence line Bob could see a roe doe grazing in the field. Does often feed during the day before they have their fawns in early May. This brings them into better condition to feed two small but hungry mouths. The doe quickly spotted Bob and Toby and bounded back into the forest, clearing the fence easily.

On the way back along the other side of the forest Bob was looking out for a displaying goshawk that he'd seen a week or so earlier. He'd almost given up on seeing the majestic raptor when suddenly it appeared. The bird was plunging down from high above the forest with its wings beating as if flying in slow motion. It then suddenly shot back up again, flew a bit further along the forest and repeated this spectacular skydance. It was eventually lost to Bob's sight but its territorial display had made his day.

The last part of the route home was a short bit of quiet country road. Some of the blackthorn bushes at the roadside were starting to come into flower and before long the lovely white curtain of blossom would contrast with the bright green of the verge. The green verge was spoiled, however, with the presence of a bright blue plastic carrier bag. Someone had carefully gathered together all their rubbish, placed it in the bag, tied the top and tossed it out on to the verge. 'Filthy inconsiderate bastards,' Bob declared loudly to Toby. Despoiling the countryside with rubbish infuriated him.

'Why the hell could they not just have taken it home.' He continued his rant, Toby, thoroughly enjoying his walk, not taking the slightest notice of his irate master. Bob was tempted to open up the bag to look for anything that might identify who had dumped it. Having found nappies and other nasty items in bags in the past he picked up the bag and carried it the last few hundred yards home to deposit it in his own rubbish bin.

Man and slightly muddy dog were home just before 8 o'clock. Toby had a long drink of water and curled up in his basket. 'It's not a bad life being a dog, Liz,' Bob observed.

'Well that maybe depends on who owns the dog,' Liz astutely replied.

Bob's anticipated quiet day at the office didn't materialise. When he checked the incidents that had occurred since he was last on duty, he saw that two men had been arrested an hour earlier for hare coursing. He studied the message on the system.

0730 – from Willie Stevens, farmer, Highgrove Farm, Forfar. 2 men presently coursing hares in one of his fields.

0733 – Echo 23, PCs Sandra Johnstone and Harry McGillivray attending

0745 – from Willie Stevens – both men have now left in a red Land Rover Discovery, first part of the VRM HS06 – heading from the farm towards the A90 Dundee to Aberdeen road

0748 – Echo 23 – on that road – vehicle now coming towards us

0852 – Echo 23 – vehicle stopped and two men detained. Dogs in the back of the vehicle

0910 – Echo 23 – men are Archibald Duncan Donaldson and Cyril Townsley Donaldson.

Bob read the full details of the two men, that a second police vehicle with another two police officers had joined Sandra Johnstone and Harry McGillivray and that the men had been taken to Dundee police station.

'Yes, got them!' he shouted, startling Shirley at the next desk.

'I take it you're pleased with something Bob,' she said, smiling.

'You could say that Shirley, I'm always pleased when hare coursers are caught. I might be going to Forfar later and if I do, I'll bring you back a bridie from McLaren the baker.' Two baker's shops in Forfar were famous for the traditional bridies, McLaren's and Saddler's and it was difficult to choose between them.

Bob used his personal radio to contact constable Sandra Johnstone. 'Sandra, Bob McKay here, what's the latest with the two Donaldsons? There's another couple of cases that could possibly be added in with yours if you have enough evidence.'

'We've interviewed them and they're denying they were coursing; they were just out for a walk with their dogs they said. The farmer is the only witness so we might struggle a wee bit to get enough to charge them.'

'One witness is sufficient under the Wildlife and Countryside Act if they've caught a hare. Did they catch a hare?'

'The farmer doesn't know. He saw the dogs chasing a hare but they went out of his sight. They ran back to the men after a while but they weren't carrying a hare.'

'Would you two be free to meet me at the farm in, say, an hour?'

'I could but Harry McGillivray is away to another job.'

'That doesn't matter, I'll make for Highgrove Farm now, it might even take me less than an hour. You'll take less time from Dundee so could you phone the farmer and see if he is free to point out where he last saw the dogs?'

Despite the likelihood of holdups caused by tractors, Bob drove to Forfar via Coupar Angus rather than take quicker but boring dual carriageway. Leonard Brown and his All-Star Band was on the CD player, the first tune being *Robbie Shepherd MBE*. Bob was a long-time fan of Scottish country dance music and a regular listener on a Saturday evening to the BBC Scotland radio programme *Take the Floor*. Robbie Shepherd had been the presenter of that programme for an amazing thirty five years and this catchy tune commemorated his lengthy service.

Just over the county boundary into Angus Bob noted the progress of the asparagus growing in the fields. This was the main asparagus-growing area in Tayside and Bob regularly stopped to buy a bunch of odd-shaped asparagus spears. They were half the price but tasted the very same as straight spears. They'd be ready in about a fortnight.

In just under an hour Bob met Sandra at Highgrove Farm steading. She had sensibly stopped off at home on route and was now wearing a pair of green wellies. Bob was impressed, even more so when she told him she'd met farmer Willie Stevens and noted a statement from him.

'Willie Stevens pointed to where he lost sight of the dogs and to where the car was parked,' Sandra said. 'He can't identify them because of the distance but he managed to get part of the car number when it passed the farm steading. We then stopped the car along the road with the two men in it so identification won't be a problem.'

'Even without a hare there's still a good chance of a conviction using the evidence of at least one of the other two cases and Moorov,' advised Bob.

'Is that doctrine not only for sexual offences Bob,' Sandra asked.

Bob felt like a tutor constable now. 'No, the Moorov doctrine was initially used in dealing with sexual offences. It allowed the court to convict a person charged with two or more separate offences, closely related in time and circumstances and where each of the offences charged is spoken to by a single credible witness. That doctrine has been accepted now in a wider range of cases so our three hare coursing cases could corroborate each other.'

'Let's try to find a hare then to simplify matters,' laughed Sandra after her impromptu lesson in crime investigation.

They trudged back and forth over the part of the large field of winter wheat where the farmer lost sight of the dogs. The crop was about five inches tall. 'It would be easy to pass within thirty yards of a dead hare here,' said Bob. 'We've seen some of the marks where dogs have turned quickly but I'm thinking the hare managed to escape. I think we'll look at where the car was parked and call it a day.' They headed for the gate.

Coursers often park at an entrance to a field. In this case they had parked at the gate leading to a grass field, crossed the field and were coursing in the much larger field with the cereal crop. The gate to the grass field was open and tractors had churned the entrance up to mud. 'We could be in luck here Sandra, there's quite a lot of footprints in the mud. Let's see if there's any worth photographing.'

'Here's a very good trainer print Bob,' said Sandra pointing from the safety of the grass at the side of the muddy tractor marks.

'Yup, that will do,' replied Bob, removing his rucksack. 'I'll get a few photos of this if you look for any others.'

'There's one on the other tractor track here,' said Sandra, with a hint of relief that she might be able to charge the Donaldson cousins after all. 'This is a larger print and looks more like a boot.'

Bob took photos of both prints and the two officers headed back to Police HQ to interview the Donaldsons, disappointed at not having a dead hare in the boot but pleased at the discovery of reasonable sole impressions. His dictum was that you can never have too much evidence. Bob went via McLaren the baker and bought three medium Forfar bridies, one for Sandra, one for Shirley and one for himself.

In one of the interview rooms at Dundee police station Bob and Sandra drank the remains of their tea and wiped the crumbs of the bridies off their chins. 'If you bring the footwear here Sandra we can compare the soles with the photos.'

Sandra collected the two pairs of footwear from outside the respective cells holding the Donaldsons and gave the soles a rinse under a tap in one of the sinks used by the prisoners for washing. Once the mud was washed off, she was hopeful of a match.

Sandra was smiling as she entered the interview room. 'The trainers are

Cyril's and the larger boots are Archie's. I think we've nailed the buggers Bob.'

They both made the comparison with the photos on Bob's camera. 'Yup, I'd say the size and pattern, plus the combination of the two sole patterns is enough to confirm their presence at Highgrove Farm. We'll still need an expert comparison of the footwear and photos but let's get them interviewed now.'

The interview turned out much as Bob had expected, with neither man admitting being involved in coursing at any of the three farms. Cyril Donaldson sat silent throughout the interview while his more aggressive cousin Archie snapped 'No comment' after every question.

After the negative interviews Bob said, 'We need to see now what evidence there is against each suspect at each incident Sandra. We'll go through the evidence and list it since it's pretty complex. You can fill me in with any missing details for this latest incident.'

After fifteen minutes Bob had made a list.

Fingowan Farm 25th February
Suspect 1 large man in yellow fluorescent jacket No positive ID
Suspect 2 smaller man in dark jacket No positive ID
Dog 1 lurcher, white
Dog 2 lurcher, tan
Vehicle Blue Suzuki SJ16 SL02MKK Driver, suspect 1
Productions (1) brown hare (2) cigarette butt (still to be examined for DNA)
Foggylea Farm 28th February
Suspect 1 large man, 40s, yellow fluorescent jacket ID – Archie Donaldson
Suspect 2 smaller man, 40s, walked with limp, dark clothing, beanie hat. No positive ID
Dog 1 lurcher, light coloured, possibly white
Dog 2 lurcher, dark brown, possibly brindle
Vehicle Blue Suzuki SJ16 SL02MKK Driver, Archie Donaldson
Productions (1) brown hare (2) photo of driver
Highgrove Farm, 2nd March
Suspect 1 47 years, 6'1, large build, yellow fluorescent jacket, brown boots ID – Archie Donaldson
Suspect 2 43 years, 5'5, slim build, walks with limp, dark clothing, beanie hat ID Cyril Donaldson
Dog 1 lurcher, male, white
Dog 2 lurcher, female, brindle
Vehicle Land Rover Discovery HS06 DRE Driver Cyril Donaldson
Productions (1) left boot (2) right boot (3) left trainer, (4) right trainer (5) photos of sole impressions

'Okay,' said Bob when he'd finished, 'now I'll summarise the list. There's clear evidence of coursing in all three. Evidence of identification, which is crucial, is perfect at Highgrove with you stopping the pair that the farmer saw driving off, but there's no corroboration of who was doing the coursing if that case is taken on its own.' He paused and looked at the list again.

'The corroboration hopefully comes from the Foggylea incident using Moorov. ID's clear against Archie Donaldson since he was photographed and the court will see the photo. It's less good against Cyril Donaldson, though there may be enough with the farmer seeing the limp and us being able to confirm that he limps. The description of both men and both dogs also matches so I think we should also charge both with that incident. If the specialist fiscal disagrees, she can always drop Cyril from this charge.'

He went on, 'Fingowan Farm is the weakest case and I think it depends on us getting DNA from the cigarette butt that matches one of the suspects. If it's negative I think we can forget that case. In the meantime I suggest we charge them both with Highgrove and Foggylea. There's an option of putting them to court tomorrow from custody or releasing them on an undertaking to appear at court in a couple of weeks.'

Sandra had been paying close attention. 'I think an undertaking is the best bet. If they're kept for court and the fiscal sees we are still awaiting a DNA result and expert sole impression comparison, she'll probably order a release before they appear in court anyway.'

'I agree, and appearing on an undertaking also lets the court impose bail conditions that should limit their coursing if they plead not guilty. Let's get the footwear prepared for examination and get them charged. We'll also need to photograph the dogs and I think we should hold on to the Discovery for forfeiture unless the fiscal disagrees and wants them to get it back. I'd love also to keep the dogs for forfeiture but I've had this out already with the force and the fiscal and neither is willing to pay for their keep for several months till a court disposal. Sandra, maybe you could arrange for someone to bring in shoes for the Donaldsons or we'll be criticised for releasing them without shoes, much as I'd like to see the buggers walking home in their stocking soles.'

Bob drove back to Perth with the setting early springtime sun in his eyes, feeling deeply satisfied with his day's work. He scanned the Sidlaw hills to his right, the River Tay on his left with the rippling surface gleaming in the fading sunshine, and the Lomond hills beyond. As he approached the magnificent Kinnoull Hill on the outskirts of Perth Bob began to whistle *The Hills of Perth,* a tune he loved especially if played on the bagpipes in 2/4 time. He'd never considered which hills around the city of Perth were the origin of the tune and wondered if it could have been Kinnoull Hill.

As he looked up to the top of the hill he recalled the pair of peregrines that successfully fledge chicks every year on one of the crags under the tower. What a wonderful place Tayside was to work, and what a wonderful job it was being a wildlife crime officer – even with a mound of office work left to do.

Chapter 8

The following morning Bob had arranged a meeting with his line manager, Detective Inspector Jonathan Sneddon. He wanted to bring him up to date with the allegations of crime on Loch Garr estate. Jonathan was well aware of Nigel Roberts and his reputation of 'improving' driven grouse moors and Bob thought that, even if Jonathan wasn't an expert in wildlife, the methods of detecting or disrupting most types of crime were pretty much the same.

Jonathan had a steaming cup of tea in front of him when Bob met him in his office on the third floor of the Perth police station. There was another cup of tea at the other side of the desk for Bob, and a three quarters-full tin of chocolate biscuits. 'Dig in Bob,' Jonathan said, 'and give me the latest on this bastard Roberts and his new keepers.'

By the time Bob had updated the senior officer the biscuits in the tin were down to the next level. 'What I'm hoping to do sir is to call on the neighbour to confirm the allegation of a stag being shot over the boundary. I've found out that the neighbour is Peter Martin, who farms Hillside Farm. It's a sheep farm of about eight hundred acres and I know Peter from a time he phoned in about a dead sparrowhawk. He was concerned that it might have been shot. I went out and collected the bird. It was an immature bird and they sometimes come a cropper hitting windows and even branches of trees. That's what happened here.

'He's a friendly chap, interested in policing and quite keen to become a special constable. We discussed policing over a cup of tea but I've never seen his name coming up in any special constable duties. I doubt a farmer would have spare time to be a special anyway. The bottom line is that I'm pretty sure that he wouldn't spread the word that we're interested in the antics of his nasty neighbours.'

'I'm in agreement with that but what would we hope to gain evidentially?'

'There's a slim chance that the bullet might still be in the stag for comparison if we get the rifle. It would also alert Peter to look out for any other illegal activity emanating from next door. If they've started their poisoning regime, as I'm sure they have, the pattern in the past for Nigel Robert's minions has been for them to put baits round the boundary of the estate to try to muddy the water if any baits or victims are found.'

'And the deer shot illegally on Loch Garr estate, what can we do about that?' Jonathan asked. 'There's no way you or any other officer will be going on to the estate at night, that's a real health and safety issue with bullets whizzing around in the dark.'

'Well Jock Scott, the previous Loch Garr headkeeper, is a witness to some of the shooting. He drove one night while one of the keepers – I'm not sure which one yet – shot deer. I suppose he's art and part involved in a crime but I'm sure we can get round that. That was the final straw for him and he handed in his notice. I've still to interview him, though even then we'd need to get corroboration from somewhere. I'm hoping once I've done a bit more groundwork that we can carry out a search of the estate and, either then or at some stage later, arrest the keepers.'

'When does Albert Curtis move out Bob; you wouldn't want to compound his problem by arresting him?'

'Albert's away in less than a week. I'm sure he said 20th March is his last day. It would take us that time to get a team together anyway. There's still a slight problem for Albert in that Nigel Roberts and his crew might blame him for going to the police but I'm sure Albert can cope with that if it crops up.'

'What sort of numbers would you need for a job on the estate Bob, bearing in mind that funding for these operations is always tight?'

'Well so far there are two keepers, though by the time we get round to an operation Roberts might have increased his staff. Most of the estates he formerly managed had at least four keepers. If we get in quick a smaller team would suffice but I'd still see four officers to each suspect, which would allow two to peel off to arrest the suspect if required. If we can use search-trained officers they could also have a member of staff from RPID with them. If we're not intending to arrest anyone the four officers at the house could search the buildings when they're finished.'

'RPID?' said slightly puzzled Jonathan.

'That's the Rural Payment Inspections Division of the Scottish Government. Part of their remit is the inspection of storage and use of pesticides. They help us quite a lot and their experience would be really helpful in identifying and handling any chemicals.'

'And the search of the estate?'

'I'll cover another aspect of the search first if that's ok: the search of vehicles and clothing. If someone is using pesticide with some regularity it is likely that there will be traces in their vehicle and on their clothing. It would be beneficial to have a member of forensic services there to collect samples.'

'This is getting to be quite a big team Bob. I'm not sure it can be justified but I'll give it my best shot.'

'And lastly the field search team. On a recent search we had the assistance of the search and rescue team. It didn't go as well as it should have done.'

'Why, what went wrong?'

'Well, the search and rescue team are good at what they do: searching for missing persons and bodies. They insisted on a line search using GPS to keep to the same contour, back and forward to cover the whole hillside. That's no bloody good when you're looking for poisoned baits. They're mostly set out in open areas, especially on ridges, and even if we had found a victim of poisoning in long heather that wouldn't have taken the investigation any further.

'Rather than having, say, ten folks in a line tramping back and forward through knee-length heather we should have been split up into groups of no more than three and each group given responsibility to search given areas of the hill, and only searching the *likely* parts of that area where baits might be set out: ridges, bare areas, either side of vehicle tracks. As it was we were all knackered, and totally unnecessarily.'

'So, what do you propose this time if we get this off the ground?'

'We can have as many teams of three – or even two – as we can get staffing for. There would need to be a police officer in each team since the power is given to the police to search with as much assistance as they need from other agencies. The rest of the team can be made up of staff from RSPB Investigations or the SSPCA.'

'It's a fair undertaking Bob. We'd probably need to consider some hired cars, provision of meals, someone based centrally controlling the operation. That would probably be me, and making sure we didn't incur too much cost in overtime.'

'I'm sure for an operation like this the wildlife crime officers wouldn't mind doing it for time off rather than payment if they incur overtime. It would be great experience for them, especially the newer ones. We could also ask the wildlife crime officers from some of the other Divisions to help out. We've helped them in the past and I'm sure they would reciprocate. That would also assist in the provision of vehicles and maybe cut the bill for hired cars.'

'Right, I'll run it by the Chief Inspector when I next see him. In the meantime you speak to Jock Scott and Peter Martin and let me know how you get on. We can decide where we go from there.' Bob was impressed that his supervisor had been taking notes and could recite the names.

'By the way do we need search warrants?' Jonathan asked.

'We'll need search warrants for any domestic premises and lockfast sheds or vehicles involved. I'll firm up on addresses and what buildings are linked to these addresses in the next day or two. I'll also make a check on PNC to see which vehicles are registered to the estate so that we don't miss any. So far as a search of the land and any open buildings are concerned there's power for us under the Wildlife and Countryside Act to search without warrant and, as I said earlier, to take other people to assist us.'

'Bloody hell, this is bigger than most drugs ops, but I'm happy you know what you're doing. I'll try to sort out permission. By the way you're on the biscuits at the next meeting, this bloody tin is nearly empty!'

The morning had flown in but Bob wanted to progress the snared badger case so that he could hand it on to Constable Stuart Robertson from Pitlochry. He'd phone Jock Scott and Peter Martin from home in the evening when there was more chance of getting them at home. Meantime he headed for the police station at Kinross.

Constable Brian Proudfoot was a stalwart in the Kinross section. He was only a year or so off retirement and had been stationed at Kinross for the past fifteen years. In that time he had got to know most of the residents that were worth knowing, either as decent citizens or as criminals. More especially, since he was originally from a farming family, he was on first name terms with every farmer in the area.

Bob explained what he was looking for and the two studied the large-scale wall map. 'This is the wood here Brian,' said Bob pointing. 'It's about twenty acres and the pheasant release pen is downhill towards the far end of the wood.'

'The nearest farm to that is Cairniehill Farm Bob. It's owned by Sid Mathieson. His farm is a mix of arable and some beef cattle. His brother, Sandy, farms next door. Between them they own about a thousand acres, which is quite sizeable for this area. So far as I know neither of them do any shooting so they might have it let out. I'm sure this wood will belong to one of them.'

'That's a great starter for ten Brian, many thanks.'

'I don't know Sandy as well as I know Sid. I'm on duty for another couple of hours so I'll nip out to see Sid and try to get more information for you. I'll give you a call later if you give me your mobile number.'

Bob was grateful that police officers were not moved around from station to station as much as they used to be. There was tremendous value in having at least a couple of officers in each area that had the knowledge that Brian had accrued during his stay at Kinross.

After an early finish, Bob's work restarted in the evening with phone calls, the first being from Constable Brian Proudfoot. 'Bob, I've spoken to Sid Mathieson at Cairniehill Farm. He rents the shooting to a syndicate. They employ a guy as a gamekeeper of sorts who used to work for Sid as a cattleman. He's Doug Butterfield, who now stays in Glenfarg. I've emailed you his full details. Sid said he's a real lazy sod, so much so that he had to sack him. He was always late to feed the beasts in the cattle courts in the wintertime and of course they roared like hell for their breakfast. He only works part-time at the gamekeeping and he uses a farm shed that the syndicate rent from Sid. It's the one with the red door. He also works part-time doing gardening jobs. I've only met him a couple of times and he comes across as quite a nasty piece of work.'

'That's great Brian, we'll give him a visit shortly.'

Bob next phoned Jock Scott and arranged to meet him the following morning. He also contacted Peter Martin and made an appointment for the afternoon. Peter helpfully promised to have a look round the fields bordering Loch Garr Estate for the dead red deer stag in advance of Bob's visit.

Chapter 9

Jock Scott was now working as gamekeeper/shepherd on a small pheasant shoot near Dunblane. Bob went to his cottage, introduced himself and they exchanged pleasantries. Jock was a short, stocky, bearded character whose lined face had a permanently grumpy expression.

Jock started the conversation. 'I was lucky to get this job at my age. It's not what I would have chosen as I know fuck all about woolly maggots but I suppose I'll have to learn. I've had to take a drop in pay and accommodation because of that bastard Roberts but given time I might be able to move to something better.'

'I'm interested in the shooting of deer at night at Loch Garr, Jock.'

'I've to put my hands up to that, but that was the final straw. I was obviously getting harassed into moving on, there was no way I would have worked under Cyril Masterfield. He's been given the title of headkeeper and he knows as fucking much about grouse as I know about bloody penguins.

'Masterfield and his sidekick Brock are out regularly shooting deer at night. Masterfield has thermal imaging on his rifle so the deer are not spooked by a spot lamp. The estate has no authority from SNH to take deer at night or out of season. There's dead deer lying all over the hill and they complain about the number of foxes, buzzards and ravens. They're providing a fucking banquet for them.'

Jock was getting angry at the thought of Cyril Masterfield's illegal antics, and he was dribbling down his chin. 'Brock wasn't available one night and Masterfield took me out to drive him. He spotted a young red deer stag and took a shot at it. He's as good at shooting as he is at rearing grouse and he hit it in the gut. The poor deer hobbled off down a steep bank of heather with its back arched. The shot would eventually kill it but that's not the way real stalkers and keepers take deer. He wanted to go on for more but I'd had enough and told him if he wanted to shoot more deer he'd need to fucking walk.'

'There was some word of him shooting a stag over the march fence one night Jock.'

'Masterfield told me that. He said it was a mature stag about 200 yards out on a grass field of Hillside Farm. He told me he let off a shot at it and it ran like hell for about fifty yards before it dropped. He thought at first

47

he'd missed it but the stupid bugger probably didn't even realise it was a heart shot.' Jock paused to explain, 'When a deer is shot in the heart it will sometimes jump up and kick out with its back legs, then run off at great speed before keeling over. The pair of them just left it. It's a wonder Pete Martin, the farmer there, hasn't phoned you about it.'

'I'm seeing him this afternoon Jock.' Bob changed the subject, 'Have you any knowledge of them killing birds of prey?'

'To be honest I haven't seen anything but I've no doubt they'll be at it. I know Masterfield gave Albert Curtis Yaltox and told him to use it. I would doubt very much that he did but these other two fuckers will be using it. Brock told me they're intending to put a pigeon loft out on the hill so that peregrines take pigeons instead of grouse. He also said that at the estate he was on in England, Flagstones Estate in Lancashire, they sometimes tied a pigeon on a long string near the loft. The pigeon could flap about and would draw in a peregrine. They'd be hidden and would shoot it when it came within range. I think it would be somebody else that would do the shooting, Brock's a hopeless shot as well as knowing fuck all about gamekeeping. He's just Nigel Robert's lackey.

'There are usually nesting peregrines on a crag at the west end of the estate, I'll show you on a map later. No doubt they'll be for the chop.'

'Has Nigel Roberts ever told you, directly or indirectly, to do anything that's illegal Jock.'

'No, I'm told he issues his instructions only through the head keeper. I was no longer the head keeper, nor did I want to be under Roberts. I only had the misfortune to meet him twice. That was enough, he's a sneaky, pompous bastard.'

'Would you give me a statement about the shooting of the deer Jock?'

Bob was surprised at the response. 'Yes, I will. The whole outfit has brought the gamekeeping profession into disrepute with their illegal practices. The fucking lot of them deserve to be in the jail.'

Bob was pleased at his morning's work. He had been shown the location of the peregrine nest site and noted a statement that took him half-way to being able to submit a case to the procurator fiscal about Masterfield. He was still no closer to nailing Roberts but at least he had made a start.

Bob moved on to Hillside Farm at Amulree and met Peter Martin. 'I'm glad you've been in touch Bob, I've been out round the fields that march with Loch Garr estate. Not only have I found the dead stag but I've found two dead buzzards as well. My neighbour's new employees clearly need to be watched more closely. Would you like to walk round the place or will we take my vehicle?'

'I think it would be better if we walked Peter, that is if you have the time. We'll have a better chance of finding signs of illegality on foot.'

'Yes, I'm clear for a couple of hours before I have to check the sheep again. They've just started to lamb. They're blackfaced ewes in lamb to a blackfaced ram. Nearly all of them manage to lamb without my help.'

'Could we take a route slightly different to the one you took earlier Peter? That way we'll have covered more ground.'

They set off for the march fence with Loch Garr estate and veered uphill when they came within about a hundred yards of the neighbouring estate. They were in a grass field when Bob said, 'We'll make for that lone tree in the field Peter. It's amazing how often I've found a victim of poisoning under a tree or having fallen off a fence post.'

As they reached the tree Peter said, 'Well your theory is right, here's another dead buzzard.' Peter suddenly noticed the orange-coloured forked tail, 'Oh no, it's a red kite.'

The kite lay on its front under the tree with its wings spread out. Its head was slightly arched over its back. Bob removed his camera from his rucksack and took several photos of the bird before turning it over. 'The head lying back like that is a possible sign of carbamate poisoning,' explained Bob. 'Another sign is clenched feet, and you can see how its feet are balled up. Later in the year we might have expected to see dead insects since carbamates, possibly carbofuran in this case, are insecticides.' Bob went through the label-signing and double-bagging procedure before putting the beautiful bird in his rucksack. He thought it would look infinitely more beautiful if it was still alive.

They continued on to the next grass field where Peter led them to the dead stag. The big stag, a ten pointer, had been in superb condition. The sight of it lying there, its skyward-pointing eye socket, emptied of its contents by a crow, shocked both men.

'This field has been empty for about ten days,' said Peter. 'I took the sheep off it at that time and there was certainly no dead stag there then, so it's been shot in the last ten days. It's just unthinkable to shoot an animal with good food value and leave it to rot.'

Bob went through his photograph and label routine, paying particular attention to a large hole in the centre of the body behind the rib cage. 'That's an exit wound. Could you give me a hand to turn the beast over Peter and we'll see what's on its other side.'

When the stag was turned there was a much smaller hole in the lower chest area. 'There's the entry wound there.' Peter pointed to the hole. 'It looks like it's been a heart shot.'

Peter muttered again, 'What a bloody waste of a good stag, and the cheek of them to shoot it on someone else's land.'

There was no way that Bob was going to seize the stag as a production; photographs and a label would suffice. There was also no chance of recovering the bullet, as there was clear evidence it had exited. He felt as angry as the farmer with deer being shot and not recovered for their venison.

'The two buzzards are about a mile or so further on,' said Peter. 'They're quite close together and at this time of year may have been a pair. It might be them that usually nest in a line of oak trees on my side of the march.'

When the men reached the buzzards and Bob saw that they were about fifty yards apart and only ten yards or so from the march fence he wondered if there might be a chance of finding the bait that killed them. After photographing, labelling and bagging he quietly said, 'Peter, I'm going to have a quick look over on the Loch Garr side of the fence to see if there is a bait. Do you want to come or would you rather stay on your side?'

Peter hesitated, then said, 'To hell with it. If they can shoot deer on my side I'm happy to help you to find evidence of wrongdoing on their side,' and began to climb the fence.

It was a short search, as buzzards killed by carbofuran seldom fly far. Bob saw the bait first, about ten yards from the fence. He rather jubilantly said, 'This will be it here Peter. It's a rabbit. The body has been picked a bit by crows or buzzards but one of the legs is well picked. I'm sure that's where the pesticide will have been placed.' As he photographed and labelled the rabbit he explained a little about the illegal use of pesticides.

'The reason I searched here near where the buzzards were lying but didn't search over on the estate where the red kite was found is that if a buzzard has a good feed of meat laced with most pesticides it seldom goes far. A red kite on the other hand doesn't gorge itself like a buzzard, or even an eagle, it picks off a morsel and usually flies to some safe place to eat it. It's much more difficult to locate a bait that's killed a red kite than one that's killed a buzzard. Having said that we'll have a quick look on Loch Garr opposite the tree where we picked up the kite. There may be a pattern in them putting their bait about ten yards from the fence.'

The second search was unsuccessful and the two climbed back over the fence and back to the farm. Bob was pleased with the results, although his pleasure was tempered by the loss of yet another four lives. As they reached the car Peter said, 'I'll be keeping an eye open now on my nasty new neighbours; I'll give you a call immediately if I come across anything else of interest.'

Bob was grateful for Peter's support, giving him his mobile number in case he needed to be in touch in the evenings or at weekends. There was plenty intelligence now to be entered on the system, intelligence that Bob hoped he might eventually be able to convert to evidence.

Chapter 10

Just as he was finishing his breakfast at 6.30am, his mobile rang. 'This is the control room here Bob. There was a call to us about 5.30am from a person who saw a small red flatbed lorry parked off the public road and beside woodland. The caller said that men were loading crates on to the lorry and it looked suspicious. One of the night shift units attended but the lorry was gone. One of the day shift traffic units spotted the lorry minutes ago heading down the M90 towards Kinross and stopped it. The crates were full of snowdrop bulbs. The traffic officers are looking for some guidance as to whether this might be illegal.'

'What are the occupants saying about the snowdrops?'

'They're saying they had permission to dig them up but have forgotten who gave them permission. There are two men with the lorry and they're from Cambridgeshire.'

Bob thought for a second, 'Okay, some interesting factors here: they can't say who gave them permission, they were digging the bulbs in the dark, they come from one of the main parts of England that trades in snowdrop bulbs and it's late-March, the perfect time to lift snowdrops in the green. If the traffic officers arrest them and bring them back to the police station, I'll be coming in shortly anyway and will help them out.'

Toby had finished his breakfast, had cleaned up any crumbs from under the table and was now wagging his tail and nuzzling Bob's leg in anticipation of his morning walk. Bob couldn't ignore the dog's enthusiasm. 'Liz, if I give this energetic old dog a shorter walk than usual could you take him out round the fields later?'

Liz had intended tidying up the garden when Bob left for work, but walking Toby in the countryside was not an onerous task. 'Of course, Toby and I will look forward to that, won't we Toby.' Her reply made Toby's tail wag even faster.

Bob arrived at the station at the same time as a traffic officer was driving the lorry into the yard. He went and spoke to the officer once he'd parked, 'At a guess there will be several thousand pounds worth of snowdrop bulbs here. I don't know too much about the types of snowdrops, but some bulbs can be valued at several pounds each. There looks to be about fifteen crates per layer and there are three layers. It's an interesting case.'

'Aye and I noticed there's a bald tyre on the lorry and the handbrake doesn't work.' the traffic officer declared.

'Who was it that stopped the lorry?' Bob asked.

'It was the other day shift crew, Willie Arbuckle and Alex Bruce. They'll be at the charge bar processing the two men.'

Bob intended to wait till the traffic officers had completed the paperwork and had the two men locked up in the cells but there was a tannoy message for him to attend at the charge bar.

He was met by Constable Willie Arbuckle. 'For completion of the forms what is the offence Bob. Is it theft?'

'The fiscal might change it to theft but we should start with the statutory offence: intentionally or recklessly and without lawful authority digging up or uprooting any wild plant not in Schedule 8 of the Wildlife and Countryside Act 1981 – Schedule 8 plants are the rarer ones with special protection. It's Section 13 of the Act.'

'Would the penalty for common law theft not be higher?

'Well, the penalty Willie is a fine of £5,000 – that's per plant or bulb – and/or six months in jail. Will that do?'

'That seems pretty good to me, I'll see you shortly in your office,' said Willie, returning to complete the paperwork associated with arresting a suspect.

Quarter of an hour later Willie and Alex appeared at Bob's desk. Alex had forms in his hand, which Bob knew were the investigating officer's copy. He also had a worried look on his face. 'Bob would you be able to take this on. We have traffic commitments we were on our way to carry out when we stopped this lorry. We'll be tied up for the rest of the day then we're off for three days.'

Bob had heard this so often and it was an unfortunate factor in policing that cases needing immediate investigation often had to be handed on. That increased the witness list if it came to a trial and often doubled the number of police officer required to prove the case. He groaned, mindful of his current workload, 'I'll start off the investigation, hopefully along with one of the wildlife crime officers if one can be freed from other duties. That officer can then take on the case for reporting to the fiscal. I believe there are road traffic offences with the lorry. Will you take those forward? The lorry won't be going anywhere anytime soon.'

'Fantastic, and thanks for that Bob. It looks like a very interesting investigation but a bit out of our league.'

'The same as proving that a handbrake is inefficient is out of my league

Alex. Horses for courses.'

Alex quipped, 'That's nay a bad answer. Get it? Neigh!' The two traffic officers left the office laughing at what Alex thought was a hilarious joke.

Bob established from the control room that there were no wildlife crime officers on duty in the subdivision covering Perth and Kinross. There was one on duty in Brechin, PC Maggie McPherson. He hoped she could be freed for this job, but he knew Dan Crawford, the Duty Inspector in that division, wasn't convinced wildlife crime was a police job. He thought that the RSPB, a charity with no official investigation powers, should investigate wildlife crime. 'He'll be retiring next year anyway, bloody dinosaur,' Bob muttered quietly to himself. He decided to ask DI Sneddon to battle with Crawford to get the authority to use Maggie McPherson.

He got his answer quarter of an hour later, 'What a moaning bastard Dan Crawford is. It took a lot of persuading for him to agree to send Maggie McPherson to take on this investigation. I'd to promise that any overtime would come out of this subdivision's budget so for God sake don't let her incur any. By the way, the Chief Inspector's okay about a team for the Loch Garr estate investigation. We'll look at preparing an operational order together when you're ready.'

Bob updated his DI on the progress with the Loch Garr estate investigation, and added, 'Right sir, I'll get as much done over the phone with the snowdrop case as I can before Maggie arrives. It's near enough an hour from Brechin to Perth so that gives me plenty time to make a start.'

'What kind of enquiries are you thinking of Bob?'

'I'll need to phone the witness who phoned in and get the exact location, then find out who owns the land there. I'll try to get some idea of the value of snowdrops. We can't count them, but I'll need to make an estimate.'

'I see the suspects are from Cambridgeshire; remember to check with NWCU to see if they're known.'

'Yes, that's on my list, and I'll check to see if the lorry has pinged any interesting ANPR cameras recently. It's a long shot but I'm as well to make use of the facility.'

Bob arranged to meet the witness, an elderly man living adjacent to where the lorry was parked. He'd phone him again when they were ready to leave Perth. He next checked the internet for prices of snowdrops 'in the green'. The most common variety was *Galanthus nivalis*, which was being offered at between £5 and £10 for twenty five bulbs. He would need to establish the variety of the bulbs on the lorry but he'd plump for the lower price meantime. He'd take random samples for identification to Cambo Estate in Fife. Their extensive grounds are covered in carpets of a large variety of snowdrop species in late winter and they specialise in selling snowdrops in the green.

Next was a call to NWCU. He heard Donald Boag, the senior intelligence officer, rattling the computer keys. 'Of the two names you gave me Mark Slattery, born 15th May 1967, has two items of intelligence on the system. The first, in 2009, relates to suspicion that he is involved in the taking of snowdrop and bluebell bulbs from the wild. The second, in 2011, is that he charged an elderly man £5,000 for an inferior tarmacking job. I'll look up his previous convictions while you're on the phone.'

More rattling of computer keys and Donald reported, 'Two previous convictions for theft, one for fraud, which was maybe the tarmac work, and one for driving over the alcohol limit. Your other chap, Declan Rafferty, born 30th November 1988, is not on the system, nor is their lorry. Rafferty has one conviction for burglary.'

'Thanks Donald, could you see if the lorry has pinged ANPR in the last month please?'

'Let's see… only once in Scotland, last week in the Borders. That doesn't take you any further with your investigation, sorry.'

Bob was aware of someone coming into the office and looked round. 'Maggie, I'm glad you could be freed up. After today the rest of the investigation can probably be carried out from Brechin. I'll bring you up to date and we'll head off to see the witness, Angus Howie.'

The two officers drove to Angus Howie's cottage near Kinkell Bridge. It was down a track lined with young birch trees just beginning to come into leaf. There was a large turning area at the cottage then the track continued past it, through a gate into open deciduous woodland down to the River Earn, some 200 yards further on. Angus was in his garden waiting for them.

'They'd opened the gate and the lorry was backed into the wood. It's a wonder I never heard them coming down the track but my wife and I sleep at the back of the house. I'm always up early and when I saw the lorry and the crates, I knew exactly what they were doing. The woodland is part of a flood plain for the river and it's full of snowdrops. It was a lovely show a month ago, though they're going back now. I've had a look and it's easy to see where they were digging. They must have been here a while as they've made a fair clearance. They probably thought they'd be away before anyone in the house was up.'

Angus led them to where the men had been digging. 'You're right, they've been busy,' Maggie said, sitting on a fallen tree trunk and taking out her notebook, 'I'll note a quick statement from you.'

Bob meantime was photographing the devastation caused to what must formerly have been a lovely display of snowdrops. He then walked part of the way up the drive and took a panoramic photograph of the crime scene.

Maggie had established who owned the woodland, which turned out to be part of Kirklands Estate. The two officers then drove to the factor's office to confirm that no-one had been given permission to dig snowdrops.

'Next job is to estimate how many snowdrops they've taken,' Bob said. 'I'm not really looking forward to that job.'

It turned out to be easier than they thought. 'There is probably an average of at least twenty five mature bulbs in each clump that they've dug up Bob,' Maggie said as she pulled a couple of clumps apart.

Bob was meantime estimating the average number of clumps in each crate. 'A conservative estimate is forty bunches per crate.' He was now counting the number of crates on the lorry. 'Forty five crates, so that's forty five times forty times £5.' He paused and brought out his mobile. 'The calculator on my phone makes it £9,000, not a bad night's work, and I'm sure we'll have underestimated the number of bulbs. I'll finish here with some photos.'

The interview of the two Cambridgeshire suspects went well, Slattery admitting that certain garden centres in Cambridgeshire were willing to take as many snowdrop bulbs as he could get. Rafferty seemed more of an assistant than a main player but admitted he had been in line for a decent cut of the profits.

'I'm not surprised both put their hands up,' said Bob, 'the evidence is stacked against them. I think they should be released on an undertaking to appear at court in the next fortnight or so. We really need to get the snowdrops seen by a botanist. We may be well out with our estimates and we need to make sure that a defence solicitor can't bargain down the value of their night's haul. That can't all be done before tomorrow's court. I think we should clear it with DI Sneddon.'

The DI agreed on the liberation of the two men since they had fixed addresses, but asked, 'What the hell are you going to do with the snowdrops?'

Bob had thought about that. 'I'm keen to hand them back to the estate, but I'm concerned that the defence solicitor might complain that they hadn't the chance to view them. I'm thinking of the stated case Anderson v Laverock, that was a salmon poaching case where the salmon had been destroyed before the solicitor had a chance to see them. That was deemed unfair to his client and the case was thrown out. I think we need the specialist fiscal's permission before we hand them back. I'd like to keep the lorry for forfeiture though.'

'You're on nodding terms with the specialist fiscal's Bob,' replied

Jonathan, 'just you make the phone call.'

Meg Runciman, one of the four specialist prosecutors in WECU, the Wildlife and Environmental Crime Unit at Crown Office, agreed with the decision to release the two men and with keeping the lorry. She was always keen to ask the court to forfeit vehicles that are used in the commission of a crime. She'd no objection to the bulbs being returned to the estate but added, 'To be on the safe side, as well as your photos, would you video the lorry and contents so that a defence solicitor might get as good a view as physically seeing them. Thanks for phoning me, I'll look forward to the case coming in.'

Maggie McPherson was able to return to her home station without incurring overtime, which might help if she ever had to carry out an investigation in another division again. As she left, Bob said, 'I'll nip down to Cambo Estate in the next couple of days to have the species identified. That will let you get your report finished.'

It had been an interesting day, but Bob really hoped that he could get free time the following day to progress the Loch Garr crimes. That was still the priority investigation.

Chapter 11

Rather than incur the cost of two trips Bob had made a late morning appointment with Dorothy Abernethy at SASA and an early afternoon appointment with Dr Joan McBride, one of the botanists at Cambo Estate. First, he made a visit to the SRUC premises in Bertha Park. Frank McArthur painstakingly took samples from the red kite, two buzzards and rabbit and Bob left for SASA in Edinburgh with a boxful of samples.

Bob chose Aly Bain on fiddle and Phil Cunningham on accordion for company on his journey south. This duo played a great selection of tunes in perfect harmony, with much of the music having been composed by Phil. Bob especially loved the slow airs and when the pair played *The Gentle Light that Wakes Me* he realised he had dropped his speed from 70 to just under 60 mph. He was back up to seventy though as Ali played *Hangman's Reel*, a really fast tune of Norwegian origin with much complicated pizzicato throughout.

At SASA Dorothy seemed pleased to get the samples. 'This new system of getting samples rather than whole carcasses is much better for us here. It's more work for the vets obviously but I used to cringe when anyone brought in a dead fox or a dead cat, especially if it had been dead for a while.'

'And it makes little difference to me Dorothy,' said Bob. 'The vetlab is virtually on my doorstep and Frank takes the samples quickly and efficiently. I worried at first about the audit trail of the samples from the carcasses to you or to anywhere else they might be taken but there have been no hiccups in court and the defence solicitors seem unable to find fault.'

'Okay,' said Dorothy, 'The good news is that I've done the buzzard, the rabbit and the tin of blue granules. The granules are a mix of carbofuran, isofenphos and bendiocarb. There's a proprietary mix of the first two that used to be available in Ireland, though never in the UK, I believe the trade name was Yaltox-combi. Whoever has been using this has also added in bendiocarb. Even without the bendiocarb it's a lethal concoction.'

'That mix has cropped up before on other estates with links to Roberts. God, would I love to see the bugger jailed. What about the rabbit and buzzard?'

'Traces of all three chemicals were in every sample. As these new samples you've brought are from the same estate I'll start by testing for carbamates first, as I did here. It makes it much quicker. As you see you had an answer within a week. Do you want me to look for any visible traces just now in advance of the lab tests?'

'I reckon we have enough for a warrant from the first samples but the stronger the evidence the better. Go for it Dorothy,'

She donned a pair of gloves and opened the beak of the red kite. 'I see nothing visible in this one.' She then repeated the procedure with the two buzzards. 'There's nothing visible in the first one but I see a couple of dark blue granules inside the mouth of the second one. Have a look here Bob,' she said, and he peered inside the unfortunate raptor's mouth.

'I'll have a look at the rabbit now.' Dorothy studied the gash in the back legs of the rabbit. 'The legs have been well picked but there are still a few – very few – granules visible. Can you see them?'

Bob again studied the carcass, 'Yeh, I can see two blue granules quite clearly. I don't think we'll have any difficulty convincing the fiscal and a sheriff to grant a search warrant.'

Bob was keen now to get back over the Queensferry Crossing to Fife and Cambo Estate. 'Thanks for that Dorothy. Maybe you could phone again once you've done the complete testing.'

At Cambo, Bob somehow was expecting an older woman and was surprised when he was met by Dr Joan McBride who barely looked thirty. She had done extremely well to have gained a PhD at such a young age and he guessed she was now fulfilling her dream as a botanist. Bob was carrying a box with a selection of twelve clumps of snowdrop bulbs.

'This sounds a fascinating case,' Dr McBride said. 'I'm really looking forward to seeing how I can help you.' She laid the clumps out in a row on a table and began to study them. Aware that Bob had guessed that the snowdrops were *Galanthus nivalis* she explained, 'Technically the UK has no native *Galanthus*. The most common one found naturalised in the UK is *Galanthus nivalis*, and this is the case here with all of these samples. It is often referred to as the common snowdrop.'

The botanist was getting into her stride now, '*Galanthus nivalis* is characterized by its applanate vernation, and the single green mark at the apex of each inner perianth segment.'

Bob was baffled and quickly stopped her, 'What is that in plain language?'

'Oh sorry. The emergence of leaves is known as vernation. This snowdrop has leaves that are pressed flat against each other as they emerge from the bud in a pattern known as applanate vernation. This is the green mark here,' she continued, pointing at a U-shaped mark at the end of each otherwise white segments of the flower.

Still not satisfied she had given Bob enough information she went on, '*Galanthus nivalis* predominantly occurs in deciduous woodlands and frequently occurs in humid places, for example near rivers and streams, by springs, on wet stony slopes, and in gorges. It often forms large colonies, spreading quickly by offsetting bulbs, and sometimes by seed.'

Bob diverted the botany lesson to a more practical aspect of the snowdrop investigation. 'How much would a clump of twenty five bulbs be worth?'

Dr McBride's answer was slightly less technical, 'Ordinary *Galanthus nivalis* sold in the green retails at £3–£5 per ten, depending on bulb size, £5 likely to be flowering size. You could say that unsorted bulbs, which is what we have here, are three for £1. I've had experience of these crates before and they hold between 750 and 1,000 bulbs, let me get my calculator.' After a short pause she continued. 'Okay, 45 crates at 750, the lower number of bulbs, that's 33,750 bulbs. Dividing that number by three gives us £11, 250.'

'Our first guess of £9,000 wasn't too far off. These two thieves were set for a massive profit at someone else's expense. Many thanks for your help Joan.'

'You're welcome Bob, and you're welcome to have a look round the estate if you have time.'

Bob's head was spinning with figures and botanical terms. He took advantage of Dr McBride's suggestion to have a walk round. The estate was covered in snowdrops of different varieties, though most were dying back. They would have been a spectacular show a couple of weeks earlier. He wandered along some of the public paths on the estate. There were Tamworth sows with piglets in some of the woodland areas excitedly uprooting the earth exactly as nature intended. In another area a boar was sound asleep, totally relaxed and maybe even dreaming of his next encounter with one of the estate's sows.

In one of the fields Bob could see three roe deer feeding at the far end; at his end there were eight herons, all standing in resting mode with their necks bent, reducing their height by more than a third. He heard a squawk emanating from some Scots pine bordering the field and could see a couple of large nests near the tops. Walking closer, he realised that this was a substantial heronry, with at least a dozen bulky nests, most of which would by now contain eggs or recently hatched chicks.

Following another path back towards his car Bob could see tracks crossing from one side of the path to the other. He suspected they were made by badgers and a close inspection on a damper area of the track revealed a clear badger pawprint, four toes almost in a line with holes made by the long claws in front of each toe. He was distracted for a minute by a great-spotted woodpecker drumming on a tree near him and at the same time a pair of bullfinches on a bush inspecting it for suitable buds. Distractions over, Bob followed the badger track and before long came to a sett on the banks of a burn that runs through the grounds. At one entrance there was fresh earth dug out during the night and at another entrance some dry grass had been brought out to be aired. Badgers are fastidious creatures and like clean bedding as much as humans do.

Bob was glad of his walk and was reluctant to leave this lovely estate to return to his office.

Earlier in the day Bob had been in touch with Constable Stuart Robertson at Pitlochry who was now back to day shift and had been progressing the snared badger investigation. Stuart phoned Bob with an update before both officers finished duty for the day.

'I teamed up with Constable Brian Proudfoot at Kinross today. I'd got a warrant yesterday for Doug Butterfield's shed on Cairniehill Farm. By good luck today was one of the days that Butterfield was doing gamekeeping rather than gardening. He obviously must have seen us at his shed and came trundling over in an old blue Fordson Dexta tractor. The tractor looked in better condition than him, Christ he's a right scruffy bugger, a week's growth on his chin and wearing an old bleached and torn boilersuit. I've seen a tidier scarecrow.'

'Did you have to use the warrant?' asked Bob.

'Yeh, we got the warrant beforehand, and it's just as well. Butterfield's as unpleasant as the farmer Sid Mathieson suggested, lots of shouting and swearing. After seeing the state of him, I wasn't surprised that the shed was a tip but we got what we were looking for.'

'The home-made wire pins to hold the snares up?' Bob had guessed correctly.

'There was half a dozen of them in a box and another three attached to snares hanging on the back of the shed door. They were made in exactly the same way as the pin we found beside the badger, with the wire at the bottom of the pin doubled up to give better grip in the ground and a wee loop at the top for the snare to go through. They're definitely made from bits of an old farm implement.'

'So, what was Butterfield saying about those?'

'He admitted he made them but denied having set any snares at the pheasant pen. He shouted and snarled at us but when we suggested we'd better continue the conversation at the police station he suddenly quietened down and remembered that he had set some snares round the perimeter of the pen. He claimed he must have missed one when he gathered them up last summer.'

'So, you have a good case of failing to check a snare and failing to attach the individual identification tag then Stuart.'

'Better than that Bob, we found a home-made hawk trap in the shed, the kind with a small compartment at the bottom to hold the decoy bird and a larger compartment at the top to catch a bird of prey. He said he only used it for jackdaws but there were some feathers in it that look suspiciously like raptor feathers and some dried blood. I've taken the feathers and a swab of the blood for DNA testing at SASA. I'd a job getting the trap into the police car but managed it eventually.'

'Great stuff Stuart, we've both had a successful day then. Could you remember to check if Butterfield ever applied for an identification tag number and when you're ready I'll nip down to SASA with your feathers and swab. Remember also to submit an intelligence entry about Butterfield.'

Chapter 12

It was a wet morning and Bob and Toby got soaked on their walk. As they passed the pond Bob noted that a mallard that had eight ducklings a couple of days earlier now just had four. The culprit could have been a mink, otter, carrion crow, gull or even a heron. The four remaining ducklings were now at a size and age they'd be more able to evade avian predators, though mink and otter still posed a threat. They buzzed around the mother like giant bumble bees, sometimes jumping in the air to catch a fly. Primroses were now blooming near the pond edge, and lesser celandines along the side of a ditch running into the pond added to the fusion of yellow. Toby was showing impatience at being on the lead but was clearly much happier when released to sniff and scrape where various mammals and birds had earlier passed and left their mark.

Back at his desk, Bob's plan was to set about drafting an operational order for a search of Loch Garr Estate and of the gamekeepers' properties and vehicles. But first he poured a cup of tea to accompany the sensation baked by Shirley Deans. But before Bob could savour a slice with raspberry jam and cream filling, his phone rang.

'Bob it's Albert Curtis here. The bastards have gone and dumped a young red deer stag in the burn a couple of hundred yards up from my house. My water supply gets drawn from that burn and that deer could have been there for a couple of weeks. The fuckers have been trying to poison me.'

'Could it just have died in the burn Albert?'

'Definitely not. There's a clear bullet wound in the head. It's probably been shot at close range and it would drop immediately. They've carted it from wherever they've shot it and thrown in into the burn. Bastards! Thank God we're away from here in a couple of days.'

'Leave it where it is Albert, I'll come right out. I want to photograph it and take a sample for DNA. If they've brought it in their Land Rover we might get blood or hair for a match. Have you a decent sharp knife?'

'Aye, I've got the knife I use for skinning deer. What is the knife for?'

'You said it was a head shot. If there is no exit wound, with a bit of luck we might manage to recover the bullet.'

Bob gulped down his tea and scoffed the cake much more hurriedly than he would have liked, barely tasting its mouth-watering delights. He was with Albert in little over half an hour.

The two tramped up the side of the burn to the deer, Albert in waders so that it could be recovered from the water. 'It's lucky that you noticed it in that deep gully Albert. I'll photograph it from the top of the bank and take a photo from here to your house to show the proximity.' These photos complete, the men clambered down the bank and Bob took another close-up photo from the edge of the burn that clearly showed the head wound.

'I'll get it out now Bob. That's quite a deep pool but I should manage to get hold of a leg and pull it closer to the bank.'

After a bit of a struggle the two men managed to get the deer to the top of the bank. By that time they were both puffing and grateful it was not a full-grown stag. Albert turned it over and both men saw that part of the stag's innards were hanging out. 'Bastards,' shouted Albert, 'It's been a gut shot first. This is the exit wound. They've gut-shot it then got closer and put a bullet in its head.' Albert looked closely at the stag's head. 'There's no exit wound Bob. The bullet should still be in the head somewhere, but it might be well fragmented.'

'We'll take a chance. Could you get your knife into action and cut the head off for me? Cut it maybe half-way down the neck. And also cut a wee piece of meat and skin from the neck, I'll use that if DNA testing is required.'

As Albert was utilising his butchering skills Bob asked if he had found a new job.

'Aye, we're not moving too far. I've got a job as a keeper/handyman on a farm on the edge of the Ochil Hills at Auchterarder. The farm's about six hundred acres with some nice woodland and the farmer seems a decent chap. I've only to rear a few hundred pheasants. Most of the job will be as a single-handed gamekeeper but I don't mind the handyman part. The farmer seems as much into conservation as shooting. He wants me to create some ponds and wetland areas and plant out some areas with native trees. It'll be a relief to get away from all the stress of this fucking estate.'

Bob placed the head and the skin fragment in separate production bags and hoped that there might be some evidence that could get these depraved gamekeepers to court. If and when, he hoped that decent, law-abiding gamekeepers would be congratulatory rather than critical. The police always seemed to be piggy in the middle with both gamekeeping and conservation interests. This thought continued to bug him on the drive to Perth Prison.

The prison staff at the gatehouse were always interested in the different dead specimens that Bob brought in and were generous in allowing him the use of the x-ray machine that was normally used to scan visitors' bags. They were especially interested in this bulky item of indeterminate shape that was in an evidence bag enclosed in a black bin liner. Bob saw from the first scan of the stag's head that, in addition to some tiny fragments of lead, there was a much larger piece that was the bullet. He photographed the scan and made two further scans which showed in three dimensions exactly where the bullet was located. Bob was pleased with his three photos, and even more pleased when one of the prison officers promised to keep a cell free for the person who shot the deer. Next stop, yet again, was the vet lab at Bertha Park View to retrieve the bullet.

When the bullet was safely recovered Bob asked Frank McArthur what risk to health there might be from the stag in the water supply, especially with part of its entrails exposed. 'There's a real risk that bacteria would be released into the water, possibly salmonella, campylobacter and maybe even ecoli. I'm not a doctor but I know that any of these can make a person really ill with a gastroenteritis type infection.'

This was a worse scenario than Bob had initially thought. 'Bloody hell, it's a good job we got it out of the burn when we did. I'll let Albert the keeper know; he'll probably want to use bottled water till he moves out.'

It was early afternoon before Bob eventually made a start to the draft operational order. His first consideration was search warrants, so he knocked on DI Sneddon's door.

'So, you'll not need a search warrant for the land as there are adequate powers for the police under the Wildlife and Countryside Act, but you'll need a search warrant for each of the new keepers' properties and vehicles. How many keepers are there Bob?'

'There's still just two, and I've found out from Albert Curtis the registration numbers of their Land Rovers and the sheds and outhouses that they use,' Bob explained. 'Albert moves out tomorrow, but he reminded me that the new keepers are out and about at first light so we'd need an early start. He also said there's a new young keeper starting but he won't be there for another couple of weeks.'

'And what exactly are you looking for?'

'Well,' began Bob, 'If the bullet recovered from the deer in the burn is suitable, we'd need to take rifles to make the comparison. The vet removed it very carefully so as not to damage any striation marks. One of the civilian drivers is taking it to the ballistics experts in Dundee as we speak so I'll know before I make out the warrant request whether rifles are relevant. I'm also getting a list of their rifles from Firearms Licensing to ensure we see them all.

'In relation to the illegal use of pesticides I'd need to include pesticides, victims of pesticides and clothing on the warrant. That would include sweepings from the vehicles and seizing relevant clothing for testing back here for pesticide traces. We'll also be looking for deer hair and blood traces to try to make a link with the deer in the burn. For the forensic aspect, two of the Scottish Police Authority forensics folks would do; they could visit each location in turn. Lastly, I'll need to ask that the warrant includes staff from the Scottish Police Authority, Bruce Bannerman from NWCU and staff from RPID.'

'Okay, so crack on with the warrant application Bob and get it to the fiscal. Now what about personnel, what do you need?'

'Well really just the numbers of police officers we spoke of at our last meeting. If the police officers are mainly wildlife crime officers that would be great. I've already asked the NWCU investigative support officer and wildlife crime officers in other Divisions if they could help and they're all up for it. Search-trained officers would be ideal for house and building searches, augmented by the RPID folks.

Bob continued, 'For the land search I think we should stick to wildlife crime officers and staff from RSPB and SSPCA. All of these folks have the appropriate gear, cameras, know exactly what they're looking for and, more importantly, where to look. If there are any issues with animal welfare we can always get one of the SSPCA folks to have a look at some stage. I'm thinking mainly about the eagle owl that Masterfield might have. Neither RSPB nor SSPCA will be searching premises so they won't need to be on the warrant. I think we'll pass on the search and rescue team. As I said before they're good at what they do but this job is different to their usual search skills.'

'Sounds like you have it pretty much under control Bob. What about a date for the operation?'

'The aspect of the investigation that's probably most urgent is finding a link to the dead deer in the burn. For that reason we should be searching as soon as possible. How about five days from now, that's a Tuesday, which might be a quieter day to get the staffing we need, and with a briefing here at 4.30am?'

'A couple of other things Bob. Could you run it past Meg Runciman, the specialist fiscal in Edinburgh, before you submit the warrant application in case we've missed anything. I'll also give you DS Gregor McIver with you, he was formerly in the Fraud Branch and if we have to go down the road of reporting vicarious liability that will give him a feel for what is required. Go for it then. Give me a look at the draft operational order when it's ready.'

Back in the office Bob was pondering the evidence needed to convict

Roberts of vicarious liability. A relevant offence would need to have been committed: the killing of a raptor or the illegal use of pesticides ticks this box. The person committing the offence would need to be an employee or agent: Masterfield. Roberts, as owner, has the legal right to kill or take a wild bird on the estate. Another tick. Roberts also needs to show that he did not know that his employee was committing the offence *and* that he had taken all reasonable steps and exercised due diligence to prevent the offence being committed. Bob knew that Roberts might well have this requirement covered. Obtaining a conviction for vicarious liability was not easy but he could see possibilities.

Clearing his head of the complexities of legislation, Bob phoned Meg Runciman, who thanked him for the update and was happy with the proposed action. She would look forward to the warrant request arriving. He intended spending an hour to get the draft warrant request and operational order underway when his phone rang.

'Hi Bob, it's DS Kevin Band, I've had a look at the bullet. It's not too badly disfigured. I can see striation marks under the magnifying glass so there's a chance it could be good enough for a comparison. If you get a possible rifle or rifles just get them down to me and I'll see what we can do.'

Great news, Bob thought to himself. He now had all the information required but completing the warrant application meant a delay in getting home. He phoned Liz, hoping that the evening meal could be delayed. Again.

Chapter 13

Internal mail was sitting on Bob's desk when he arrived at his office in the morning. He opened it to find a sealed brown envelope inside. Opening that, he found it was forensic reports from the Scottish Police Authority. He was surprised the results hadn't taken longer but assumed that the forensics staff weren't overloaded as the Division hadn't had any murders since the previous October. A murder enquiry can really create substantial backlogs for work on less serious investigations. He read the first report, which confirmed that the cigarette end found at Fingowan Farm bore the DNA of Archie Donaldson. That was a great start.

The second report wasn't as conclusive as he would have liked; the forensic folks weren't able to say that the marks Bob photographed were made by Archie and Cyril Donaldson's footwear, but could state that they were similar size and pattern. Bob wasn't too bothered; if the case came to trial the sheriff could look at the photos and footwear and make a decision on the visual evidence. Archie Donaldson could now be charged with the first incident, Fingowan Farm, and it should clinch the case against both for the third incident, Highgrove Farm. He'd pass on details to PC Sandra Johnstone, who could now get the case reported to the fiscal.

Bob's first telephone call of the day was to be to Scottish Natural Heritage in Inverness in relation to the illegal shooting of the deer on Loch Garr Estate, but first he wanted to double-check the legislation. Ten minutes later he was talking to one of the SNH Deer Officers, Murdo Morrison. He explained some of the details of the case, 'Could you please check if any authority has been sought by or given to Loch Garr Estate in Perthshire.'

'You'll know Bob that we issue a general licence for the shooting of deer out of season,' Murdo replied, 'but the general licence would only allow them to be shot – wait, I'll read it out to you – "to prevent damage to any crops, pasture or human or animal foodstuffs on any agricultural land which forms part of that land, or to prevent damage to any enclosed woodland which forms part of that land, and that no other means of control which might reasonably be adopted in the circumstances would be adequate." I'm sure none of these conditions apply in your case since it's moorland.

'So far as shooting deer at night is concerned,' Murdo continued, 'that estate has never applied for a licence so if they've shot any species of deer at night they've committed an offence.'

Bob had been working on the draft operational order all morning and it was almost completed when he received a call from the control room. 'Bob, one of our young officers in Dundee, PC Jim Davidson, is attending a call where a teenage girl and her mother are alleging that the father deliberately kicked the girl's pet hamster against the sitting room wall. He then stood on the injured creature and killed it. The father's drunk and is sleeping on the settee and there's a very dead and very squashed hamster on the floor. Jim Davidson is looking for a bit of guidance.'

'Jim has power to arrest the father if he thinks that's necessary. It's his call but I'd advise that course of action as in a drunken state he may well pose a risk to the family. Whether or not arrested he should be charged under Section 19 of the Animal Health and Welfare (Scotland) Act 2006 for causing unnecessary suffering to a protected animal. To be on the safe side he should take possession of the hamster and get it to me for examination by a veterinary pathologist.'

The control room operator was puzzled, 'But PC Davidson said the hamster is dead, why would it need to go to a vet?'

Bob muttered, 'Oh for fuck sake' under his breath before answering, 'Because we need to prove the hamster was alive before all this kicked off – sorry, no pun intended. It's not an offence to kick or squash a dead hamster. Even though the mother and daughter might have witnessed what happened it saves any arguments in court from an awkward defence solicitor. Remind him to send a production label signed by the witnesses and himself along with the hamster.' This instruction from Bob arose out of frustration of the number of police officers who diligently had production labels signed for stolen items that had been recovered, offensive weapons seized or tools used to break into properties but never considered doing so for dead animals.

Bob had eventually managed to put the finishing touches to the operational order when one of the drug squad officers, DC Martin Moore, appeared in his office. Bob had worked in the same team as Martin some years before and knew him as a very competent and enthusiastic officer who, once he got his teeth into an investigation, held on like a terrier.

After a few short pleasantries, Martin got to the point. 'We turned a house in one of the Dundee schemes yesterday. The occupant is Pete Wilson, Peter Ramsay Wilson, a well-known drug dealer. We were a bit unlucky; the information was that he had a kilo of cannabis resin a couple of days ago but he seemed just to have an ounce left when we searched. You'll be interested in what's on his mobile phone. Have a look at this.'

Martin switched on the phone and both officers watched the film. Martin commented, 'There seems to be four men involved, I don't know the other three and I assume since it's Pete Wilson's phone that he is the person doing the recording. They're digging what must be a badger sett. One of them is head first down the hole now and just about out of sight. You'll see in a minute he pulls out a black terrier which has hold of a badger – or the badger has hold of the terrier. There's other dogs there too, one is a great big brute of a thing.'

Martin paused for breath before continuing. 'That's the badger making a run for it across the field but one of the guys has a shotgun. Though the film doesn't show the man with the gun he fires at the badger and obviously injures it as the badger rolls over then tries to get away again but you can see that it's now dragging both back legs. The dogs are let go and the black terrier, a brown terrier, a lurcher and the massive dog go after it. They catch up quickly and start to maul the poor badger.'

The film clearly distresses Martin, but he carries on, 'The guy filming, probably Pete, and two of the others run up to the badger and are shouting encouragement to the dogs to kill the badger. In a minute or so one of the men whacks the badger with a spade but I think it's probably dead by that time anyway. It's unbelievable that folk can do that to an animal. Look at the bloody mess of that black dog's face, the skin's ripped off its jaw. I think it only has one eye as well.'

'Bloody hell, that's frightening Martin. How will these bastards be treating their family? Does Pete have any kids? There's a proven link between cruelty to animals and domestic violence.'

'We didn't see any kids but they could have been at the school. The wife looks pretty cowed but she still managed to shout and swear at us for searching the house.'

'Were there any dogs in the house?'

'There were none in the house but I could hear dogs barking out the back, and there were dirty dogs' dishes lying in the sink. By the way, the date of that film is just three weeks ago.'

'Can you get forensics to save it and put it on a DVD for me Martin? We'll need to get a search warrant and go back to see what evidence there might be of badger digging or animal cruelty. When I get a warrant do you want to be in the team in case there are any drugs found during that search?'

'That would be perfect. We couldn't justify drugs being listed on the warrant but if any are found we could quickly get another warrant to seize them.'

'I'll keep in touch then. I've just sent a warrant request to the fiscal, this will be another one.'

When Martin had left Bob phoned Meg Runciman to alert her to the investigation and to tell her to expect another search warrant request in a day or two. He'd spend the final hour of his day on SID to get up to date with Pete Wilson and trying to work out who his associates might be. It would be a bonus to identify them and get the whole lot to court. It was a toss-up who was worse, badger digging Pete Wilson or grouse moor owner Nigel Roberts.

Chapter 14

The intelligence listed on SID mostly related to drugs, but also clearly indicated that Peter Ramsay Wilson was involved in a range of illegal activities. He was suspected of digging out foxes and badgers, hare coursing and poaching deer. The entries spanned eight years. He was also suspected of carrying an offensive weapon. His previous convictions listed on the Scottish Criminal Records Office database included driving under the influence of drugs, possession of an offensive weapon, serious assault and assault on his wife.

Bob looked at his associates, nine in all. The one that cropped up most regularly was Clint Wayne McLeish. 'Christ, his parents must have been into western movies,' gasped Bob aloud, yet again attracting baffled looks from Shirley Deans.

He flicked over to McLeish on the screen. The intelligence listed against him was remarkably similar to that of Wilson: drugs, violence and cruelty. There was also an entry about him keeping a large fierce dog, thought to be a bull lurcher, in a kennel in the garden. Bob studied a photo of McLeish and instantly recognised him as one of the morons who were urging on the dogs to kill the badger in the film clip. It was McLeish who whacked the badger over the head with the spade. 'Gotcha!' he shouted.

Shirley called over, 'You seem to be having a good morning.'

'It's always good when I get evidence against criminals Shirley. This is a particularly vicious group I'm looking at. I'm trying to arrange for them to get a free holiday.' He added quietly, 'at Her Majesty's expense.'

He trawled the rest of the associates of the two badger diggers but drew a blank at finding the other pair that were present when the badger was mercilessly dragged from its sett, shot and savaged by dogs. He especially wanted to trace the man with the shotgun and would circulate a short bulletin on the incident to all of the officers in the force to see if anyone had a suggestion. He wasn't hopeful, as the man with the shotgun didn't appear on the film. His last check was with the firearms licensing department; neither man was the holder of a shotgun certificate.

Bob began to type yet another search warrant request for the premises of Pete Wilson and Clint McLeish. This time he'd include SSPCA officers on the search warrant. If the other two men were identified he'd make out further warrant requests. It was going to be an exceptionally busy couple of weeks. March to June were always Bob's busiest months. It looked like this year was going to be no exception.

His phone rang as he was making a cup of tea and he recognised the number. 'Good morning Ralph.' Ralph Murdoch was the Senior Investigations Officer with RSPB Scotland and he and Bob regularly communicated about bird crime, especially crime committed against raptors.

'Bob, there's a problem with an eagle in the Enochdhu area of Perthshire. It's one that's fitted with a satellite tag and the raptor group folks had noted that it was favouring one of three different eyries it has on Aberurgan Estate. It should be laying about now but it's gone off the radar. It's been keeping pretty much to its home range recently and the tracking device has been working perfectly. It suddenly stopped yesterday about a mile east of its favoured eyrie and there's been nothing since. It's highly suspicious, especially in view of the other recent problem on that estate.'

'Yeh, that cage trap that the bird watcher found with goshawk feathers in it can't be far from there. I've got other urgent stuff to do but I know that PC Jake Williamson is on duty in Crieff just now. I'll see if he can be freed to help you to search. How many would be free from your team?'

'There's three of us Bob, we're ready to leave. If Jake's free we could meet him at Blairgowrie.'

Bob would have loved to be on that search. He loved tramping the hills and very nearly relented, but just in time he accepted that he was too busy. 'I'll get back to you shortly Ralph.'

Constable Jake Williamson was a community constable and less likely to be tied up with reactive policing. He had been a wildlife crime officer for the past five years and was extremely competent. Bob was hopeful when he called his mobile number.

'I've nothing that can't wait,' Jake replied. 'The sergeant is here so I'll clear it with her. Just hang on.' He was back on the phone in minutes, 'Yes that's fine Bob. I'll nip home to get changed and head for Enochdhu. Ralph can phone my mobile when he's nearly there.'

That was a relief for Bob, he was glad that most of the supervisory staff in the Division were cooperative. He updated Ralph and got back to his admin work. He didn't dislike being in the office since part of his role was to co-ordinate and delegate wildlife crime investigation across the Tayside Division. Nevertheless, he liked to be involved in as much as possible.

By the end of the afternoon the operational order for Loch Garr Estate was completed in draft form and he took it to DI Jonathan Sneddon. 'One aspect of this job we never sorted out sir was who would run the op. Would you be doing that?

'I thought you'd be doing that Bob.'

'I'd really like to be in the team that deals with Masterfield,' Bob hesitated 'If that's possible.'

'Well, I suppose I could have a radio switched on in my office, listen in and make whatever decisions are necessary.'

'And would you be taking the briefing at 0430?'

'You'll soon have me in your team as a bloody wildlife crime officer.' Jonathan drew a deep breath, 'Oh well, since I'm your line manager I suppose so.'

'Thanks. I'm owing you a dram sometime.'

'A bloody bottle of malt more like.'

Chapter 15

In the days before the Loch Garr Estate operation Bob had prepared the search warrant applications for Peter Ramsay Wilson and Clint Wayne McLeish. In a strange way he looked forward to meeting McLeish to see if he looked as weird as his name. He'd apply for the warrants after the present operation was completed. By that time he might even have the names of the other two men involved.

The search for the missing satellite-tagged golden eagle had taken place over three days and had failed to find any trace. Bob had put out a press release since he'd no doubt that the keepers on the estate would have seen the search. He'd left it to Constable Jake Williamson to interview the landowner and various employees but the chances were slim of establishing what had happened to the bird. Past experience of the sudden failure of a satellite tag which had been working perfectly fine led Jake to record the incident as a crime.

On the morning of the Loch Garr Estate operation Bob arrived first at the meeting room where the briefing was to take place. DI Sneddon arrived shortly after and sounded remarkably enthusiastic considering the early start and his initial reluctance to take the briefing.

Bob had been considering the options for dealing with the two suspects and sought the senior officer's view. 'Sir, unless circumstances change during the search, I think we should leave any arrest of the two keepers until we have all the evidence to hand.'

'I think I know where you're coming from Bob but why is that?'

'Well, the best evidence might come from traces in a vehicle either of pesticide or a link to the deer in the water supply, pesticide traces in their clothing or any other forensic tests that might be required of anything recovered today. They'd be better interviewed at a police station about that type of evidence and of course we can't do that today as we don't know yet what we'll find. They'll probably just make no comment interviews today but if we have stronger evidence the interviews are more likely to go in our favour.'

'Yep, I agree. We'll be in touch by radio and mobile phone anyway and if circumstances change then we can change tactics. The other advantage, of course – and I'm sorry to bring budget issues into this – is that we'll finish the operation earlier and we're much less likely to incur a huge overtime bill.'

Staff for the operation were arriving now and at 4.30am DI Jonathan Sneddon started his briefing. 'Good morning ladies and gents, thanks for all arriving on time. The police officers amongst you got a numbered copy of the operation yesterday so you should be up to date with the background to the op, details of the two suspects, what your particular duties are and who you'll be working with. Please make sure these copies are returned to Bob McKay at the end of the day.

'I won't take too long over this as it's essential to get to the two suspects before they disappear on to the estate,' Jonathan continued. 'The search trained officers detailed to search at the two addresses can head off in advance of everyone else and ensure the suspects remain at the addresses till the rest of the group catch up. You'll have copies of the search warrants; Bob will have the original if there's any argument of the warrant's authenticity. Bear in mind when searching to note anything that might help with the suspects' line management as we may go down the road of vicarious liability at a later date. If there's anything that's particularly relevant and not covered by the warrant, we can speak to the fiscal and make a quick application for an additional warrant if she thinks that's necessary. There will be packed lunches delivered around lunch time, I don't think any of you will die of starvation before then. There's plenty of bottled water available here so make sure you take some with you. Bob will give a quick recap on what you'll be looking for but before that the four officers going to the addresses can get away now. The rest will follow shortly. Bob…'

Bob began his part of the briefing, 'Charlie Galbraith and Lena Spencer from RPID will help the search teams at the two keepers' addresses. Illegal pesticides will be the main focus of the search for these teams. Seize any clothing that is likely to have traces of pesticides, that will include the jacket and trousers that the suspect is wearing. Concentrate on working clothing, probably just stuff that's hanging in the hallway or wherever they keep their working clothing. Search working vehicles and quad bikes. Look for knives or game bags but remember that our forensic experts will be taking sweepings from the vehicles so let them have first go at vehicles. If there are any welfare issues with dogs the SSPCA inspectors can have a look when they finish the land search. Masterfield may have an eagle owl. Have a look at the conditions it's being kept in as well. The team searching Brock the under-keeper's house, would you remember to take any rifles for test firing, bearing in mind the bullet recovered from the deer. Ensure first they're unloaded.

'For the land search there will be four teams of three, each made up of wildlife crime officers, and either a member of RSPB Investigations or SSPCA. You'll see from the maps which part of the estate you have to search. You all know the type of places to search and what you should be seizing, whether baits, victims or illegal traps or snares. Bear in mind health and safety, especially near water, any crags, the handling of traps or from pesticides. Thankfully there will be low risk from ticks just now.

'Lastly forensics. Any blood or deer hair in vehicles may well help prove through DNA who threw the dead deer in the burn. That would be a great aspect of this case to solve. Everyone should be wearing nitrile gloves when handling anything that they might be seizing. Thanks everyone, keep DI Sneddon updated with progress, happy hunting and we'll meet here again at the conclusion for a debrief.'

The different teams set off for their respective duties. The teams totalled twenty one, made up of seven wildlife crime officers, four search-trained officers, two forensic staff, the NWCU investigative support officer, DS Gregor McIver, two RPID staff, two members of RSPB Scotland investigations and two SSPCA specialist inspectors.

Bob and DS Gregor McIver, plus Bruce Bannerman from NWCU went to Masterfield's house, noting when they arrived that Lena Spencer was sitting in her vehicle outside. She'd be called in if any suspected pesticides were found, otherwise she'd wait to assist with the search of the outbuildings.

The two search-trained officers, PCs Joan Steele and Danny Pirie, arrived twenty minutes before the others. Masterfield had clearly heard the sound of their vehicle arriving and came out of the house before the officers had even opened the car doors. Any person committing crime, gamekeeper or otherwise, must expect the police to knock on the door and in that regard Masterfield showed no surprise at the early morning visit.

When the second part of the team came into the house Joan and Danny had already started searching a cupboard in the hallway. Masterfield was watching their every move, which didn't bother them; if they found anything of interest, they would show it to him and see what his reaction was.

'Could you label and bag the work clothes hanging here in the hallway Joan,' said Bob. 'When you're finished in the hall have a brief look in the rest of the rooms and use your discretion as to what to search. You might decide against searching the bedrooms and living room.' Bob took DS Gregor McIver aside and said quietly, 'There's a small room here Gregor which might serve as an office. Can I leave it with you to search this room in case there is anything that might show ownership of the estate or any chain of command?' Bob then turned his attention to Masterfield, 'Cyril, would you unlock the gun cupboard please.'

'How can I do that and still watch what's happening here?' retorted Masterfield. He was full of bravado but Bob could see the beads of sweat on his brow. And an almost imperceptible quivering of the back of his shirt revealed that he was trembling. Masterfield was having a bad day. And it had barely started.

'You'll just have to go back and forward between us. If any of us are taking anything away we'll tell you.'

Masterfield reluctantly opened the walk-in gun cupboard. It was a substantial size, with space for many more weapons than it held. Bob eyed up the weapons. 'So, you've got a double-barrelled shotgun, a semi-auto shotgun, a .22 BSA rifle with a sound moderator, a .243 Remington rifle and – what's that heavy calibre rifle Cyril?'

'A .270 Winchester,' replied Masterfield.

'That'll be for the deer then,' stated Bruce Bannerman.

'It's perfect for deer, a heavy enough calibre without too much of a recoil.' Masterfield was caught off guard by Bruce's question, probably not intending to give away anything to the police.

Bob lifted the .270 and checked it was empty. 'We'll be taking this Cyril.'

'What the fuck are you taking that for?'

Before Masterfield got a response Bruce lifted the .243. 'And we'll be taking this as well.'

'Is this covered by the warrant? You don't have the right to take my rifles.'

Bob took the original warrant from his pocket. 'You'd see the copy warrant when the first two officers arrived. I have the original here.' Bob unfolded the warrant and held it where Masterfield could see it. 'Look here,' he said, pointing at the wording. 'It says, amongst the other items we're searching for, *rifles.*'

Masterfield snorted, 'They better not come back damaged. You'll pay for them if they are.' He stomped off to watch the other officers, who had completed placing three jackets in evidence bags.

'Are these your jackets Cyril?' Joan Steele asked.

'No comment,' replied Masterfield.

'Do they belong to anyone other than you?'

'No comment.'

'Does any other man live here?'

'No comment.'

Masterfield was wearing a pair of grubby trousers. 'Well need these Cyril, my colleague will go with you to collect them.' Masterfield gave a grunt as he and PC Danny Pirie left the hallway.

Meantime, to finish off the search of the gun cupboard, Bob and Bruce made a check of the floor and shelves as they could be a safe place to store illegal pesticides, though most rogue keepers hide any illegal products well away from the house. When Bob opened one of the drawers there was a metal cash box inside. His mouth opened in a gasp. 'Look at this Bruce, it's absolutely stuffed with money.' He flicked through the notes, 'There must be thousands here, could you get Cyril through.'

When Cyril appeared his face was ashen. Bob held out the thick wad of notes. 'What's this money Cyril?'

'It's nothing to do with you. It's my money. I've been saving up.'

'Do you know how much is there, Cyril?'

'There's twelve thousand pounds,' he answered.

'Well I've been saving up for a lot longer than you,' said Bob, 'and I've got nothing like this amount. We'll need to count it and we'll be taking it with us.'

'What right have you to take my money?' Masterfield was sounding desperate.

'Under the Proceeds of Crime Act 2002 we have power to seize cash amounts over £1000 if we suspect it has come from crime or is intended to be used to commit crime.' Bob continued, 'We'll need to count it now in front of you.'

The two officers went to the kitchen and, with Masterfield present, laboriously counted the cash, which was in a mix of £50, £20 and £10 notes. There was £12,120, a sum that the officers noted in their notebooks. At the conclusion it was placed in an evidence bag and the money and rifles were locked in the boot of the police vehicle. Minutes later PCs Joan Steele, Danny Pirie and DS Gregor McIver joined Bob and Bruce at the vehicle.

'What did you folks find then?' asked Bob.

Joan was loading the clothing into the boot and Gregor showed Bob several documents that were on Loch Garr Estate's headed paper and signed by Roberts. They were a series of instruction to Masterfield, though Gregor, having scrutinised them all, stated that there was nothing in them indicating illegal practices. 'What a bloody pity,' said Bob.

There were four outbuildings now to be searched. Bob, as the team leader, instructed Joan and Danny to collect Lena, who had been patiently waiting in her car, and search the two larger buildings. Packed lunches had just arrived though, so the searches would just have to wait a bit.

Once he'd had a bite to eat Bob gave an update on his radio to DI Sneddon. He'd heard the other house search team updating the DI that they had seized a rifle, clothing and also a shotgun that had been left unattended in a cradle over the handlebars of a quad bike. The forensics team had also finished with the vehicles at Brock's house and had left to join Bob. He'd heard no update at that point from any of the land search teams.

Minutes later the two forensic officers, Madeleine Smith and DC Mark Anderson arrived at Masterfield's address. Masterfield had been in the house on the telephone to Nigel Roberts. He rushed out on seeing the new vehicle arrive. 'Mr Roberts said that you've to stop any further searching until my solicitor gets here.'

Bob was getting fed up with Masterfield only speaking when it was to complain. 'We don't take orders from Roberts. We've a search warrant here signed by a sheriff and it says nothing on it about not searching till a solicitor is present. You can phone Roberts back and tell him that if you like.' He addressed Madeleine and Mark. 'Could you make a search of the Land Rover and quad bike please. We're going to get on with the buildings. You'll get us there if you need us.' He turned to Masterfield again, 'You can observe what the forensics officers are doing at the vehicles or watch us in the sheds, but don't touch anything.' Masterfield stomped over to the forensics team about to make a start on the Land Rover. That indicated to Bob that there may be little to progress the case in the sheds.

After an hour and a half searching the outbuildings the teams drew a blank. They did, however, find an eagle owl in a small and barely legal cage in one of the sheds. It was in pretty cramped conditions but the cage was clean and it had food and water. It wasn't any quality of life for such a magnificent raptor as an eagle owl. Bob was aware of the limitations of animal welfare legislation and knew there was no offence that they could charge him with. He also knew that the only reason such a bird was kept by gamekeepers was to draw in birds some keepers considered as 'vermin' and shoot them, whether protected or not. He was also sure that when Masterfield was using it for this purpose the owl would be tethered, an offence under section 5 of the Wildlife and Countryside Act. He muttered to Bruce, 'I wish we could catch Masterfield using this poor bird and we could take it off him. We'll get hold of him and see what he says about it.'

Forensics had finished with the Land Rover and were taking sweepings from any likely part of the quad bike. Masterfield was watching them intently. Bob approached him, 'What's the eagle owl for Cyril?' There was no response.

'Is it your eagle owl?' Still no response

'Do you use it to lure in other birds, maybe hen harriers for instance, to shoot?' Masterfield still remained silent.

'Why are you not answering?' Bob asked.

'Mr Roberts said I'd not to answer any questions,' was the curt response this time.

'Then you've failed,' said Bob, a smile of satisfaction spreading across his face.

There was little more that Bob could interview Masterfield about; it was the right decision not to arrest him until later. At this early stage he didn't want to show his hand about the recovery of the bullet from the deer in the burn. He suspected that the keeper would be thinking that the taking of the rifles would be linked to illegal shooting of deer out of season and at night. Even with suspects that are likely to give no comment interviews, the police are much more likely to have success if the suspect is out of his comfort zone and at a police station. He'd look forward to that day once they had more evidence. It was time to head back to the police station for the debriefing.

Chapter 16

The group searching Brock's premises were first to arrive back at the police station, closely followed by the two forensic officers. All were busy sorting out and labelling the items they'd taken as productions or for further examination. Bob's team did likewise while they all waited for the arrival of the search teams.

It was a further hour and a half before everyone was back at the police station and Bob looked into DI Jonathan Sneddon's office to see if he was ready for the debrief.

The DI asked every team to give a run down on what they had found, where the search had gone to plan and where there had been issues that could be resolved for future searches. Bob started with the report from his team. He was happy that the search had gone smoothly but suggested that the officers from RPID may have been better helping with the land search rather than having to wait until the house search had been completed. They could always have been called in at some stage if something had been found that needed their expert opinion.

DI Sneddon asked, 'Where do you think the £12,000 came from Bob?'

'They're probably tips he got on his previous estate. He's not been long enough on Loch Garr Estate to get tips as the shooting season was all but finished when he started.'

'Is there a chance we can justify that the money's proceeds of crime Bob?'

'I think we were justified in taking the money under POCA. If protected species are being killed on an estate to increase the bag and hence the profitability, that would also reflect in the amount given as tips. I doubt if we'll ever prove that, but I think it's worth running it by the financial investigation officers. We might need to give it back again before forty eight hours is up but if we do, the income tax folks might go after a share of it as I doubt if he'd pay tax on his tips.'

Constable Stuart Robertson, the wildlife crime officer based in Pitlochry had led the team searching Brock's premises. He began with what items they had taken during the search. 'Brock is a young lad and although he's no doubt been schooled by Nigel Roberts, he appeared to be in a real state of panic during most of the search. The two search-trained officers, who were first to arrive, noticed a quad bike in a shed with a Browning semi-automatic shotgun in a cradle over the handlebars. It was just starting to get light and there was a good chance it had been left there overnight. Brock denied this and said he had taken it out just before we arrived as he was about to set off on rounds of his traps. Either way it was unattended and not under lock and key.

'When we searched the house we took a .243 Tikka rifle. He also had a side-by side shotgun and a .22 rifle, which we left. Brock had a jacket hanging in the hallway, which we took. We also took possession of the trousers and jacket that he was wearing.

'In one of the sheds there was a dead cat which initially looked like a wildcat but when I inspected it more closely I'm happy it was a hybrid. Much more interesting was a dead pine marten. He initially tried to say he knew nothing about it but eventually admitted that he had caught it in a live-catch cat trap and put the trap and the animal in a burn to drown it. The pine marten was soaking so that tied in with his admission. There was also a partially built trap in the shed which, when it was completed, looked like it would finish up as a hawk trap.'

Stuart continued, 'If the two keepers are arrested at a later date, Brock will definitely be the weak link. I had quite a good rapport with him and would be happy to interview him if we get to that stage. I'd also agree with Bob about better use of the RPID staff as Charlie Galbraith who was with us had to sit for nearly an hour twiddling his thumbs.'

DC Mark Anderson, one of the forensic officers, was next. 'We started off at Brock's address. We took possession of a game bag from his quad bike and also some sweepings from a wooden box that was fitted to the back of the bike. There was quite a lot of dried blood in the box. We took a couple of samples but the box wouldn't have been big enough to hold a red deer so I don't think that would be the transport used to take the deer to the burn.'

Mark went on, 'In the Land Rover there were two knives in a dashboard shelf at the passenger side. There was also a short, thin stick beside the knives. We took those and took samples of dust from the shelf. We took sweepings from the floor at the driver and passenger side and from the back of the vehicle. There was some blood, though not a lot, in the back and we have a couple of samples.

'We then moved on to Masterfield's address. The quad there had an identical box fitted to the back. It was covered in blood and lots of white and grey fur. I think he'd been shooting mountain hares. In his Land Rover there was a knife in the dashboard shelf. We took that and again took dust samples from the shelf. There was a game bag on the passenger seat, which we took, plus sweepings from the floor on the driver and passenger side. There were also a couple of bullet cases, probably from his .270 or .243 but I don't suppose that's unusual in keepers' vehicles.

'The back of the Land Rover was interesting. It was reasonably clean apart from a pool of dried blood near the door and a couple of small tufts of what I'm sure is red deer hair. That may turn out to be our transport for the deer in the burn.'

The four land search teams gave the account of their searches in sequence. Three of the four teams had found dead deer on their search, the total being five red deer and two roe deer. Most were well predated and there was no point in taking possession of any of them. Dozens of rail traps over waterways were found; all new DOC 150 traps, all legal. Two of the teams brought in a total of four rabbits that may have been poisoned baits, with a recently dead buzzard lying near to one of them. One team found a dead woodpigeon that was almost certainly a bait, with a dead sparrowhawk lying beside it.

The team led by Crieff PC Jake Williamson had most success. Jake narrated the day's work. 'We started off up the side of larch wood on our way to the hill. The fence was netted but there were a number of holes in the netting. There was a fox snare at almost every hole, eight in all. Each was set where an animal caught could be partially or fully suspended. One in fact had caught a fox. It had jumped over the fence and was hanging down the other side. It had clearly been dead for several days. We bagged all the snares carefully for DNA examination.'

Jake went on, 'We also had a look inside a double size multi-catch cage trap. It wasn't being used and the door was padlocked open but Ralph Murdoch used his RSPB skills to identify a golden eagle feather inside the trap. We'll never know whether it was killed or released.'

The Sub-Divisional Commander, Chief Inspector Sandy Thomson, had popped his head into the room just as DI Sneddon had started addressing the group, He listened in to the DI's remarks. 'Thanks to all of you for your great work today, especially those of you from other agencies or other divisions who've been helping us out. We should manage to get at least one of the keepers to court and it's early days yet to see if we get a vicarious liability case. Could you make sure all the relevant production labels are signed before you leave and, for the officers who have copies of the operational order, remember to leave them with Bob.' He paused to draw breath, 'Bob, you've a lot of follow-up work with this, and of course you've the badger-digging pair to get sorted out as well. I'll try to get you one of the divisional wcos for a few days to help out as we've potentially got a good result here.'

Chief Inspector Thomson added to DI Sneddon's thanks. 'We're lucky in Tayside Division that there is tremendous support for wildlife crime from the Chief Superintendent. He's well aware that wildlife crime is closely linked with many other types of crime and that it often gets as much publicity as a rape or murder. This has been a great start to this operation today. All of you have my thanks as well as those from the DI. I've a meeting with the chief super tomorrow and I'll update him on today's operation. Bob, you *will* get some assistance. DI Sneddon will let you know in the morning who that will be.'

Bob was well chuffed, not only at the results of their work today, but that it was commented on positively by senior officers. He was heading home for a dram of his best malt. He thought of the fiddler Niel Gow again who composed several tunes about the drinking of whisky. He'd love to know the story behind the writing of *Niel Gow's Farewell to Whisky*, then his later tune *Whisky Back Again*.

Chapter 17

The Chief Inspector had been as good as his word; DI Sneddon phoned just after he'd arrived at the office. 'Bob, you can have PC Jenny Watson for the next four days. The Chief Inspector has cleared it with her inspector. She's day shift in Perth in any case. Just get her to work whatever hours you are going to work.'

Bob started to organise the workload and Jenny walked into his office half an hour later. She was one of the newer wildlife crime officers In Perth. She'd been desperate since she started to get involved in some of the investigations. She beamed with pleasure. 'Hi Bob, I'm at your disposal. Four days full-time on wildlife crime work, fantastic.'

'Great Jenny, I'll certainly keep you busy, and we might even manage an operation on badger diggers if things go as I'd like them to. I'll give you more details later but first of all there's a forensic job for you that you'll not have done before.'

He had Jenny's full attention. Her eyes were wide open in anticipation as he continued, 'Madeleine Smith of forensics will be here shortly. She'll be taking samples from clothing we seized yesterday. You can help her and sign the relevant productions and labels.'

'What does that entail?' she asked.

'Well, she'll vacuum samples from the pockets of the different items of clothing. The vacuum cleaner will have a filter that catches the dust. The dust will be put in containers, with the filter being changed for each item of clothing so that there is no cross-contamination. We're looking of course for traces of pesticides that may have been used on the estate.'

Bob continued, 'After that I'll get you to take some rifles to Dundee police station for test-firing.' Meantime I'm going to the SAC vetlab to get samples from the dead beasties we picked up yesterday. I'll also get a post-mortem examination done on a dead pine marten that's probably been deliberately drowned.'

Once Jenny and Joan had started on the vacuuming Bob headed to Bertha Park View to see Frank McArthur. Frank took the usual samples from the four rabbits, wood pigeon, buzzard and sparrowhawk and these were placed in containers, then labelled and signed.

Frank then carried out a post-mortem examination of the pine marten. He opened the body up, starting from the chin and finishing three quarters way along the underside. 'Have a look at this here Bob,' he said, pointing to the head, 'there's frothy foam in the nasal cavity and pharynx. There's also fluid in the trachea and main bronchi. These are all signs of drowning, though they are not always present. There are no other injuries to the pine marten. It's inhaled water while still alive and death is from drowning.'

Bob was photographing the signs that Frank was pointing out. 'Normally we'd need a second veterinary pathologist to speak to this but since the suspect has admitted drowning the pine marten your evidence should be enough. Could I get you to look at this fox now and see if you can estimate how long it has been dead?' Bob placed the fox up on the bench and Frank studied it.

'If it had been further into springtime Bob my estimate of how long it has been dead might have been easier with the presence of maggots and beetles. Meantime the most interesting external feature to age it are the eyes. The eyes are glazed over, are a blue/grey colour and well sunk into the head. In addition, rigor mortis, in an average situation, occurs approximately twelve hours after death and lasts approximately thirty six to forty eight hours. At that time the rigor relaxes and the body once again goes limp. This fox has gone beyond rigor and is now limp again.'

Frank opened up the fox. 'If you look here there is red watery fluid leaking into the body cavity. You wouldn't normally see this during the first twenty four hours. I couldn't tell you with accuracy how long it has been dead but with the signs we have I'd say at least two days.'

'Minimum two days is fine Frank. I think I have enough knowledge of the changes in the eyes of dead creatures to be able to corroborate that, so unless the fiscal wants corroboration from a second veterinary pathologist that will do in the meantime.'

Bob returned to the police station, by which time Jenny and Joan had completed their examination of the clothing. They all had a quick cup of tea before the next tasks. In Jenny's case this was to head off to Dundee with the three rifles for test firing. Before she left Bob told her, 'I'm going to get the application for a search warrant for the two badger diggers away to the specialist wildlife fiscal. By the time you come back I'll have everything in the car ready to set off to SASA. I'd like you to come along so you can see what is available there free of charge to Police Scotland for wildlife crime investigation.'

Jenny was back with Bob just after 1pm and they set off with a mix of sweepings, dust samples, knives, a stick, two game bags and ten various

CALLS FROM THE WILD

containers with different samples from the possible baits and victims recovered. In addition, they had a variety of blood samples and deer hair samples for Dr Jane Jackson, who was in charge of the wildlife DNA lab. This only left the snares that had been removed from the fence at Glen Garr Estate. They could be examined by forensics at Dundee but Bob wouldn't send them for human DNA testing until he had DNA samples for comparison from the two gamekeepers. These would be taken when they were arrested, but everything had to be done in sequence and they wouldn't be arrested until the result from all of the other tests had been done.

At SASA, Dorothy Abernethy seemed pleased to get a case that was just a bit more complex than normal to work on. 'We're actually not too burdened with work just now Bob so I'll be able to make a start on these in a couple of days. The gamebags will be the most awkward to do as I'll have to flush them out and test the resultant liquid for pesticides. I'll carry out the test for carbamates first and give you a verbal result. I'll test for other pesticides after that and give you the written report at that time.'

The next stop, in a different part of the same building, was Dr Jane Jackson's DNA lab. Wildlife DNA testing was one of SASA's newer facilities. Jane signed in the blood samples and the deer hair. 'These are more than adequate samples to work from,' she said. 'Especially the samples you've taken from the deer in the burn. It should be simple to tell if they're all from the same deer. We've considerably expanded our database of DNA from different species, though the deer and raptor species have been done for some time as they are the animals most likely to have crime committed against them. As usual I'll give you a call followed up in due course with a written result for court purposes.'

The drive back to Perth passed in no time. Jenny was fascinated with the variety of wildlife crime investigative work and bombarded Bob with questions. She was going to make a first-class wildlife crime officer. She'd no taste in music though. After listening to most of Bob's CD of Capercaillie, with the sensational voice of the lead singer, Karen Matheson, mostly singing in Gaelic, she declared a preference for jazz.

Chapter 18

The next couple of days gave Bob a bit of breathing space and were filled submitting intelligence to SID. He also had to return the £12,120 to Masterfield as the financial investigation officers couldn't justify keeping it and going for forfeiture as proceeds of crime.

Bob had spent time planning the search of the two badger diggers' houses. He had obtained search warrants for both addresses and they were now about to execute them. Two of the four men involved had yet to be identified but Bob had decided to move in on the two that were known. Not as early as the Loch Garr Operation but Bob wanted to be at their Dundee addresses by about 7.30am. There was no intelligence to suggest that the suspects were in employment, but Bob didn't want to take a chance.

The briefing was set for 7am at the Tayside Division's training centre at Baluniefield, situated in Douglas near where the suspects lived. The teams arrived and Bob took the briefing.

'There are two targets, Peter Ramsay Wilson and Clint Wayne McLeish. For Wilson's address there will be Jenny and I, the Dundee wildlife crime officer, Peter Bruce, plus DC Martin Moore. Martin is there partly because of the drugs interest in this target but will be helping with the search for animal welfare-related evidence. SSPCA inspectors Campbell Crawford and Sheila McInally will also attend and will concentrate on any dogs at the address. There is a strong chance that they will have to be removed for veterinary examination and possibly treatment. I've spoken to one of the vets in the Dundee practice, McInroy and Grant, who'll be at his surgery all day and is happy to look at the dogs.

'At McLeish's address will be two of the wildlife crime officers from Angus, PCs Maggie McPherson and Mike Timms, and PC Bruce Bannerman from NWCU. DC Cathy Smart from the drug squad will be there for the same reason as Martin in the first group. The two SSPCA inspectors will be Roddy Smith and Betty Morrison. Maggie, will you keep me updated with progress at McLeish's address please. At the conclusion of the search, unless they are awkward and we have to do it beforehand, the two suspects will be arrested and taken to Dundee police station. Remember that a shotgun was used in the badger incident, though not by any of these two. The ownership of the shotgun is not known but it's included on the warrant just in case.' He paused in case there were any questions, then continued, 'They're only a few streets away so let's get going.'

Entry was easy to Wilson's house. He had still been in bed and answered the door wearing only a pair of grey underpants, which looked as if their original colour had been white. Bob cautioned him and explained the purpose of their search. As they were entering the house Bob asked, 'Who else is in the house Pete?'

'Just my two cousins. They're from Stirling but they're here for a couple of days.'

PC Peter Bruce and DC Martin Moore went with Wilson to an upstairs bedroom to allow him to get some clothes on while Bob and Jenny went into the next-door bedroom where two men, alerted by the sounds of talking, were nearly fully clothed. The smell of cannabis in the room was overpowering. Bob immediately recognised one of the men as the third man in the video. He wondered if the other man would have been the fourth, the man who was unseen but who shot the badger.

He addressed the man he'd recognised, who looked the younger of the two. 'What's your name?'

'Mitchell Clark, I get called Mitch,' he answered quite pleasantly.

Bob noted Mitch's full details. He was surprised that he was twenty years old; he looked much younger. He then addressed the other man. 'What's your name?'

It was a different story this time. The second man was aggressive and refused to give his name and address. Bob had read the man's mood and was ready for this. 'This place stinks of cannabis. I'm going to search you both under section twenty three of the Misuse of Drugs Act 1971.' Addressing Mr Nasty, Bob asked, 'Have you anything on you that you shouldn't have?'

Mr Nasty was silent.

Bob began a search of his clothing, removing an expensive mobile phone from his back pocket then a tobacco tin from his side pocket. 'What's this then?' Bob asked, holding up a small block of brown resin that was in the tin along with tobacco and some cigarette papers.

'I could arrest you right now and take you to the police station. That might yet happen, but I can defer it if you give me your details now.'

Mr Nasty quickly lost much of his spark, 'Alastair Black, I'm Mitch's cousin,' he said, pointing at Mitch. 'I'm Pete's cousin as well.' He gave his age as twenty five. Both had addresses in Stirling.

'How did you get here from Stirling Alastair? Bob asked.

'We both came in my car. It's outside on the street.'

Having got Black's details, Bob searched Mitch, but his search was negative. 'I've never used any kind of drugs,' he said when Bob was finished with him.

Bob addressed the two suspects, 'We have a warrant to search Pete's house for anything that might be connected with badger digging or animal welfare offences. We'll be keeping your phone meantime.' Turning now to his colleague, 'Jenny, we might as well start with the search in this room while we're here.'

The room was sparsely furnished, with little more than a couple of single beds. Jenny was down on her knees and reaching under one of the beds. 'Bob, look at this.' She was carefully pulling out a double-barrelled shotgun that had been covered by a sheet. Jenny was well acquainted with guns, having regularly handled them when she was checking firearms against firearm and shotgun certificates. 'At least it's not loaded,' she said as she moved the lever to the side to allow the gun to open.

Mitch was now whiter than the sheet that had seconds before covered the gun. 'That's nothing to do with me.' He was looking in desperation at cousin Alastair for some response.

'It's mine,' admitted Alastair. Black was showing a modicum of decency, though he'd shown none to the badger, thought Bob.

'Where are the cartridges?' Bob demanded.

'They're further back under the bed, under another sheet,' was the reply.

Jenny reached under the bed again and this time produced a red cardboard cartridge box of Eley brand cartridges, No. 4 shot size. The box originally would have held twenty five cartridges but now only contained five.

Bob took Jenny aside. 'We need to get Mitch and Black detained and down to the police station, but we'll need to search Black's car first while he's here with the keys. We'll formally arrest and handcuff them and do that now. Could you arrange for a van to come and pick them up while I quickly speak to Peter Bruce next door?'

Bob called Peter out into the hallway and updated him on their progress. They had found personal cannabis on their suspect when they searched him but nothing so far in the bedroom that helped with the badger case.

The search of the car was negative and as Bob and Jenny finished the search the van arrived to take the two arrested men away. With just one suspect left in the house supervision and containment would be much easier.

While the three police officers were continuing the search of the house Bob went out to the back garden to see how the two SSPCA inspectors were getting on. Now that there was sufficient light Campbell Crawford was photographing the kennels that held two dogs, a brown terrier and a lurcher. He gave Bob an update. 'The kennels as you'll see are pretty dirty.

The lurcher is really thin and I'd say there will be an animal welfare charge there. The wee brown Lakeland terrier is in better physical condition but it has recent damage to the underside of its jaw where the skin is badly torn and the bone is exposed. It's certainly not been treated professionally as the skin would have been stitched back on.'

Bob was well aware that this type of damage was typical of that inflicted by a badger. 'I can see that Campbell. There's some scarring around its face as well which is no doubt old damage from encounters with badgers. Would you take them both to the vet please. He'll certainly need to do something to help the poor wee terrier. You'll get decent photographs of the injuries there under better lighting.'

Bob re-joined his colleagues in the house. They had taken possession of Pete Wilson's laptop and had also found a book entitled *Badger Digging with Terriers*, by an author David Harcombe. 'Why the hell would anyone be allowed to publish a book that gives advice on breaking the law?' Bob asked, mostly to himself.

'We'll need to search his car now.' He looked at Wilson, 'Is yours the grey Subaru Forester in the street next to your cousin's car Pete?'

'Yeah, the keys are beside the sink in the kitchen,' he answered somewhat reluctantly.

Bob and Jenny made a search of the car and returned to the house with several items of interest. Bob showed Wilson a spade with traces of blood and a large knife. 'Are they yours Pete?'

Pete Wilson was well aware of the trouble he was now in. 'No comment.'

When both search teams were finished, and all four suspects were languishing in cells at Dundee police station, the officers met up again at Baluniefield. Bob gave an update of how his team had progressed. Maggie McPherson then spoke on behalf of her team.

'McLeish is a complete brute. He wouldn't let us in but he'll need to be buying a new door now. We arrested him and put him in handcuffs right from the start. He'd a bit of personal cannabis on him when we searched him. His wife is a poor soul, obviously terrified of him. There is also a child of about a year old in the house. The wife told me quietly when McLeish wasn't about that she was making plans to leave with the kid. I'll make sure social services are aware of the situation.

'We took possession of McLeish's laptop and mobile phone. Would you believe he had a framed photo on the wall of him holding a dead fox in one hand and holding his poor black Patterdale terrier by the scruff of the neck in the other hand? It's not on the wall now, it's in the back of my car.

'His car was the most interesting. We took possession of a spade and a knife, which seem to be common tools for badger diggers. He also had a wire crate and a coal sack which were both bloodstained. I suspect at some stage he's taken a live badger or fox away to face a horrific end.'

Maggie stopped momentarily to gather her thoughts, then continued. 'The SSPCA inspectors are away to the vet with two dogs. McLeish had a black Patterdale terrier, maybe the same one as in the photo with only the one eye. The bottom jaw had recently been ripped open, part of the gum was missing, and you could see the roots of its teeth. It was in a terrible state. The other dog was a massive bull lurcher, a horrible looking thing but surprisingly it was quite friendly. It had an abscess on the side of its face which looked like it needed urgent treatment.'

Bob had been taking notes, 'Thanks Maggie. I'll see if I can get one of the SSPCA inspectors or the vet on the phone. We could do with knowing the state of the dogs before we interview our four detainees. We could do with the dogs either being signed over to the SSPCA or the court forfeiting them. I'll see if SSPCA can kennel them meantime.'

Bob looked at Jenny now. 'You and I will interview the three detainees from our search. Maggie and Mike, would you interview McLeish? The others are free to go now. Make sure you've signed labels for everything that you've taken and many thanks for your help. Could you submit statements as early as possible, and I'll give you an update in due course?'

When the duty solicitor arrived Bob and Jenny decided to interview Mitchell Clark first since he was the weakest link in the group. He didn't seem to be into badger-related crime as deep as the others and, unusually, didn't want the solicitor present. But Mitch had a surprise for them when he was interviewed.

'Look, I didn't come to Dundee expecting to be involved in this badger stuff. I knew that my cousin Pete was into cruelty to animals and I was kinda dragged into going along. I'd no idea it was going to be as bad as it turned out to be, especially when I saw that Alastair had taken along a shotgun.

'Tell us exactly what happened that day Mitch, who did what,' Bob said quietly.

'We went to a wood near a big antique centre not far from Dundee on the road to Perth. The badgers' hole was near a burn. Clint did most of the digging. Pete was filming everything on his phone and when Clint hauled the badger out of the hole Alastair shot it as it was running away. It wasn't dead and the two terriers and that bull lurcher ran after it and began to bite it. Clint then whacked the badger on the head with a spade, but I think it was dead by that time anyway.

Tears were welling up in Mitch's eyes and he dabbed them with a dirty hankie. 'What do you think will happen to us at court?'

Bob didn't think that Mitch would get as severe a punishment as the others but wasn't prepared to tell him that at this stage. 'Most times folk convicted of badger digging get a jail sentence.'

Mitch's complexion went even more pale and he thought for a minute. 'If I could tell you something about a drugs stash do you think I might get off?'

'I can't second-guess what the fiscal might say Mitch. It also depends on what you might have to tell us, but I'd be prepared to speak to the fiscal if it was worthwhile.'

'If it was to find a kilo block of cannabis and some bags of speed?'

'I'd certainly speak with the fiscal. I can't say you'd get off but you might just get a fine.' Bob gave Mitch some thinking time before he answered.

'Pete has a big block of cannabis and a couple of dozen deals of speed in a poly bag in the garden. He's dug a shallow hole under a bin, put a bit of plywood across and the bin's on top. It's hidden under there.'

If this was true the fiscal might well go lightly on Mitch, Bob thought.' okay we'll see if we can get it and I'll let you know. If it's as you say I'll see what the fiscal says.'

When the officers were finished the four men had been charged with various offences under the Protection of Badgers Act 1992. Peter Wilson and Clint McLeish had additional charges under the Animal Health and Welfare (Scotland) Act 2006, the most serious of which were causing an animal fight to take place and keeping dogs for the purpose of fights. The other two were charged with taking part in an animal fight. Alastair Black had no shotgun certificate and was charged with that offence.

Bob made the decision to have the four liberated on an undertaking to appear at court later, though wanted them kept in custody until the drugs stash could be recovered from Pete Wilson's garden. Keeping Jenny up to date he said, 'There are still enquiries to be completed here yet so there's no point in keeping them for court tomorrow. We'll need to get the spades, knives, wire cage and coal bag away to SASA for DNA testing. We'll also need to get the laptops and mobile phone examined. I'll have a look tomorrow to see if I can find the sett that has been dug as well. You can report the case to the fiscal, I'll give you a hand with it.'

'Bob, I'm off tomorrow but I'd be happy to come out on my day off to help you look for the sett. Now that I know how to get to SASA I could maybe help by taking the productions to Dr Jane Jackson.'

Bob jumped at the chance, 'That would be great Jenny. Now for the last job, to tell Martin Moore and his drug squad colleagues where they can get a good drug recovery.'

Chapter 19

Jenny was in the office even before Bob the following morning. They studied the map and identified the burn that Mitch had been speaking about. They were of the view that the easiest way to find the sett was to follow the burn down, one on either side. It was a miserable day of rain but both officers were well equipped for the foulest of weather. They had the foresight to appreciate that they may not be able to cross the burn due to the rainfall, so Jenny took a spare camera so that she could work independently from Bob.

The plan worked, and less than an hour after they started Bob had a call on his radio from Jenny. 'I've found the sett Bob, it's near to a single oak tree which you'll easily see from your side. There are five entrances so far as I can see. Two of the entrances have been dug. At one entrance they've gone down really deep, about five feet down. This might be the one in the film on Peter Wilson's phone where the badger was pulled out.'

Bob was pleased that they didn't have to spend the whole morning looking for the sett. 'Are there any footprints or any physical evidence around the sett Jenny?'

'No, I've had a look and there's nothing. If there had been any footprints probably the rain has spoiled them. I've looked in the hole that's been dug and there's no trace of any blood or hair or anything that could link in with the dog.'

'Could you have a look around the area and see if you can find a spent cartridge?'

'Okay, I'll get back to you shortly.'

Ten minutes later Jenny came back on the radio sounding quite excited, 'Bob I've found a red cartridge. The brass case says Eley and the red plastic casing has a number 4 on it. I've bagged it.'

'That's great Jenny. The more evidence the better. We don't want the buggers getting off.' He suddenly remembered radio etiquette; he shouldn't have said buggers. Bugger it, he was pleased at the result anyway. It had been a successful morning and it was just after 9 o'clock. Some folk wouldn't even be up yet, he thought.

Back at the office he helped Jenny load her car. She would go via Divisional Headquarters in Dundee and drop off the laptops and mobile phones for analysis by the technicians. She would then continue via the Tay Bridge on to SASA and hand over the spades, knives, wire cage and sack to Jane Jackson for DNA testing. Just before she left, Bob answered a call on his mobile.

'Bob, this is Martin, Martin Moore. We got a drugs warrant yesterday and went back to Pete Wilson's address. Eureka, exactly where you told me we recovered not one but two kilo blocks of cannabis resin and fourteen £10 bags of amphetamine. Wilson didn't have a good day yesterday.'

'That's fantastic Martin. So many criminals involved in offences against wildlife are involved in other types of crime.'

Bob was barely back in his office when his phone rang. 'I don't want to give my name,' said a man with an English accent, 'but you should take a look at Long Ridge Farm in Glen Clova. The chap there who does the rabbit trapping is a Neil Crombie. He lives in a cottage just as you go up the farm road. He's unemployed and only catches the rabbits on the farm part-time. He goes on drinking binges for three or four days at a time and when he's on a binge he's not checking the traps and the rabbits starve to death.'

'Do you know what kind of traps he's using?' asked Bob.

'They're drop traps. I found one just now that was full of dead rabbits. There was one still alive. I lifted it out and it hopped away but it was skeletal and probably won't make it. The trap was at the south side of a wood above the farm. There's a big rocky crag in the middle of the wood. You can identify it by that, but all of the places where there are big numbers of rabbits are netted and there's rabbit boxes round all of these netted areas.'

'Thanks for that,' replied Bob, 'I'll have it looked at as a matter of urgency.'

Bob had intended to have one of the wildlife crime officers from the county of Angus take on this investigation but when he checked with the control room none were on duty. He decided to take along one of the beat officers if one could be freed and phoned the duty inspector to arrange this. The inspector was helpful and said that Bob could have a brand-new probationary officer to go with him, PC Matt Scobie, and to pick him up at Kirriemuir police station. Bob checked the map for the location of the farm, then set off for Kirriemuir.

Matt Scobie turned out to be a tall gangly chap in his early twenties. He had spent all his life in Edinburgh and seemed to know little about country life. He would be a round peg in a square hole, at least for a while, in what was the most rural station in Angus.

'So, what are drop traps?' asked Matt.

Bob hoped the next question wouldn't be 'what are rabbits?' but he began to explain how drop traps worked. 'When rabbits are in high numbers they can cause a lot of damage to crops, and of course eat a lot of grass as well. It's often worth fencing them in but leaving holes in the net at intervals. Where these holes are left a wooden, fibre glass or metal box is buried in the ground with a wooden tunnel running over the top of the box. The roof of the buried box is a treadle so that a rabbit crossing it would slip off it into the box. The roof is prevented from tipping until the rabbits get used to going through the tunnel. It can be locked with a bolt and padlock but sometimes just a large stone is placed on it to prevent it tipping. The traps are normally only used for a few days at a time then made inoperative with the bolt or rock till the next time it's required. They're very effective and it's not uncommon with a high volume of rabbits for a box to catch over twenty rabbits in a night.'

Bob continued the lesson to the interested young officer, 'If the boxes are operating but not being checked the rabbits have no food or water and lose condition very quickly, eventually starving to death.'

At the farm the officers had to pass the suspect's cottage and saw that the curtains were still drawn. Bob easily identified the wood a couple of fields away and parked at the farm. There was no-one around so the officers set off up the hill. When they reached the fence between the two fields Bob put his left hand on a fence post, his right foot on the top strand of barbed wire and hopped easily over the fence. He looked round expecting Matt, who was taller and younger than him, to be over the fence but Matt was totally unable to master the technique of climbing a fence. He tried several times but gave up after he jabbed his hand on one of the barbs. There were plenty of training courses in the police but none for climbing fences.

'Matt, I see a gate along there a bit. Go along and either climb the gate or go through it. I'll carry on and you can catch up.'

Bob made for a corner of the wood and started to go clockwise round it. Matt caught up as they reached the first drop box. The stone that should have been used to prevent the treadle operating had been placed to the side so the box was in catching mode. Bob lifted the inspection hatch and gasped. 'There are six or seven rabbits in here. They all look to be dead. I'll get some photos before we take them out.'

Bob removed seven dead rabbits from the drop box and laid them side by side on the ground for another photo. The rabbits were extremely thin, little more than half the weight that they should have been. He placed the stone in position so that no other rabbits would be caught, and they continued round the wood intending to collect the seven rabbits at the end.

The circuit of the wood showed that there were eight drop boxes in all.

All were in the catching mode and the officers took a total of thirty five dead rabbits and eight barely alive rabbits out of the drop traps, taking photos as they went but leaving the dead rabbits beside the traps.

When they returned to the first drop box Bob put the seven rabbits into two evidence bags and they shared the load back towards the car.

'Why are we taking these seven rabbits?' Matt asked.

'I want a veterinary pathologist to have a look at them to prove they have died of starvation rather than disease. I don't think for a minute there is any doubt about that but the charge under the Animal Health and Welfare (Scotland) Act will relate to causing unnecessary suffering. We need to prove that.'

'And why are you not taking the dead rabbits from the other drop boxes?'

Bob was pleased that Matt was showing interest. 'There's no point in taking all of them; we have photos and you can corroborate their poor condition. A sample from one drop box will be enough.'

At the farm they were met by the farmer. When Bob explained the position to him the farmer was furious. 'I should never have allowed that bloody drunk anywhere near the drop traps. I did see him up at that wood last week but come to think of it I've never seen him since. I'm sorry about this but that will be the last. His house is a bloody pig sty and this is the last straw. He's getting his marching orders.'

'Where else on the farm are there drop boxes?' Bob asked.

'There are another four netted areas with boxes. Do you want to go round them or will I get my son to do that and sort them out?'

'If you could get your son to empty and secure them that would be helpful. We have enough evidence here. We'll see Neil Crombie on the way past and interview him.'

Crombie was reeking of drink when Bob and Matt interviewed him. He admitted that he had set the drop traps but couldn't remember when, only that it was a Monday. This was now Thursday, so the chances are that many of the rabbits had been in the boxes for nine or ten days; little wonder they had starved to death. The officers charged him with the animal welfare offence and he promised he would plead guilty. In Bob's experience many suspects say that; that is until they speak to a solicitor. A solicitor will make more money if a case is dragged out. That wastes everyone's time and it really pissed him off.

The officers headed to Kirriemuir, back to PC Matt Scobie's base. Bob was thinking about the shambolic mess in Crombie's house. Matt was quiet, then asked, 'That's a catchy Scottish tune you're whistling Bob. I've never heard it before. What's it called?'

'*The Wind that Shakes the Piggery,*' replied Bob, laughing.

Bob dropped into Frank McArthur on the way back to Perth. Frank looked at all of the rabbits and did a quick post-mortem examination on two of them. 'Definitely starvation Bob,' he said with obvious anger at the cruelty involved. 'No sign of any disease and there has been very little lasting snow over the winter so the rabbits should have been in very good condition. Look at this one here, it's a doe with five young rabbits inside it. They've only been developing for about half of the twenty-eight-day gestation period. Very unlikely a rabbit would conceive in such poor condition.'

Back in the office Bob checked his emails. One was from a firearms enquiry officer. Loch Garr Estate had started another two gamekeepers and the firearm enquiry officer was due to check their firearms and their security in the next few days. Nigel Roberts was clearly spending big bucks to make the estate a high intensity driven grouse shoot. That was bad news for any wildlife other than red grouse.

Chapter 20

Bob yawned as he switched on his office computer in the morning. He'd had a poor sleep wondering about how he could get evidence to get Roberts to court. Liz complained in the morning that she kept getting wakened up because of his restlessness. Even Toby, in his basket in a corner of the bedroom and normally raring to go, slept on to try to catch up on lost sleep. It was as if Bob had anticipated the bombshell that awaited him when he got to work.

DI Sneddon had left a note on Bob's desk for him to look in to see him. 'There's been a letter of complaint from Nigel Robert's solicitor. He is claiming it was completely out of order for so many police officers to descend on his estate and his gamekeepers for pesticide abuse matters which they claim were nothing to do with them and which they totally deny.' That didn't bother Bob unduly as he knew the operation and the number of officers were justified, but the next part of the complaint was upsetting.

The DI continued, 'The solicitor is saying that Masterfield claims that when the money was counted when it was taken from the gun room it was at least £500 short of what it should have been. He claims money had gone missing between when it was found by the police and when it was counted. He says that he didn't realise till later. I don't believe that for a minute Bob, but the matter will need to be referred to Professional Standards. Could you prepare an operational statement and I'll get the others who were involved with the money at that stage to do likewise. No doubt you'll all be interviewed by Professional Standards once they read the statements.'

Though Bob knew that complaints were often made to muddy the waters and to make the police look disorganised and dishonest, they did cast unjustified suspicion on him and his fellow-officers. They now had to try to prove their innocence. This was going to vex him until it was resolved. He tried to put it out of his mind while he continued his investigation against Roberts and his keepers.

Bob met DI Sneddon later in the day. 'I've been studying the intelligence on SID relating to Roberts,' Bob began. 'Until recently he was advisor to five grouse moors in Scotland. According to NWCU, he advised on at least another two in England. He now owns Loch Garr Estate and is trying to buy another in Inverness-shire. When you look at the intelligence listed against the estates collectively, the number of shot raptors, trapped raptors, poisoned raptors, and poisoned baits that have been found is horrendous. Add to that formerly active badger setts that are no longer occupied and there's a clear course of conduct throughout these estates to eliminate any species, whether protected or otherwise, that interfere with producing large bags of grouse. The additional volume of profit for the landowner, and presumably Roberts in his former occupation, is most definitely proceeds of crime. If that could be proved either he, the landowners or both would have to pay back hundreds of thousands. He is probably the most relevant person to be targeted under POCA as he is the common link throughout.'

Jonathan cut in, 'I agree Bob, but I don't see an easy way of estimating the financial value resulting from killing protected species, and of course we'd have to prove that he was responsible for this.'

'I think that's the crux of the problem sir. We need to prove his responsibility, either through vicarious liability or even conspiracy. Conspiracy needs more than one person so we'd need to look at his close involvement in giving instructions to act illegally to at least one of the head keepers, and the head keeper agreeing to the demands.'

'In theory that sounds fine Bob, but how do you suggest we achieve that?'

'I think we need to trawl through all the intelligence to look for options to convert intelligence to evidence. The best place to start is with keepers who formerly worked on the estates he had links with.' Bob was considering all of the raptors that had been found dead. Worse, he was thinking of the much greater number that had been killed and never found. He realised that he hated Roberts and all that he stood for, and of course memories came flooding back of his one and only encounter with him. 'Fuck knows why, but many keepers think that working under Roberts' direction is a plum job. If they've been kicked out they're likely to hold a grudge. If so, we might be able to persuade them to speak up, that is of course if they've been privy to any illegal instructions from Roberts.'

'How many keepers, or maybe ex-keepers, do you think we might be talking about?'

'There was always a turnover of young keepers, with some being moved to other estates by Roberts. There will probably be a dozen that have left for whatever reason, plus the older keepers that were kicked out shortly after he became involved with a new estate. That's probably, at a guess, at least twenty. All of them can be traced through firearms licensing, but I know some from Scotland have gone back to England.' Bob was in his stride,

'I know we can't dictate what forces in England do but I'd hope Police Scotland might be up for this.'

'And who'd do the interviewing Bob?'

'For Scotland I think we'd need two teams of two officers, a CID officer and a wildlife crime officer. They'd need to have a roving commission, including going over the border to chase up keepers that worked here at some stage, maybe even linking up with investigative support officers from NWCU in England to do this.'

Jonathan seemed supportive, though Bob knew the agreement would need to come from much higher up the chain of command, probably at least at Assistant Chief Constable level. He thought for a minute. 'I'll start with the Divisional Commander. He was pleased with the result of the recent Loch Garr operation and I know he spoke of it to the ACC. If we can get him on side, he might speak with ACC Hugh McIntosh in Glasgow who you know is the lead for Scotland on wildlife crime. Before he can be persuaded he might need a target profile and an analysis of the intelligence. Maybe NWCU would be prepared to put an analyst on to that.'

'Thanks sir. If they get the chance I'm sure NWCU will do a good job. As you well know, this is where it's crucial that officers always submit intelligence to the system. Some are bloody hopeless at that and I know one wco who just keeps intelligence in his head. Missing intelligence could be what lets a proposal like this down.'

Bob was pleased that there was a ray of hope, but it was no more than that.

Chapter 21

Three weeks had passed since the letter of complaint from Robert's solicitor. All the officers involved in the search of Mastefield's house had been interviewed by Professional Standards. All were convinced the allegation of missing money was just to stir up trouble but there had been no final word yet from Professional Standards, so they were all still under suspicion. Most police officers go through this at some time in their service and it makes some physically ill.

There had been no word either on what ACC Hugh McIntosh thought of a Scotland-wide – or better still, UK-wide – operation to gather evidence against Bob's nemesis. Maybe it was taking longer for NWCU to prepare a target file; or maybe they hadn't been asked. In the intervening time Bob saw from the intelligence on SID that in other parts of Scotland three further poisoned raptors and two poisoned baits had been picked up on estates which Roberts had formerly worked with. At one of these estates two buzzards had also been found dead just outside the boundary. When x-rayed lead shot was clearly visible in both. All of these incidents were under investigation by police colleagues.

Bob was frustrated, though not surprised, that no-one had been charged with any of these crimes. He thought of the pair of peregrines on Loch Garr Estate and wondered if they were on eggs. He would love to have set up a surveillance camera on the nest site but of course the law said he couldn't do that without the permission of the landowner. 'That's a lot of fucking good.' he said aloud.

'You talking to yourself again Bob?' Shirley Deans shouted over.

'Sorry Shirley, but can you believe that the police have to get permission from a landowner to go on to his land to set up a covert camera to catch a criminal? A criminal that you suspect is his gamekeeper. He either gives you permission and tips off the gamekeeper or tells you to bugger off. How is that in the public interest?' He groaned, 'Sorry, I'm not looking for an answer to that.'

Bob had gathered together the various productions to take to the court for the trial against the Donaldson hare coursers, which was due to take place that morning. He wouldn't have to wait in court as police officers can usually get on with work as long as they are a phone call away.

He dropped off the productions with the fiscal and noted that the farmers from the three different farms were waiting in the witness room. 'Good morning guys,' he said cheerily as he popped his head into the witness room. 'Hopefully we'll get an early start and get this over with today.'

None of the three smiled back. Tom Burt from Fingowan Farm was looking particularly fed up. 'It's a great sunny morning, the first dry day for about a week and I'm sitting here when I could be getting my last field of oats into the ground. It's not your fault Bob but sometimes I think it's better just to frighten these buggers off and not call the police. We could be stuck here for the whole day, and it could be pissing with rain tomorrow.'

'I understand how the three of you must feel. It's a good case so we'll just have to hope that they get a decent penalty.' Bob never let on that the fiscal had told him that there were seven other trials scheduled and if most of the accused in these trials maintained a not guilty plea the farmers might find themselves back sitting in the witness room again and losing another day's work.

Bob was back in the office when his phone rang just after 1pm. 'Hi Bob.' He recognised the voice of Meg Runciman, the specialist fiscal. 'There was a plea offered by the two defence solicitors just before lunch time. Archie Donaldson, the big fellow, pleaded guilty to charges 1 and 3, those were the incidents at Fingowan Farm and Highgrove Farm. His cousin Cyril pleaded guilty to charge 3. I accepted the pleas. Archie was fined £800 and Cyril was fined £400.'

She paused. 'The sheriff was considering disqualifying both from driving for using their vehicles in the commission of a crime but their solicitors claimed that as travellers with families, this would cause them undue hardship. They said they went berry picking and tattie dressing in different parts of Scotland. One said that his client, Archie, went to the Hebrides to gather freshwater pearl mussels. The sheriff's eyebrows raised and there was an audible gasp from someone in the public benches, but Archie quickly whispered in panic to his solicitor that it was whelks and cockles they gathered. The sheriff relented on the disqualification but they certainly got a fright.'

Bob had a snigger at the mention of freshwater pearl mussels, which might indeed have been accurate. 'Well, it's not too bad a sentence Meg. It's just a pity they didn't change their plea yesterday and save the witnesses wasting time coming to court. Do the witnesses know the outcome?'

'Yes, I went into the witness room and told them. I think they were thankful they only lost half a day. One muttered something about going away now to sow his oats. God knows what he meant by that.'

Bob returned to his admin work but had a call later in the afternoon from Willie McLaren, the tenant of Hilltop Farm on Loch Garr Estate. 'I'm sorry to be a pest Bob but I thought you should know things are getting pretty bad for me here. They're keen to take the farm back in hand and have offered me a deal to move out. I've told them I'm not going, and they can't put me out as I've still got a good chunk of my tenancy agreement to run. Two of the sheds are old and either need re-roofed or replaced but they are refusing to do any repairs, yet they're spending thousands on doing up houses for the gamekeepers.'

Bob could hear from Willie's voice that he was upset. 'The keepers are idiots. They fly around in their new Land Rovers and quads and have no respect for the in-bye grass fields, tracking over them on even the wettest of days. I got a blackfaced ewe the other day caught by the front leg in a fox snare. It had probably been in for at least a day and had dislocated its leg. I'd to shoot it. It had a lamb which I've now either to rear as an orphan or try to twin on to another ewe. There's no way they should be setting snares on the hill when the sheep are there.'

'I'm sorry to hear all that Willie. I know hill farmers have a hard enough life without all this grief. We've an investigation ongoing just now and might manage to get a court case but if one of the Loch Garr keepers is convicted, he'll just be replaced by a young keeper who is equally malleable and obedient.'

'And I'm sure they're still shooting deer at night,' said Willie. 'I found a shot red deer hind on the hill yesterday. It wasn't there the day before. I can't prove which one shot it or that it was shot at night but we're well into the close season for hinds. They'll be calving in a week or two. This one was shot at the top of the front leg, which was shattered, so they're not great shots.'

'I'll record that as a crime Willie, but I'll not come out to see the deer as we have plenty of evidence of other deer being shot illegally. If you're able to photograph it and send me the photo that would be helpful.'

'I'll do that. I'll be back up there in the early evening to check there's no more sheep in snares.'

Bob felt heart sorry for Willie and his family and wished there was more that he could do. It was a David and Goliath situation. The unfairness was that Goliath had money. Lots of money.

Chapter 22

Several forensic results were now coming in relating to the Loch Garr Estate investigation. The ballistics experts at force headquarters had phoned Bob a few days earlier to say that they were really interested in comparing the bullet removed from the young stag in the burn to the keepers' three rifles submitted. The report now in front of him confirmed that the bullet had been fired from the .270 rifle belonging to Masterfield. That was a great start, but it was still necessary to prove who pulled the trigger, and who flung the deer in the burn.

There was also a long report in front of him from Dorothy Abernethy at the chemistry lab at SASA. It made for very interesting reading so he took it to DI Jonathan Sneddon's office.

'I was just about to come and see you Bob,' the DI said. 'The DCI from Professional Standards is just off the phone. They are satisfied that Masterfield's allegation of stolen money is false. They're sure it has been a malicious complaint emanating from Roberts but unfortunately they're unable to prove that, otherwise they'd be charging him and Masterfield with public mischief. That would have been a serious charge and most likely would have been a jail term for both of them.'

'The bastard put us under suspicion of a serious theft,' spat Bob. 'As you know sir complaints like that can sometimes ruin an officer's career, even if they are false. And more so if there's not a satisfactory conclusion.'

The DI nodded in agreement. 'Anyway, I'm glad that you and the other officers have been cleared by Professional Standards. It demonstrates Roberts' complete lack of scruples. A rich man who doesn't like interference with anything he does. Are those some reports you want to show me?'

They read Dorothy Abernethy's report together.

BIRDS AND BAITS
Buzzard found buried on Loch Garr Estate: traces of carbofuran,
isofenphos and bendiocarb found in gullet and liver
Rabbit bait found buried on Loch Garr Estate: traces of carbofuran,
isofenphos and bendiocarb in cuts on back legs
Tub of dark blue crystals found buried on Loch Garr Estate: contained a
mix of carbofuran, isofenphos and bendiocarb

Red kite found under tree on Hillside Farm: traces of carbofuran, isofenphos and bendiocarb found in crop, liver and kidneys

Buzzard 1 found on Hillside Farm: traces of carbofuran, isofenphos and bendiocarb found in crop, liver and kidneys

Buzzard 2 found on Hillside Farm: traces of carbofuran, isofenphos and bendiocarb found in gullet

Rabbit bait found on Loch Garr Estate: traces of carbofuran, isofenphos and bendiocarb in cuts on back legs

Rabbit 1 found during operation on Loch Garr Estate: no traces found

Rabbit 2 found during operation on Loch Garr Estate: traces of carbofuran, isofenphos and bendiocarb found in body cavity

Rabbit 3 found during operation on Loch Garr Estate: no traces found

Rabbit 4 found during operation on Loch Garr Estate: traces of carbofuran, isofenphos and bendiocarb found in body cavity

Buzzard found beside rabbit 4: traces of carbofuran, isofenphos and bendiocarb found in gullet, liver and kidneys

Woodpigeon found during operation on Loch Garr Estate: traces of carbofuran, isofenphos and bendiocarb found in cuts to breast

Sparrowhawk found during operation on Loch Garr Estate: traces of carbofuran, isofenphos and bendiocarb found in gullet, crop and liver

HOOVERINGS

Jacket 1 – Masterfield: no traces found

Jacket 2 – Masterfield: traces of carbofuran and isofenphos found in right-hand pocket

Jacket 3 – Masterfield: no traces found

Trousers – worn by Masterfield: traces of carbofuran, isofenphos and bendiocarb found in left and right-hand pockets

Jacket 1 – Brock: no traces found

Jacket 2 – worn by Brock: no traces found

Trousers – worn by Brock: no traces found

VEHICLES AND CONTENTS

Land Rover at Masterfield's address:

Sweepings from floor at driver's side: traces of carbofuran, isofenphos and bendiocarb

Sweepings from floor at passenger's side: no traces found

Sweepings from rear compartment floor: traces of carbofuran, isofenphos and bendiocarb

Game bag: traces of carbofuran, isofenphos and bendiocarb; traces of chloralose

Knife: traces of chloralose

Quad bike at Masterfield's address:

Sweepings from wooden box on rear of quad: no traces found

Land Rover at Brock's address:
Sweepings from floor at driver's side: no traces found
Sweepings from floor at passenger's side: no traces found
Sweepings from rear compartment floor: no traces found
Game bag: no traces found
Knife 1: traces of chloralose
Knife 2: no traces found
Stick: no traces found
Quad bike at Brocks's address:
Sweepings from wooden box on rear of quad: no traces found

Both officers were amazed at the results. Jonathan Sneddon was first to speak. 'Interesting that both keepers have items with traces of chloralose. Were there any chloralose baits found, or victims?'

'No, nothing with chloralose sir. It's most often used in colder weather, though it was still just early spring when we found most of the dead raptors and baits. They'd maybe been using it earlier and changed to carbofuran. Maybe it had come from their previous estates. I'm just guessing.'

'Why is chloralose used more in cold weather?'

'It kills by lowering the body temperature and the victim effectively dies of hypothermia. Once or twice birds have been picked up that are almost dead but have fully recovered when they are warmed up.'

'Do you think there is enough evidence there to nail them?'

'Proving the link between the baits and victims and the traces is always the hardest part. Even if they give no comment interviews when we interview them it's still worth reporting the case to the fiscal. There have been similar cases in the past that have been marked no proceedings, but the traces in the pockets of clothing being worn by Masterfield might swing it in our favour. What we haven't tried is a charge of possession of the pesticides. I know it's miniscule amounts but if the sweepings were put in water and someone drank it, I suspect they could become very ill.' Bob added, 'There's also the tub of the carbofuran cocktail that Masterfield gave to Albert Curtis, but of course he doesn't want to give a statement.'

'I'm just wondering if the common law crime of conspiracy might be relevant for Masterfield and Brock,' mused the DI. 'Let's see if what they did constitutes conspiracy. The definition is roughly *when two or more people get together and plan to carry out a course of conduct which will necessarily involve the commission of an offence.* In other words, more than one person agrees to do something which will involve committing a crime. I doubt at this stage if we can prove that they did conspire, which is a pity.'

'They were shooting deer at night and out of season,' Bob added, 'so I think we'll need to look at that offence under the Deer (Scotland) Act 1996. There's the evidence of Jock Scott being there when Masterfield shot a deer at night. That's uncorroborated so far. Only one witness is required under the Act for being in possession of a deer taken illegally but since they don't seem to pick them up we'd struggle to even prove constructive possession. The exception being, of course, the deer that was dumped in the burn. The DNA report is also here from Jane Jackson, let's see what it says.'

Bob flicked through the papers till he came to Jane's report and scanned through it. 'This report is terrific. There is confirmation that blood and hair in the back of Masterfield's Land Rover is from a red deer and that it matches the samples that I took from the deer in the burn. We now have that deer shot by Masterfield's .270 rifle and at some stage between being shot and dumped in the burn, being in the back of his Land Rover. We're just a fraction short yet of being able to prove Masterfield shot it but I think we have enough to prove illegal possession since it was taken out of season.'

'But still not enough yet to prove who dumped it in the burn,' added Jonathan. He paused for a few seconds while he reached into his drawer and brought out a box of biscuits, 'When are you thinking of arresting the two keepers?' He munched a biscuit while awaiting an answer and shoved the box across to Bob.

'Well, this is Tuesday. I think we could go for them on Friday. Stuart Robertson seemed to get on well with Brock so I think he and I should arrest Brock but interview both of them. If I could get another two officers to arrest Masterfield and leave him in the cells for us that would be perfect. Ideally I'd like Brock to think he is the only one being arrested.'

'For all the time it will take them I'll give you two of my detective officers to arrest Masterfield. You can brief them beforehand. So, Friday morning it is.

Chapter 23

There were three emails needing Bob's attention the next morning, and all three related to casualties: a buzzard, an otter and a badger.

He dealt with the badger incident first as it was the most straightforward. A retired police officer had spotted a dead badger at the side of the road on the A9 near the village of Ballinluig in Highland Perthshire. He had obviously looked at the ordnance survey map for the area and had given a map reference. Bob considered the options. There was always a chance that someone had killed the badger by some illegal means and dumped it on the road to look like a road casualty; he thought this unlikely in this part of Perthshire. If he went to look at every dead creature the time and expense would be disproportionate to any result by way of confirming a crime. He decided on simply phoning Scottish Badgers, a group of dedicated and experienced folks who are invaluable to the police with their assistance in badger crime investigations. They are always interested in the location of dead badgers since they are seldom killed far from their sett. In this part of Perthshire, where there are relatively few badgers, it might help the group to identify the location of a previously unknown sett.

The badger dealt with, Bob phoned the person who had reported the roadkill otter, a Mr George Smiley.

'I saw the otter lying at the roadside,' said Mr Smiley, 'where the road runs by the River South Esk near Brechin. I'm a taxidermist but I'm well aware that I can't pick up a dead otter for taxidermy unless I have a licence from Scottish Natural Heritage, and I'm unlikely to get that unless the otter is for educational purposes. Seeing the dead otter reminded me of a chap I met at a conference recently who was bragging about having found two roadkill otters that he intended to stuff. I also overheard him saying to another taxidermist that he had quite a few dead specimens in his freezer and he was keen to take up taxidermy.'

'When was it you spoke to this person Mr Smiley?' queried Bob. If there was going to be an application for a search warrant it would need to be based on recent intelligence.

'It was two weeks ago, in fact less than that. It was on a Saturday so it would have been a week past Saturday. I was meaning to report it but completely forgot until I saw the dead otter on the road yesterday.'

'Can you give me a name and address Mr Smiley?'

'His name is Gordon Gregor. I don't know his address, but I know he lives in the village of Wellbank just outside Dundee. He's a chap of about sixty and I think he's into clay pigeon shooting if that helps.'

Bob had never been to Wellbank but he knew it as the home village of the late John Ellis, leader of the John Ellis Highland Country Band. It was one of Bob's favourite bands and was unique in that the tunes started without any introduction. For the band members to manage that consistently demanded immaculate timing. He began to whistle one of his favourite John Ellis tunes, *Captain Cameron's March*.

The clay pigeon shooting information certainly helped. A quick call to the firearms licensing department showed that he was Gordon Campbell Gregor, aged sixty two years, of 7 The Crescent, Wellbank. Now for the third casualty: the buzzard.

The message indicated that the buzzard had been reported by a Ms Annie Smyth and gave her phone number. Bob phoned her and asked a series of questions aimed at identifying whether or not the buzzard could have met an accidental death, a natural death or had been the victim of crime. The first question related to when she had found it and where it was.

'It was yesterday evening,' Ms Smyth said, 'when I was walking my dog in the field behind my house. I saw Lady sniffing at something and went over to have a look. That's when I saw it was a dead buzzard.'

'Have you any idea if the bird was thin, Ms Smyth?'

'Sorry, I don't, I didn't want to touch it, even to kick it over.'

'Were there any power cables or electricity poles near the bird?'

'There's a line of poles running through the field. It was under one of these poles.'

'Was there anything at the top of the pole, like a transformer maybe?'

'I never noticed, but I'll look out the window if you hang on.'

Ms Smyth put the phone down and Bob heard the footsteps on a hard floor clip-clopping into the distance, then growing louder as she returned. 'Yes, there's a big grey metal thingy at the top of the pole. That's the pole in fact that my electricity must come from as there's a wire leading from it to my house. I'd never noticed that before.'

'That's great Ms Smyth. It's most likely that the buzzard has been electrocuted. Unfortunately it's not uncommon to find large birds such as a buzzard at the bottom of these poles. I don't know which part is live but clearly if they come in contact with it, it electrocutes them. I'm as happy as I can be that the bird isn't the victim of a crime. You're as well to leave it there and nature will take its course. It might provide a hearty meal for a fox. Many thanks for letting us know about it.'

Bob entered an intelligence log on SID about the suspicion that the taxidermist Gordon Campbell Gregor had dead mammals and birds that were illegal to possess. He next phoned PC Peter Bruce, the wco covering the Dundee area.

'Peter, if you look on SID later you'll find intelligence that I've just put on about a Gordon Campbell Gregor in Wellbank. It might not be sanitised and available to you yet but it will be shortly. Could you apply for a search warrant and get one of the other wildlife crime officers to go with you to execute it please.'

Peter was happy to get the job. Bob was equally unhappy that he couldn't go on the job. Since it was Bob who had received the information from a member of the public who wouldn't want to be identified as the informant, that excluded Bob from the investigation in case he had to give evidence. If Bob had been in the witness box a defence solicitor might legitimately insist that he tell the court who had passed on the information. He'd be obliged to do that, and that might not turn out too well for Mr Smiley. If the solicitor asked Peter Bruce the same question, Peter would have no idea who gave the information since that would not be available to him on SID.

Now that Bob had dealt with the casualties of the day he got down to thinking about an interview strategy for Masterfield and Brock on Friday. It looked like it was going to be a full day in the office. Maybe just as well; the rain had come on and it was now bucketing down.

Chapter 24

On Friday morning Bob and PC Stuart Robertson arrested Charles Brock and took him to Dundee police station. With cells arranged in separate blocks, he would have no idea that Cyril Masterfield was also in custody. Masterfield arrived with two detective officers an hour later. The duty solicitor was called for Brock, the first of the pair to be interviewed.

The solicitor was allowed a word with his client before Bob switched on the tape and Stuart began the interview. Brock began with 'no comment' replies as no doubt instructed by the solicitor. It is difficult, even for a seasoned criminal to maintain this stance and this was the teenager's first time in a police cell and interview room. He was pale and visibly shaken with beads of sweat on his forehead. He asked for a glass of water.

Bob left the room and returned with water for the suspect, who seemed relieved that the police had agreed to his request. Stuart continued with the questioning, keeping to easy questions initially.

PC Stuart Robertson: How long have you been a gamekeeper, Charles?
Charles Brock: Just two years.
SR: How long at Loch Garr Estate?
CB: Seven months
SR: Enjoy it?
CB: Suppose so.
SR: Good conditions?
CB: Yup, nice cottage, Cyril and I got brand new Land Rovers when we started.
SR: Good rate of pay?
CB: Yup, better than the average keeper's wage.
SR: Do you have your own beat on Loch Garr Estate?
CB: No, we work over the whole area.
SR: How many keepers now?
CB: Cyril the headkeeper, me and two new keepers
SR: Who do you get your orders from?
CB: Cyril.
SR: Do you ever get orders from Nigel Roberts?

112

CB: No, I seldom see Mr Roberts. He deals with Cyril.

SR: When I spoke to you the day we searched your house and sheds you said you'd caught the pine marten we found in a shed in a trap. Is that right?

CB: Yup.

SR: What kind of trap?

CB: It was a wire cage trap I'd set for a feral cat I'd seen near the main burn that runs through the hill. It was a legal trap.

SR: And was the pine marten alive when you checked the trap?

CB: Yup

SR: You said that you drowned it.

CB: I didn't have my rifle so that was the only way of killing it.

SR: Pine martens are protected. Why did you not let it go?

Brock suddenly realised he had said something he shouldn't have. He went quiet and Stuart repeated the question.

CB: No comment.

SR: Have you been told to kill pine martens Charles?

CB: No comment.

Stuart realised he needed to get Brock speaking again. He noticed that his water was finished. 'Do you want more water Charles?'

'Yup, that would be good.'

The tape was turned off and Bob left the room again for water. Stuart took advantage of the time to get Brock going again. 'You're in a wee bit of bother here Charles but I know fine that you're just following orders. You're just a young chap and no doubt feel you have to do what you're told.'

The solicitor raised his eyebrows at these comments off tape but said nothing.

Brock sighed, 'I work probably sixteen hours most days, seven days a week. I really enjoy the job and I'm trying to show the headkeeper and Mr Roberts that I'm a good gamekeeper and doing more than my share.'

'Nevertheless you have to stay within the law. When you leave here you need to remember that and do what is right,' Stuart told him.

'Will I get jailed for this?' Brock was clearly worried, not just about what he had admitted but about what else the police might know.

'I think that's unlikely Charles,' replied Stuart. 'You're young, in a very junior position and probably acting under the orders of others. I've no doubt a court will take that into consideration, especially if they see by your answers during this interview that you're being truthful and unlikely to offend in the future.'

Bob had returned with another glass of water. He turned the tape back on and Stuart continued where he left off, testing Brock's attitude with his next question.

SR: When officers searched the hill they found eight fox snares set on a fence up the side of a larch wood. Was it you who set them?
CB: Yup, they're legal snares. They're not self-locking.
SR: I agree they're not self-locking. How often do you check them?
CB: Every day.
SR: Are you sure you check them every single day?
CB: Most of the time yes, though we were busy building grouse butts on the days before you came to raid the estate.
SR: So how long might they have gone without being checked Charles.
CB: No more than three days, probably just two days.

Suspects always downplay their degree of guilt, whether that be in relation to drink drivers stating they have just had a 'couple' of drinks or a suspect for embezzlement claiming the amount taken was only half of what was really stolen. In any case he was admitting that at least one more day elapsed than was permitted by law.

SR: Do you know that snares are not allowed to be set where the animal caught is likely to be fully or partially suspended?
CB: But these were on a netting fence. It was too high for the fox to jump over if it was caught.
SR: Afraid not Charles. One snare had caught a fox which was hanging over the top of the fence. In the terms of the legislation it had been fully suspended. The officers tried the other snares and they all reached over the top of the fence.

Tears were now forming in Brock's eyes.

SR: Were you told to set snares there Charles?
CB: Cyril told me to snare that side of the wood. He said it would be a good place to catch foxes.
SR: There was a dead deer dumped in the burn just up from Albert Curtis's house. What do you know about that?
CB: Nothing at all.
SR: Are you sure?
CB: Look, if there was a dead stag in the burn it was nothing to do with me.
SR: How do you know it was a stag Charles?

CB: You said.

SR: I never said stag, I just said a dead deer. Remember what I said about telling the truth. Interviews of suspects are read out to the sheriff.

Brock's head fell forward, then he reached for the glass of water.

SR: Are you going to be truthful Charles?

CB: Cyril shot the young stag out on the hill with his .270. I was driving and we were out on the hill near Albert's cottage. Cyril said to drive down to the burn near Albert's house. He got me to help him to throw the stag in the burn.

SR: Did he kill it first shot?

CB: No, the first shot hit it in the guts. I drove closer and he finished it off with a shot in the head.

SR: Did you know that was Albert's water supply that you flung it in to?

CB: I didn't at the time. Cyril told me as we were driving away. He was laughing and said that would get rid of the bugger.

SR: You mean get rid of him off the estate?

CB: Yup.

SR: Have you shot any deer on the estate?

CB: No.

SR: Has Cyril shot other deer, either out of season or at night?

CB: No comment.

SR: When you say 'no comment' can I take it that is yes?

CB: No comment.

SR: You were driving him one night when he shot a stag over the boundary on Hillside Farm, weren't you?

CB: How do you know that?

SR: I can't say but it's true, isn't it?

CB: He doesn't like deer because of the ticks they carry. The ticks spread to grouse. He just loves using his .270 as well I suppose.

SR: Did he just leave the deer lying or go and get it?

CB: Just left it.

SR: We took two knives and a small stick from the front of your Land Rover. Were they yours?

CB: No comment.

SR. There were traces of a pesticide on one of the knives. Can you explain that?

CB: I brought these knives with me when I moved to Loch Garr Estate. I got one of them from the head keeper on my previous estate. That's maybe the one with the pesticide. I've never used poison of any kind.

SR: We recovered a number of baits and poisoned raptors on the hill during the search. They were laced with or killed by pesticides. What can you tell me about that?
CB: No comment.

The two officers could see that they had gone as far as they could with Brock. They had charges prepared and charged him with leaving a firearm unattended on his quad bike, killing a pine marten, cruelly killing it by drowning it, setting eight snares where an animal caught was likely to be fully or partially suspended, failing to check snares within twenty four hours, shooting a red deer stag out of season and at night without authority, illegal possession of a red deer stag, shooting a red deer stag without lawful authority or written permission, illegal possession of a firearm and ammunition used to commit an offence, being two or more persons acting together to commit these deer-related offences, and culpable and reckless conduct by knowingly placing a deer in a water supply.

Once Brock was charged Stuart told him, 'It may be that the fiscal will want to use you as a witness in relation to the deer charges. Have a think about the illegal use of the pesticides and if you change your mind about your 'no comment' answers get back to us. You'll now get your fingerprints, photograph and a DNA sample taken.'

Once Brock was back in his cell Bob and Stuart had a break before interviewing Masterfield. It was nearly lunch time and the duty solicitor had agreed to come back in an hour. Bob was disappointed that Brock dried up when the pesticide abuse questions were put to him. 'It's so bloody difficult to get a conviction for poisoning wildlife. We've got evidence of poisoned baits, poisoned birds, the same unique mix of pesticides in Masterfield's vehicle, his game bag and his clothing. Because of the unique mix we can probably link the pesticide traces to the baits and victims, but we can't prove that either of them set out these baits. This is the case with just about every pesticide abuse investigation. I'm going out to get us a couple of pies. Masterfield can enjoy the discomfort of the cells for a wee while longer.'

Chapter 25

After Masterfield had a few minutes with the duty solicitor, it was Bob's turn to carry out the questioning. He thought that, as a rule, it is better if only one of the officers present does the questioning. The interviewing officer may be going down a particular track with the interview, and this can be spoiled if the second officer butts in. The second officer is usually better trying to note anything the first officer might have missed and coming in with that line of questioning when given the nod. When he took Masterfield into the interview room Bob noticed that the back of his shirt was soaked with sweat, and he knew the cells were not exactly saunas.

Bob went through a long list of questions with Masterfield but always the answer was 'No comment.' He had been better schooled than Brock though this was the first time he had been in a police cell. Bob continued the questioning irrespective of Masterfield's lack of answers, hoping to get a break eventually.

PC Bob McKay: The rifles that you own, do you ever give them to anyone else?
Cyril Masterfield: No.

Bob was happy at the first sign of a chink in Masterfield's armour.

BM: Why not?
CM: You're not allowed to unless that person has it on their firearm certificate. You should know that.

A wee bit of confidence from Masterfield, that might work against him.

BM: So you never lend your rifles to anyone or allow anyone else to use them?
CM: No. I've told you that. You cops are always looking at a breach of a firearm certificate to take firearms away from keepers.
BM: Remember when we searched your house we took away your rifles, including the .270?
CM: Yeh, it's about time I got them back. If there's any damage to them

you'll pay for it.

BM: Do you ever shoot deer on the estate?

CM: That's part of my job. I shot one or two roe does when I came to the estate at first. I've shot a couple of bucks since they came into season.

BM: When did roe bucks come into season?

CM: Are you trying to catch me out or what? They came into season on 1st April.

BM: What about red deer, have you shot any red deer?

CM: I was too late to shoot hinds, I'd other things to do when I took over as head keeper. I'm waiting to get some stags when the season opens on 1st July.

BM: So you've only shot roe, no red deer yet?

CM: That's what I've just told you. Do you need everything repeated?

BM: I'm just making sure Cyril because a bullet found in a stag on the estate was fired by your .270 rifle. That's one of the rifles you're not allowed to give to anyone else.

The colour drained from Masterfield's face. He was not so cocky now. Bob let him sweat for a wee while. He knew from experience in interviews that the suspect often feels the need to break the silence; to fill the void. After almost a minute Masterfield spoke.

CM: I'd forgotten about that one. I left it where it dropped for the ravens and eagles. I appreciate I shouldn't have shot it.

BM: You were also out one night with Jock Scott, the former headkeeper, when you shot a young stag. It was a gut shot and the deer went off injured.

CM: Jock moved and the Land Rover shook just as I was pulling the trigger. That's why it wasn't a clean kill.

BM: Was that with the .270 as well?

CM: No, that was with my .243 Remington.

BM: Going back to the first stag, the one you said you left for the eagles and ravens, did you not bring it off the hill?

CM: No I just left it as I said.

BM: So it was never in your Land Rover?

CM: You're asking me to repeat myself again. I left it where I dropped it.

BM: Strange that we got blood and hair in the back of your Land Rover with a DNA match to a stag. You shot that stag with your .270 rifle and carted it in your Land Rover to the burn just up from Albert Curtis's house and dumped it in the burn there, didn't you?

There was silence again, broken half a minute later by Masterfield's 'No comment.'

BM: You dumped it in the burn because you knew that was Albert Curtis's water supply, didn't you?
CM: No comment.

Bob went over the line of questioning that covered the pesticide on Masterfield's clothing, in his vehicle and the baits and victims found on the moorland. The suspect was probably thinking he had said enough and the answers until the end of the interview remained 'no comment.'

Masterfield listened in silence to the charges: shooting two red deer stags out of season and at night without authority, illegal possession of a red deer stag, shooting a red deer stag without lawful authority or written permission, illegal possession of a firearm and ammunition used to commit an offence, being two or more persons acting together to commit these deer-related offences, and culpable and reckless conduct. The pesticide abuse charge of possessing the mix of carbofuran, isofenphos and bendiocarb was also added in. By the time Bob had finished Masterfield looked completely deflated.

With Masterfield back in his cell Bob and Stuart were having a relaxing cup of tea and a cake from the canteen. Stuart wondered about the likelihood of the charges being proved.

'Well,' said Bob, 'I still think the fiscal might not take up the deer-related charges against Brock. However, the beauty of the illegal possession of deer or firearms and ammunition is that a person can be convicted on the evidence of one witness. Even if there's no further evidence comes to light Masterfield should be sunk by these charges. I'm thinking too of the pesticide offences which could pave the way for a vicarious liability charge against Roberts.'

'Do Masterfield or Brock need to be convicted for a vicarious liability charge to be proved against Roberts?'

'No Stuart, that's not necessary, but there's an escape route for Roberts if he could show that he didn't know that they were committing the offence and – the 'and' is important – *and* that he took all reasonable steps and exercised all due diligence to prevent the offence being committed. I suppose it's a reverse burden of proof, but I'd be surprised if Roberts hasn't devised a way of covering his arse.'

'What about the culpable and reckless conduct charge?'

'The way I see it, what Masterfield has done falls within the definition of culpable and reckless conduct: it's most certainly a deliberate act and

I'm sure with the risk of bacteria getting into the water supply it will have exposed Albert Curtis and his wife Lizzie to significant risk to health, if not life. I'll have a word with Meg Runciman for some direction.'

Masterfield and Brock were later released and Bob would now submit a report to the procurator fiscal. When he returned to his office there was a note on his desk to look in and see his DI.

'Bob, unfortunately we're not going to get authority for any teams to look at Roberts. I'm told that money is too tight; budgets have been slashed. The ACC never said it in so many words but wildlife crime is still not a high enough priority.'

Bob was disappointed but not surprised. 'Maybe wildlife crime is not as high a priority as drugs and human trafficking but we're talking about trying to convict probably one of the worst wildlife criminals in the UK. It's really frustrating but thanks for giving it your best shot sir.'

'Anyway, how did this morning go Bob?'

'It went pretty well, probably better than I expected. Neither admitted the setting of poisoned baits or killing the birds of prey but they said enough to let us charge them with the deer offences.'

'What about the culpable and reckless conduct?'

'There's enough to report Masterfield for that, especially with the evidence from the veterinary pathologist about the possible health effects of a deer with its guts hanging out put in a water supply. I'm going to speak with Meg Runciman about a possible charge against both of being in possession of a pesticide, albeit just traces, or whether she might want to use Brock as a witness against Masterfield in some of the charges. I wonder if we should consider a vicarious liability charge against Roberts?'

'I think the documents seized during the search show that Roberts is clearly in a supervisory position regarding the keepers. If the fiscal doesn't go ahead with the possession of pesticides charge it might be a pretty thin vicarious liability charge on traces alone. Wait and see what Meg says first. Well done anyway. I think we should be looking at revocation of their firearm and shotgun certificates. Would you do a report on that please. I'll sign it off and send it to firearms licensing. We still have most of their rifles anyway.'

Bob phoned Meg Runciman before he finished duty. She quickly grasped what was a fairly complex investigation. 'I'm not sure about the possession of pesticides charge with just traces. I'll speak to Crown Office and see what view they have. If we don't run with that I don't see a possibility of a vicarious liability charge being possible against Roberts. I agree that the culpable and reckless conduct charge is relevant, and I tend towards using

Brock as a witness in some of the charges, but I'd rather read the whole case on the system first. When is it likely to be with me Bob?'

'A couple of weeks at the latest.' He was pleased with his day's work but exasperated that he was still unable to nail the man at the top of the tree.

Chapter 26

Bob was in his office going over the evidence for the trial of the snowdrop bulb thieves, Mark Slattery and Declan Rafferty, which was due to take place later that morning. He was awaiting a call from the court officer for his attendance when Shirley Deans appeared with a delicious-looking slice of home-made lemon Madeira cake, complete with candied peel. 'What was annoying you yesterday then Bob?' she asked, grinning.

'Och it was just frustration that the top criminals, the ones making all the money, seldom seem to get caught and convicted. They're usually smart enough to keep their distance from the crimes they instigate. They reap the rewards and their minions get caught and fined. Anyway, this lovely bit of cake will cheer me up.'

Bob's phone interrupted the conversation and Shirley went back to her desk. The caller was PC Maggie McPherson, the Brechin wildlife crime officer who had reported the snowdrop bulb case to the procurator fiscal. 'Bob, some good news. The two Cambridgeshire snowdrop thieves have changed their plea to guilty. I'm going to sit in on the case to hear what is said. I'll give you an update later.'

'That's great Maggie. With their record they might be looking at a jail term, but we'll just have to wait and see.'

He was wiping the crumbs off his desk when PC Peter Bruce, the wildlife crime officer from Dundee, arrived with an update for the investigation into the two dead otters.

'Gordon Campbell was a pleasant enough chap to deal with,' said Peter. 'He's just taken early retirement and wanted to concentrate more on taxidermy, which he claimed he is just about to start out on. On the evidence we found he's not a taxidermist as yet; just a chap collecting dead specimens with a view to taxidermy in the future. He also intends to do dog training. He has some lovely dogs: a liver and white springer spaniel and two black Labradors. He had one or two stuffed specimens he'd bought in his sitting room, but we started on the freezer.'

'Did two otters jump out and bite you?' interjected Bob.

'Just about, the two otters were right at the top. He'd quite a lot of other birds and mammals that were okay, including a lovely big dog fox. The interesting birds were a female sparrowhawk, a very light-coloured buzzard and a tawny owl. He also had what could be a polecat but I'll need to get expert identification on that.'

Peter took a slurp of tea and continued, 'The stuffed specimens in the sitting room were okay, they were all common birds: a song thrush, a lapwing and a cock pheasant. I ran the things we took from the freezer through the scanner at Dundee Airport on the way here and the three raptors have been shot with a shotgun, with plenty of pellets visible. I've taken photos of all the scans. There were no pellets in the polecat and the two otters seem to be roadkill.'

'Any idea where the three stuffed birds came from Peter?'

'He said he bought the cock pheasant in an auction. The two other birds apparently came from a taxidermist friend. They're pretty crap and don't say much for his friend's skill. There's no evidence in the house or shed that he's stuffed anything or sold any specimens yet.'

Peter finished the last of his tea. 'What do you propose I do now to continue the investigation?'

'For the raptors I think we're okay with the photographs of the scans unless the fiscal says otherwise and wants x-rays done by a vet. Despite you and I knowing what the birds are, I suggest you phone Ralph Murdoch at RSPB Investigations and ask him to look in sometime to positively identify the species. That way there will be no argument from an awkward defence solicitor. The polecat is really interesting. You could have it identified by the curator of mammals either at Perth or Dundee museum. If it really is a polecat and not a feral polecat ferret then take it to Frank McArthur and see if he can give a cause of death. It might be quite hard though to differentiate between being deliberately hit over the head with a stick and being hit by a car on the road. So far then he's got possession of three raptors which have been shot, a strict liability offence, possession of two otters, which are on Schedule 2 of the Habitats Regulations, and possibly a polecat, which is on Schedule 3 of these Regs.'

'I wondered how he came by the raptors Bob. I asked him when we interviewed him if he had shot them and he said he hadn't. He is a shotgun certificate holder though. I asked if he had got them from someone else. That was the only time he answered, 'No comment.' That's probably the truth of the matter but there was no way he was prepared to say.'

Peter headed off to Perth Museum to have the polecat identified and Bob continued preparing the case against Masterfield and Brock. Just after lunch time Maggie McPherson phoned him. She sounded excited. 'Bob, Mark Slattery, the snowdrop thief with the worst record, was almost jailed. The sheriff said he was minded to jail him but since the maximum imprisonment under the Act was only six months and he'd have to get one third off for a guilty plea he'd be going against the guidelines for courts to hand out sentences of less than a year. He sentenced him to carry out two hundred and forty hours of community payback as an alternative to imprisonment.'

Bob butted in, 'I'd rather have seen him jailed.'

'But I'm not finished yet, wait for it. The sheriff forfeited his lorry as well.'

'Oh well, that's not so bad,' said Bob with a degree of relief.

'And the other bulb thief, Declan Rafferty, was fined £3,500."

'All in all that was a good result Maggie. And a pretty disappointing visit to Scotland for the Cambridge Two. Hopefully that has put them off coming up here again.'

Bob made good progress preparing the Loch Garr Estate case in the remaining hours of his shift. He heard from Peter Bruce just before he finished duty. The 'polecat' was indeed a feral polecat ferret and there was no offence with its possession.

As Bob was about to head home his phone rang. 'Mr McKay, this is a Mr Calum Brookes here. I live near Carnoustie. My neighbour had workmen at the house two days ago tidying up cement work under the gutters of his house roof. They filled in two holes with cement under the gutter where there are swifts nesting. I hesitated about phoning you, but it's been on my conscience that they might have blocked a bird in.'

'Since it's your neighbour do you want to remain anonymous to save any trouble?' Bob asked.

'That was why I've delayed phoning but he's selling the house, hence the tidying up of cement work, so I'm not bothered about being identified as the person contacting the police. He's a pretty horrible character anyway and his wife is not much better. I'll be glad when they go.'

'If you give me your address, I'll come to see you first thing in the morning Mr Brookes.'

Mr Brookes gave his address and added, 'It's the second of the two farm cottages as you come up the farm road.'

Bob suspected if a swift had been deprived of food for two days it may well be dead. He would find out in the morning. He hoped the investigation wouldn't take too long and he'd get back to the Loch Garr report to the fiscal after lunch.

In the middle of the afternoon he took a phone call from PC Jenny Watson, who had been working diligently on the badger digging case and was in a position to get it reported to the procurator fiscal.

'Bob, the results have come through on the phone and laptop examination and from Jane Jackson at SASA re the badger blood on DNA testing of the stuff we took from McLeish and his co-accused. I'll deal with Alastair Black first. There was nothing of interest on his phone. The shotgun he had was stolen during a break-in to a house in Carlisle five years ago. There's no evidence to suggest that he was the person who stole it.'

'That's a good start Jenny, though I'm surprised there's nothing on his phone,' Bob replied.

'Peter Wilson now,' said Jenny, 'There were traces of badger blood on his knife and there was some badger hair adhering to the spade. These were the items we found in his car. The only thing of interest on his laptop was a short clip of a dead badger that was absolutely covered in blood and photos of his lurcher and a couple of dead hares at its feet. Nothing we can get extra charges from, though the incident will help show the court what sort of a brute he is.'

'Okay,' said Bob, 'and the horrible Mr McLeish?'

'There was nothing on the spade, but the knife, wire cage and coal sack were all contaminated with badger blood.'

'Good results Jenny, that makes a strong case overall. These three should get jail sentences. Meg Runciman had no problem deciding not to prosecute Mitch. He played a minor part and of course it was a good recovery of cannabis and speed as a result of his information. That should be another jail sentence for McLeish.'

As Bob was driving home his thoughts returned to the report of the swifts being blocked in. If it were true how the hell would he manage to prove that?

Chapters 27

In the morning Bob drove to Carnoustie in the company of the rousing Bobby MacLeod's band. The late Bobby MacLeod ran the popular Mishnish Hotel in Tobermory on the Isle of Mull. Bob had once had a pint of Guinness in the Mishnish bar; sitting there he had tried to imagine the incredible atmosphere when Bobby regularly entertained guests with his accordion music well into the night.

Mr Brookes was still in his pyjamas and just about to have breakfast. 'Come in and have a cup of tea while I get changed Mr McKay. Would you like a slice of toast?'

Bob had not long finished a hearty breakfast. 'No, I'm fine with a cup of tea thanks. Just milk and no sugar.'

In no time a mug of tea was placed in front of Bob, and Mr Brookes went off to get dressed. He was back a few minutes later and sat down at the kitchen table opposite Bob.

Without prompting he began to elaborate on the issue with the swifts.

'The swifts have nested in gaps under my gutters and next door under Mr Jones' gutters for at least the last five years. There are two places they nest at my house and two at Vince Jones's house. He has regularly moaned about 'these bloody swifts' as he calls them making a mess of his windows with their droppings as they come into the gaps in the brickwork where their nests are. He's always saying he intends to block up the gaps so they don't get in.'

Mr Brookes took a bite of his toast and marmalade before continuing, 'That would be fair enough if he had carried out the cement work when the swifts had left for the winter. My two nest sites are occupied by swifts and one of his is occupied by swifts. I'm sure they'll have young by this time. I think the other gap in his wall is occupied by sparrows this year as swifts seem to be scarcer. My wife and I love to watch them coming and going.'

After another bite of toast and drink of tea Mr Brookes continued his tale. 'On Monday, that's three days ago now, two workmen appeared in a white van. They mixed up cement on a board and began to seal the two holes the birds use, and generally tidy up the rest of the brickwork. They were here for about two hours. I've never seen the swifts near the nest site since that, nor the sparrows for that matter. I've no way of knowing whether they got out before the work or if they're blocked in.'

'Do you know where the workmen came from?' Bob queried.

'The van had McEwan and Rutherford, Dundee, on the side. They've got a website; I'll get you their address and phone number.'

Bob finished his tea and thanked Mr Brookes for his help. He made him aware of how he would progress the investigation and told him he would update him in due course.

After a phone call to the company Bob discovered the names of the two workmen and where they were currently working, which was at an address not many miles away in Monifieth.

The visit to the workmen served to answer important aspects of the investigation. They were pleasant young lads but appeared to have little knowledge of birds and were much more interested in which football team Bob supported and had he watched a particular game at the weekend.

'The holes under the gutter you were filling, did you see any birds either flying in or out at any time?' Bob asked.

The older of the two responded. 'I take it that it's wee birds you're asking about, like robins?'

'It's wee birds right enough, particularly sparrows or swifts.'

'I know of sparrows as I saw a sparrow's nest in a bush once when I was young. I don't know what swifts are like, are they the same size as sparrows?'

Bob could see there was no point in a lesson in ornithology. 'Did any birds at all come out of the holes you were filling?'

'There was one bird came out of the biggest hole when I put the ladder up. It probably got a fright when the ladder clattered against the wall.'

'What did it look like?'

'Sorry, it came out so fast I didn't get much of a look at it.'

'Who did you get your instructions from in relation to the job you were doing?'

'It was the chap in the house, I think he's called Vince as I heard his wife shouting to him to come in as someone was on the phone.'

'What were your instructions?'

'Just to repair all the cement work under the gutters.'

'Was there any instruction to leave alone any part of the wall?'

'No, just to go right round the house and make it as tidy as possible.'

'In relation to the bird that came flying out did you have any idea what it might have been doing in the gap in the wall?'

'I never gave it much thought. Would that be the place that it sleeps?'

'No, that's where it would have been nesting.'

'You mean that there could be eggs on the inside and the bird on the outside unable to get in? That's terrible, that's just not right. I'm not sure what I would have done if I had known that but it's just not right at all.'

Bob thought about the next part of the investigation and called into the office of the Fire and Rescue Service when he returned to Perth. Police and fire officers always work well together, and Bob knew some of the staff from having attended various grades of fires and serious road accidents earlier in his service. He left particularly pleased with the offer given to him by the station officer.

An application for a search warrant was next on the list. Bob stressed the urgency of this since it was still possible there was a live bird entombed behind the new cement. He was promised the warrant would be available by late afternoon, in time to catch one of the sheriffs before they finished for the day.

The procurator fiscal at Forfar had appreciated the urgency and Bob had collected the warrant by mid-afternoon. He'd arranged with the court officer to give him a call when there was a sheriff available and just after 4 o'clock he was shown into Sheriff Iain Holcroft's chambers in Forfar Sheriff Court.

'This sounds an interesting investigation Constable McKay, and I see you have included an officer of the fire and rescue service on the search warrant. That's quite unusual, why is that?'

Bob explained the requirement for this specialism as Sheriff Holcroft signed the legal document. 'Well, I'm more than satisfied with the grounds for a search warrant and I wish you the best of luck. In due course will you please let the court officer know the outcome, I'd be very interested.'

Bob now arranged to meet the designated fire and rescue officer, Jim McNab, first thing in the morning and also arranged for Constable Mike Timms, wildlife crime officer from Forfar, to meet him at Carnoustie police station.

Bob had just arrived home when his mobile phone rang. It was PC Stuart Robertson. 'Bob, I've just seen in the paper that Doug Butterfield pleaded guilty.'

'Who was Doug Butterfield again Stuart?' Bob had forgotten.

'The part-time gamekeeper from Cairniehill Farm at Glenfarg who caught the badger in a snare he'd left behind. He was fined £250 for not checking the snare, £100 for not having a tag on it with his registration number and another £100 for having an item that could be used to commit an offence.'

Bob remembered every detail of the offence now. 'That would be the home-made hawk trap with blood and feathers in it. What bird were they from Stuart?'

'The DNA testing done by Jane Jackson at SASA showed they were from a sparrowhawk. So, it was a good result overall.'

Chapter 28

By 9.45am the two police officers and fire officer were at Vince Jones' house at Carnoustie. Jones and his wife Cynthia came to the door.

'I have a search warrant here to allow us to remove the new cement where swifts or sparrows had been nesting.' Bob explained politely to Vince Jones. 'They may be blocked in, which puts them at real risk of dying of starvation.'

'Nah, you're okay,' Jones replied confidently, 'I hit the wall a few times with a stick just before the workmen arrived and they flew out. They're safe.'

Bob quizzed him, 'Do you know what kind of birds they are Mr Jones?'

'They're just sparrows,' Jones replied, maintaining his air of self-assurance.

'Could they not have been swifts Mr Jones?'

'Look constable, I know about birds. They're sparrows. Common everyday sparrows.'

'The search warrant entitles us to remove the cement and investigate what is inside.'

Jones was getting annoyed. 'You're not damaging this new work; not for bloody sparrows.'

'I'm afraid we are Mr Jones. We'll try to minimise the mess but that's what we're just about to do.'

Cynthia Jones waded in to defend her husband. 'This is absolutely ridiculous. Threatening to damage our property because of birds.' Her face was reddening, 'Because of sparrows that are ten a penny.'

Bob took an extendable ladder from the boot of his car and put it against the wall where Mr Brookes had earlier identified the nest site of a swift. Fire officer Jim McNab climbed the ladder and began to drill through the cement, chipping it away until he had a hole right through it. He came back down and swapped the drill for an endoscope camera.

'Why is this chap damaging my house?' asked Jones. 'He's not a policeman, he's a fireman. He's not entitled to do that.'

'Mr Jones,' Bob answered quietly, 'he is named on the warrant and he can carry out any necessary actions under my direction.'

'You'll pay for any damage,' the red-faced Cynthia Jones shouted. 'You'll pay the bill for the workers to come back to make good this damage.'

Meantime Jim McNab had climbed the ladder again and was feeding the endoscope in through the hole and looking at the screen on the laptop attached to the other end of the cable. He moved the endoscope about and announced matter-of-factly, 'There are no live birds in here. There are two dead young swifts that are almost fully fledged. There's no real nest to speak of, just one or two bits of hay or straw and some feathers. I'm recording this so you can verify it when I come down.'

Bob had a look at what the endoscope had revealed and knew that Jim's assessment had been accurate. For corroboration he had PC Mike Timms look as well. By this time, Jim had moved on to the next cemented area and had begun drilling. Bob moved along with the endoscope, Jim swapped the drill for the endoscope and climbed the ladder.

After a few minutes examining the interior of the cavity Jim said, 'This is different from the last place. There is a lot of nest material here, mainly straw and feathers. I'll poke the endoscope into the middle and see what might be there.' A few minutes later he announced, 'I see some eggs here. It's hard to see how many but there are at least four. I'll let you look at them when I come down.'

Bob and Mike studied the eggs and were confident they were house sparrow eggs. Bob would later let Ralph Murdoch from RSPB Investigations study the recordings to confirm their identification.

Mr and Mrs Jones had been closely following what was happening and saw the ladder being collapsed and stored away in Bob's car. 'Who do I send the bill to for this damage,' Vince Jones demanded.

'Afraid you'll have to pay for it yourself Mr Jones,' Bob responded, continuing with a caution to Jones and details of the charge arising from his unlawful actions: obstructing or preventing a wild bird from using its nest.

Jones was a lot less confident now and he and his wife stomped off into their house as Bob, Mike and Jim got into Bob's car to drive off. 'Would you mind reporting this case Mike?' asked Bob as they drove down the farm road, 'I've a lot on just now and want to get the Loch Garr Estate case on the system and to the fiscal if possible tomorrow.'

'No problem,' answered Mike, 'I'd love to assist in getting Jones before the court. He knew exactly what he was doing and didn't give a damn about these birds, especially the swifts that had flown all the way from Africa to nest.'

'Remember to add into the report that the house sparrow is a red-listed bird and that the swift is amber-listed. Give some detail of what the lists mean.'

Bob returned to his office and by 4.30pm he had put the finishing touches to the cases against the two Loch Garr Estate keepers and had sent the case to the report checking section for onward transmission to the procurator fiscal. He headed home but later, just after he had finished his evening meal, he had a phone call from DI Sneddon.

'Bob, I've just heard from the control room that a nine-year-old girl from a farm on Loch Garr Estate has been admitted to Ninewells Hospital in Dundee. She's critically ill and the doctors suspect she has been poisoned. I'm heading back into the office to meet the Chief Inspector. Could you come back in as well and we'll discuss what action we need to take.'

'Hell,' Bob said aloud as he put on his boots and jacket, 'this was inevitable, but to happen to a nine-year-old. What a bloody disaster, and of course no budget to try to put a stop to it.'

Chapter 29

By the time Bob got to Chief Inspector Thomson's office the situation had escalated. DI Sneddon was just putting down the phone after having called the doctor in the casualty department at Ninewells.

'Bastards,' he said quietly. 'The girl died just minutes ago. The doctor I spoke to told me they really had no time to try anything to save her but there are very few options available anyway where fast acting poisons are concerned.'

Bob wondered about the origin of the poison. Could it have been a pesticide stored incorrectly on the farm or could it be related to Roberts and his gamekeepers. He had seen buzzards in the same condition, having ingested one of several pesticides that are regularly abused. They survive a short time, many enduring excruciating muscle spasms then, often in a final agonising contraction, succumb to the gamekeeper's or pigeon fancier's pesticide-laced bait. He hoped the wee girl's end was a bit more merciful than that.

'Who was she?' Bob asked.

'She was a Susan McLaren,' answered the DI.

'Christ, that's Willie McLaren of Hilltop Farm's daughter. They have a wee boy as well. They're a really nice couple but have been getting some grief recently. The estate wants them out so the farm can be taken back in-hand.'

'What does in-hand mean?' asked the Chief Inspector, who had transferred on promotion from Lothian and Borders Division three years earlier and had spent most of his police career in Edinburgh.

'The estate no longer wants to lease the farm to a tenant sir, they want it run by the estate, probably with a farm manager,' explained Bob.

That maybe didn't mean much to Chief Inspector Thomson but he thanked Bob and continued, 'We still don't know how Susan came to be poisoned. Since you know the family Bob could you go out and make initial enquiries. Take PC Jane Dalgleish with you. She's a family liaison officer and she can stay with the family. You're used to these poisoning cases, albeit against wildlife, but obtaining the evidence will be the same. What suggestions can you make here?'

'Well, it's most likely Susan has handled a poisoned bait or a victim,' guessed Bob, 'maybe even found a hidden stash of pesticides. We'd need a search to see if whatever it was can be found, though to be honest linking it to the poisoning of a person will be no easier than linking a bait to the poisoning of a fox or raptor. It's nearly dark now. I'd suggest a team to search first thing in the morning, wildlife crime officers preferably as they know where to search, what they're looking for and have the proper PPE.'

The Chief Inspector took a deep breath. 'Right, we'll get some wcos organised for just after first light tomorrow. Could you go out now and see exactly what has happened and when you come back what you've learned will inform the next steps.'

The McLaren family was in turmoil when Bob and PC Jane Dalgleish arrived at their door. It was pitch dark by now. Willie's wife, Marjorie, was in tears and barely able to speak. Susan's older brother, Andrew, was in bed. Jane remained with Marjorie, and Bob went with Willie to the kitchen to get an account of the events leading to Susan's tragic death.

Willie related the timeline of what happened. 'Andrew and Susan went out to have a walk round the in-bye land about 4pm. They were to be back by 5pm for their tea. Andrew said that they found a buzzard that was unwell. It could stagger about but couldn't fly. They wondered what to do with it and decided to bring it home so that I could maybe help it.'

Willie wiped his eyes with his hankie, paused for a minute, then managed to continue. 'Though Susan is a year and a half younger than Andrew she is more willing to tackle difficult issues. She'd picked it up and the two started to head home with the bird. Andrew said that after a while Susan needed to put the buzzard down to blow her nose. She did that, then after a wee rest they carried on again with Susan still carrying the buzzard.'

Willie stopped again to gather his thoughts. 'After walking a bit further Susan said she felt unwell and dizzy. She kept going but a few minutes later she collapsed. Andrew said that she was unable to speak. By this time they were less than a quarter of a mile from the farm and Andrew ran home to tell us what had happened. Knowing about the dying buzzard and my daughter suddenly becoming unwell I pretty much guessed what was wrong. I told Marjorie to phone an ambulance while I ran out with Andrew to see Susan.'

He stopped again before describing what must have been a horrifying experience for him. Bob remained quiet waiting for him to continue; he could see this was really difficult for Willie. In his own time Willie began again. 'Susan was lying on the ground. She was barely conscious. I could see a buzzard beside her. I think it was dead. I lifted Susan and carried her back to the house as fast as I could go. Marjorie confirmed an ambulance was on its way but I was to phone the ambulance service as soon as I got back to update them. I did that and they told me that they would send the air ambulance, which would get Susan to Ninewells Hospital much quicker than the ambulance. By now Susan had lost consciousness.'

Tears were running down Willie's cheeks and he had to stop for a break again. 'I went with Susan in the ambulance. It took no time to get to Ninewells. Susan died five minutes after we arrived.'

Bob gave Willie time to compose himself. 'This is a heart-breaking incident Willie and I'm desperately sorry about the loss of Susan. Would you mind if I go over what the police role here now is?'

'Do whatever you can to bring these Loch Garr gamekeeper bastards to justice Bob. What do you need me to do?'

'I'd like to recover the dead buzzard now, just in case the keepers have been alerted by the arrival of the air ambulance or it's maybe taken by a fox. Would you be able to take me to it in the dark?'

'Aye, that's no problem, I know every inch of this farm.'

'I'd also like to get the outer clothing that Susan was wearing. It's possible that the buzzard has been sick, which often happens, and Susan somehow got some of it on her clothing or hands, which could have been transferred to her mouth when she blew her nose. Are the clothes at Ninewells?'

'Yes, they're still there. You can have them if you need them.'

'Thanks Willie. I'll arrange for them to be collected. After we get the buzzard I'll go back and report to the Chief Inspector and DI who have both come back on duty. We'll arrange a search of the area first thing in the morning as there is likely also to be a bait – or maybe more than one bait – lying somewhere near where Susan and Andrew found the buzzard. Could you find out from Andrew where this was and let me know when we come out in the morning. If possible, could you also keep an eye on the in-bye hill in case the keepers come to clear up and remove any evidence.'

'That's no problem. I'll probably not sleep tonight anyway, and I'll keep an eye on the area till you come back. Is this likely to be treated as murder Bob?'

'No, even with such a despicable act as leaving out a deadly bait where a person can access it there would be no intent to kill someone. I suspect it will be treated, at least in the early stages, as culpable and reckless conduct. That's a common law crime that can be heard in the High Court with an unlimited sentence.'

It was nearly 11pm before Bob got back to Perth with the dead buzzard. The Chief Inspector and DI were still there, and the DI had called out a staff member of the firearms licensing section to get an up-to-date list of the keepers on Loch Garr Estate. The plan in the morning was for Bob and three of the wildlife crime officers to do a search of the estate where they were most likely to find the bait which the buzzard had eaten. A civilian driver was to take the buzzard to SASA to establish what pesticide was involved and a team of detective officers would arrest the keepers on suspicion of culpable and reckless conduct and take them to Perth police station for interview.

Bob headed home for a few hours sleep before a 6 o'clock start the following morning. It had been a devastating end to the day and, like the McLaren family, he doubted if he would sleep much either.

Chapter 30

When Bob got out of bed at 4.30am neither Liz nor Toby stirred. He arrived at DI Sneddon's office an hour later. The DI was already in, as were some of the officers that were detailed to arrest and interview the keepers. Pairs of detective officers were allocated to each gamekeeper, of which there were now five in total.

The DI came over to Bob. 'I've enough going on with the arrest and interview of the gamekeepers Bob. I'll leave you and the three other wildlife crime officers for the ground search. That's your area of expertise so I'll not interfere, just keep me up to date by phone if and when you find anything relevant as it might be important for the interview teams. I'm treating this the same as we would a murder investigation. I'll set up a mini incident room and of course we'll be arresting Nigel Roberts at some stage, but there's no point at this time till we see what his keepers are prepared to say.'

'Did you want me to take statements from the McLaren family sir?' 'Bob asked.

Jonathan Sneddon thought for a minute, 'No, I'll send one of the officers out to link in with the family liaison officer, Jane Dalgleish, to do that. You've enough to do. You could warn Jane and the family of my intentions though.'

'Did someone pick up Susan's outer clothing from Ninewells sir?'

'Yes, they're here. I'll leave you to liaise with SASA as to the best way to test them. There's a post-mortem examination tomorrow morning with two pathologists, just as we'd have in a murder investigation. Any thoughts on where samples could be analysed for pesticides?'

Bob thought for a minute. 'The chemistry section at SASA are the experts in agricultural chemicals, I'd imagine that's the best bet. I'll find out later.'

First in Bob's thoughts was how to get sufficient evidence to convict Nigel Roberts. 'I think it might help sir if the officers interviewing the keepers ask if they've ever had any training, either from Roberts, Masterfield or anyone else, in the use and storage of pesticides or chemicals, or if they'd been instructed verbally or in writing that they should not break the law. The answers might improve, or maybe exclude, the chance of a vicarious liability charge.'

The DI smiled, 'You're right Bob, I'll make sure they include that in the questioning. You're a shrewd bugger and you're determined to get Roberts jailed.'

The three wildlife crime officers had arrived for the search of the estate near Willie McLaren's farm and Bob quickly briefed them. He wanted to get on to the estate before the keepers had a chance to move any incriminating evidence. He also didn't want to have Willie McLaren keeping an eye out for too long; he'd plenty on his mind and he'd be needing a sleep.

Twenty five minutes after leaving the police station the four officers were with Willie McLaren. The poor man looked exhausted. 'There's nobody been near the area Bob. I'll leave it with you now, will you remember where we went in the dark last night?'

'Yeh, I should be okay Willie. I noticed a group of three larch trees growing beside a big rock. It wasn't far from there.'

'That's not bad for being in the dark Bob. There's actually four larches but you still would have found the place.'

Bob told Jane about the situation with interviews and left it with her to arrange a mutually convenient time for the family. He set out for the moorland with Stuart Robertson, having allocated a separate area to Constables Bob Brewster from Blairgowrie and Brian Proudfoot from Kinross.

The four larch trees appeared as Bob and Stuart crossed the first ridge and Bob made for them, keeping them on his right as he and Willie McLaren did the previous evening. The two officers were about twenty yards apart and paid particular attention to the most likely places for a bait to be set: on ridges, on top of rocks and on areas of ground clear of heather. It was a lovely morning to be out; the sun was up, there were meadow pipits everywhere, plenty of extremely smart looking wheatears in the rockier parts of the hill and even one or two whinchats. Bob almost stepped on an adder that was warming up in the morning sun. He saw it in time and backtracked a few yards to go around it without disturbing it. The bubbling call of a curlew came from Bob's left, and as he looked round he saw the bird starting to fall vertically towards the ground, wings held in the air above it, as curlews often do in their territorial display. Bob was halfway through whistling the pipe jig *The Curlew* but the tune came to an abrupt end when he remembered why they were out on the moorland.

After about half an hour of searching Stuart shouted, 'There's a dead woodpigeon here Bob. It's been partly eaten and is almost certainly a bait.'

Bob walked over and joined him. 'Yeh, it looks like the breast has been cut open, though a good lot of the breast meat has been eaten.' Bob got down on his knees beside the woodpigeon for a closer look, 'I can see a couple of dark blue granules and there's also a dead bluebottle just beside the carcass. It's definitely a bait and a carbamate-based pesticide has been used. It's very fresh, I think only dead two or maybe three days. Would you give the DI an update while I take some photos and bag the bird?'

They moved on again to find they were only fifty yards from a rough vehicle track used by the keepers and probably Willie McLaren. 'Stuart, in the past I've found baits quite regularly not far from tracks that the estate vehicles use. Let's search along one side of the track and come back up the other side.'

Bob spotted a patch of exposed peat on the track and bent down to inspect it. 'There's fresh Land Rover tracks here. We had heavy rain three days ago and there's no sign of the tracks being eroded in any way by the rain. Looks like the vehicle has been here since the rain. We'll sign a production label and place it beside the tread mark as a scale and I'll take some photos. Could you update the DI again and ask if he wants to send out a scene of crime officer to take plaster casts. They'd be much better than a photo.'

A SOCO was being dispatched and the officers continued their search. They found nothing else of interest but the other two officers found a woodpigeon bait with a dead buzzard lying almost on top of it. They were several hundred yards from Bob and Stuart and it was hardly coincidental that their find was close to a hill track.

By midday the search was complete and the SOCO had taken several plaster casts of the tyre marks. Bob looked into the farmhouse to update the family. Willie McLaren still hadn't been to bed. When told of the tyre tracks on the hill track he gave a valuable piece of information. 'Bob, the only person I've seen driving on that track is the so-called head keeper, Cyril Masterfield. There's a bit of the track further down that's really dodgy, the track has been partly washed away and it may be that he doesn't let the other younger keepers go past there.'

'Thanks Willie, that could be really important. When you give a statement later could you remember to include that please?'

The DI was pleased when Bob phoned him. 'I'll get someone to go out to the estate and bring Masterfield's Land Rover in for comparison. If we can put the Land Rover near the site that Susan picked up the buzzard that would be a major step forward.'

'Just a thought sir, I've suspected for a while on another problem estate that it's only the head keeper that gets supplied with the pesticide and he's the only one who uses it. That probably keeps the risk of being caught tighter. That might apply on Loch Garr Estate, and it might be worth the detective officers doing the interviewing being aware of that.'

'You could be right Bob. I'll let them know.'

'It might also be helpful if the interviewing teams ask their respective suspect about the use of the Land Rovers – to establish that they only use their own vehicles and not another keeper's. It would help the case if we can eliminate or at least minimise the possibility of any of the under keepers using Masterfied's vehicle.'

'Good suggestion Bob, I'll do that.' Half-jokingly he said, 'Would you like a job with me in CID?'

The other officers returned to the police station at Perth while Bob went to deliver the two woodpigeon baits and dead buzzard to the vet lab to have Frank McArthur take samples on which SASA could work their magic. He would take all these plus Susan's outer clothing to Dorothy Abernethy later in the afternoon.

Chapter 31

It was after 5pm when Bob returned to Perth from SASA and he was not surprised that the DI was still on duty. 'Bob, let's go to Chief Inspector Thomson's office and I'll brief you both at the same time.'

The two officers sat round the table with the Chief Inspector. Jonathan Sneddon began. 'The interviews were interesting. Masterfield made no comment throughout. The newer under keepers, who just came in on a voluntary basis rather than being arrested, answered the questions but with their recent arrival on the estate the interviewers tended to believe they knew very little, though one admitted driving the Land Rover one night when Masterfield shot a red deer hind and a calf. He seemed pretty disgusted that the hind was shot out of season and with a calf, and that they were just left lying in the heather. He also said that one of the new keepers, a Mark Mason, had just lasted a week and left. Apparently he didn't like the idea of shooting deer at night and out of season, plus he hadn't appreciated the exceptionally long hours they were asked to work. Firearms licensing gave his new address, a village in the north of England, and he's being interviewed as we speak by one of the investigative support officers of the NWCU.

'On Bob's suggestion the underkeepers were asked if they'd ever had any training, either from Roberts, Masterfield or anyone else, in the use and storage of pesticides or chemicals, or if they'd been instructed not to break the law. None had any such training or instruction on Loch Garr Estate, though one underkeeper said he had quite extensive training on the first estate he worked on in Norfolk before he moved to the north of England. Masterfield was asked the same question but he made no comment.'

The DI took a minute to compose his thoughts and began again. 'Now for the best bit. The under keeper that has been there longest, Brock, was shitting himself at being in a cell for a second time. He asked the interviewing officers that if he spoke up and told the whole truth might he get off with your charges Bob. He was told, quite honestly, that the matter would be discussed with the fiscal but no promises could be made. What are your thoughts Bob before I go on?'

Bob had no hesitation, 'Brock's just a young lad and is a very small cog in a big wheel. He's already spoken up to a degree against Masterfield. If he can substantially add to that or say anything that puts Roberts before a court, it's well worth using him as a witness. I suspect Meg Runciman will see it that way as well.'

'Well, I think he will be in luck.' The DI was smiling, 'He witnessed Masterfield mixing what he is sure were pesticides. There was a small tub and a larger tub. He poured the contents of the small tub into the larger one and stirred with a stick. He got a fright when Brock came into the shed he was working in and there was a slight spillage on to the bench. Brock describes the spillage as dark blue granules, about granulated sugar-sized. Brock has never seen him putting out any baits but a couple of times he has seen baits, a rabbit one time and a woodpigeon the second time, in an area where Masterfield was working earlier the same day. Brock is also upfront about the shooting of the red and roe deer out of season and at night. He's driven Masterfield four or five times when deer have been shot.'

Bob interjected, 'Can we find out from Brock which shed this is, and if it's normally locked or unlocked.'

'I'm sure we can. We still have all the suspects in custody.'

Chief Inspector Thomson came in now, 'Why the difference if it's locked Bob?'

'If it's locked sir we need a warrant. If it's unlocked the powers under the Wildlife and Countryside Act are sufficient.'

Bob doubted that the Chief Inspector had ever read the Wildlife and Countryside Act, but he clearly had a grasp of the chain of command on Loch Garr Estate with his next question. 'Some good evidence against Masterfield but nothing yet against the bugger who's driving the whole chain of criminality.'

'Nothing yet,' Jonathan sighed, 'but we're not finished, though I'm not hopeful. Roberts will need to be arrested and interviewed in any case. Did you find out about the examination of any samples taken by the pathologists Bob?'

'Yeh, they can be done at SASA. Dorothy Abernethy told me that they have carried out analysis for chemicals used in agriculture for the police in other cases of human death, though not in relation to carbofuran. She said she'd give any samples in this case priority.'

'That's great, thanks Bob.'

Bob's phone rang and he could see who was calling. 'That's Albert Curtis, one of the former gamekeepers from Loch Garr Estate. I'll take it outside.'

He returned a few minutes later and was beaming from ear to ear. 'Albert Curtis is now prepared to give evidence. Albert, if you remember, was handed a tub of pesticide by Masterfield and told to get on with killing some *vermin.'* Bob emphasised the word. 'He buried the tub and contents and took me to it later. It was a mix of carbofuran, isofenphos and bendiocarb. He didn't want to give a statement and I respected that. Now of course he's heard of the death of wee Susan McLaren. He knew the family well and is more than happy now to give a statement if it helps. I'm seeing him tomorrow.'

DI Sneddon blew his cheeks out. 'That will be a major piece of evidence in a circumstantial case against Masterfield for setting out the bait for the buzzard that eventually killed Susan, especially if the tyre marks near the pigeon bait you got this morning match Masterfield's Land Rover.'

'How is that going sir?' asked Bob.

'The Land Rover's been taken on a lorry to Dundee. I got it picked up, I didn't want to add to any chance damage marks or change the wear pattern by having it driven there. We should have the result tomorrow.' He paused briefly. 'In relation to reporting this case, DC Hamish McColl is collating the evidence gained from the interviews. He'll charge Masterfield with culpable and reckless conduct before he is released. Any other charges can follow. Would you liaise with Hamish and between you get this case to Meg Runciman as soon as all evidence is available?'

Chief Inspector Thomson concluded the meeting. 'It's been a very sad investigation with the death of a young girl, but everyone has worked extremely well and we've got the makings of a pretty solid case against Masterfield. There are a few strands to tie up yet so we'll see what tomorrow brings. Thanks to both of you for your professionalism and Jonathan, would you pass on my thanks to everyone else in the team today.'

Bob had now worked nearly fourteen hours with little sustenance. He headed home to see if Liz had left him anything to eat and if she had already walked the wee Westie.

Chapter 32

Incident No. 71 read that about 1.30am a farmer at Sunnybank Farm near the village of Comrie in Perthshire was disturbed by his sheepdog barking. He looked out the window and saw a spotlamp being used in one of his fields. He quickly got dressed and tried to intercept a Subaru 4WD pick-up charging out of the field. He ran towards the car but stopped short when the passenger threw a bottle at him. Police units had searched for the car but had been unable to find it. There was nothing on the incident that indicated a statement had been taken from the farmer or that a crime report had been submitted.

Bob was annoyed when he read this type of incident. Night shift are always short-staffed and have plenty to keep them busy but investigations into hare coursing, rabbit poaching or whatever the men had been after mostly get discontinued if no-one is caught at the time. He got the farmer's number and phoned him to get more details.

'Have you given a statement to the police regarding this incident?'

'No, I spoke on the phone to report it, phoned again when the passenger threw a bottle at me, and I received a phone call later to say that the police had searched the roads in the area but there was no trace of the Subaru. No-one has been to see me. I'm bloody annoyed at that. I could have been hit and injured by the bottle.'

'Where is the bottle now?' Bob asked.

'It's still where it landed. I ran after the pick-up but I had to give up after about a hundred yards.'

Bob could hardly believe that a crucial piece of evidence in the identification of the passenger hadn't been recovered by the police. He had arranged to see Albert Curtis at lunch time, but he had the morning free. 'Leave the bottle where it is then. I'll head out to see you and we'll have a look in the field where they were.'

In a little over half an hour Bob was with Tam Bain, the farmer. 'Let's see if we can get this bottle first Tam. It could be really important.'

'It should be lying in the grass field that they were in,' said Tam. 'It's the only grass field I have just now that has no stock, which is maybe why they picked that one. Thankfully it's dry so it won't be too badly tracked by them driving around.'

The small green bottle was easily found. It had originally held beer and because the grass was dry there was a fair chance of obtaining fingerprints or DNA from it.

'Let's see if we can find what they were up to Tam. You never know what evidence there might be.'

They made a thorough search of the field, following the route the men had taken by following the tracks wherever possible.

'The driver's been a bit heavy on the brakes,' Tam observed. 'Most of the time when he has stopped you can see a slight skid mark.'

The skid marks helped locate when the vehicle had stopped to pick up a hare, the type of mammal being identifiable by some of the hare's fur left on the grass.

'The fur from a hare comes away from its body very easily,' said Bob, 'far more so than that of a rabbit. That's certainly helping us here. There's not enough fur though for the hare to have been taken by a dog'.

Tam Bain was a sharp-eyed character and spotted a glint in the short grass. 'Here's a .22 rimfire bullet case Bob. They've been shooting the hares. It would be like shooting fish in a barrel. When I've been out checking the sheep in the dark at lambing time the hares hardly bother with the lamp or the headlights; they just continue eating grass.'

'Well done Tam. That's another possibility for DNA when they've fed the bullet either into the clip or the chamber of the rife.'

The two men found evidence of where three hares had been shot. There were no injured or dead hares in the field. Bob observed, 'It's clear from the car marks and the traces of fur that the men lifted the hares as they shot them and put them in the car. If we ever get them to court it will be a battle with the defence to prove the killing of the hares without having recovered them, but I think between us, with the experience we have, we'd just about manage that.'

By the time Bob had noted a statement from Tam Bain and photographed the view of the field the farmer would have had from the farmhouse it was time to set off to see Albert Curtis. As he drove away from the farm Bob glanced up at the chimneys on Tam's farmhouse and began to whistle the tune *Tam Bain's Lum*. Absolutely no connection of course as the tune originated from the Tam Bain Pub in Laurieston near Falkirk. Though Bob didn't know it at the time, there was a police connection: the tune was written by the late Donald Shaw Ramsay, ex Pipe Major of Edinburgh City Police Pipe Band.

Albert looked a different man when Bob met him on the farm which was his new place of employment. Morningside Farm at Auchterarder nestles on the north edges of the Ochil Hills, a chain of hills running from Perth to Stirling and rather resembling humpback whales rising out of the sea. A massive weight had clearly been taken off Albert's shoulders and he was smiling.

'Jump into the Toyota Bob and I'll take you round to see what a great place I'm working in now. What a bloody change from the last place, night and day.'

They drove off towards the Ochils. 'Look at these strips of woodland running up from the foot of the hill. The present farmer's father planted them. Not your usual crappy spruce but a mix of native woodland: some Scots pine, birch, rowan, wild cherry, aspen, whitebeam and some oak at the bottom. There are fencers coming in shortly and there will be another three areas fenced off for planting in the autumn. I've got 500 pheasant poults due to arrive shortly. By the time they spread out through these woodland strips there will plenty for the four shoots we have over the winter. Best of all the boss has no interest in big bags or commercial shooting, only about four guns each day, made up of friends and family so nothing too fancy.'

'You've landed on your feet here Albert. What's your new house like?'

'Pretty good. It's a bit smaller than the last one we had but there's only me and Lizzie. It's easy to heat. We've a woodburning stove and I've plenty access to logs. Now look at this crop here.' Albert had driven further along the foot of the hills to a field of about ten acres. 'This crop is for the wild birds. No doubt the pheasants will use it as well but the boss wants to encourage the wee birds. It's sown with mustard, forage rape, quinoa, sunflowers and millet. There's phacelia round the edges to encourage insects. Magic, absolutely magic.'

Bob was impressed. 'That's great Albert. It's not a huge amount out of the acreage of the farm but if every farmer did that what a difference it would make to finch populations. You might even bring back the corn bunting to this area.'

'And look at this.' Albert had moved across on to flatter land. 'One of the first things I was asked to do when I came here was to create some ponds on this marshier land.' I've made two already and I'll make another couple over the winter.' He pointed at the nearest pond. 'Look, there's young mallard already and a couple of moorhens. Their first nest failed, I think the crows got the eggs, but they'll probably try another clutch, there's time yet. There were one or two teal for a while on the third pond but they never stayed. It might be better for them when there are some trees round the edges.'

'I'm really pleased for you Albert. You had a bad experience at Loch

Garr Estate. Hopefully you'll enjoy bringing this farm on as you and the owner would like it to be.'

'The boss knows what he is doing but he listens to me as well. I suggested more hedging, probably hawthorn with trees interspersed. That's now on the list of things to do. If all these are handyman jobs, I'm all for it.'

At the end of the tour of the farm Bob sat in the Toyota with Albert and noted a statement about Masterfield giving him a tub of pesticide. There was little to add to the statement that he hadn't told Bob at the outset. If a case came to court Albert's statement and the recovery and analysis of the tub of pesticide would make a massive difference.

Back at the station Bob looked in on DI Sneddon to update him. The DI also had an update for Bob. 'Mark Mason, the under keeper who had left Loch Garr Estate in disgust gave a statement when he was interviewed by the NWCU investigative support officer. He said that he realised very quickly that Masterfield is a hopeless head keeper. It's Nigel Roberts that's pulling the strings and telling him exactly what to do. He was there twice during the week Mason was on the estate and was mostly out on the hill with Masterfield in his Land Rover.'

Before he continued the DI pointed to the biscuit tin and Bob removed the lid and dipped in for a chocolate biscuit. 'He's putting Masterfield in the frame for shooting red and roe deer at night. He was also there when Masterfield shot a buzzard roosting in a tree, but there's no corroboration of that. Most interesting of all he helped lower Masterfield down to a peregrine nest. Masterfield placed a dead pigeon on the ledge where the nest was. He can't say that this was a poison bait but the pigeon, or the remains, may still be there.'

'I know the location of the peregrine nest scrape,' said Bob, 'Jock Scott the former head keeper pointed it out to me on a map. It's at the west end of the estate. I'm clear to go in there tomorrow to pick it up sir. I could also take sweepings from the bench that Brock mentioned. Do we know which shed it's in yet?'

'Sorry Bob, with so much going on I'd forgotten to tell you. Brock drew a wee map pinpointing the shed.' He reached into his desk and brought out a sheet of paper which he handed to Bob. 'About the nest, if Masterfield had to be lowered down on a rope I'm not having you doing that. Health and safety and all that. I'll arrange for two of the search and rescue team to go with you. They're trained for that and have the equipment. They can recover it under your direction. I've also spoken to Meg Runciman about the possibility of using Brock as a witness. She's got your report against Masterfield and Brock and will get back to me when she reads it.'

The DI had a puzzled look on his face when he asked the next question. 'Why do you talk about the peregrine's scrape rather than its nest?'

'Ah, peregrines don't make nests, they just shuffle with their feet and body and make a wee scrape on a ledge into which they lay their eggs.'

'Every day is a school day. I'll pass my wildlife crime officer's exam yet.'

A good case against Masterfield was now beginning to come together. Bob was looking forward to another visit to Loch Garr Estate and there were more than sufficient grounds to carry out the search without the need to apply for a search warrant.

Chapter 33

The .22 rimfire bullet case and bottle were packed and away to forensics. Bob had high hopes of a result. He still had an hour before PCs Simon Bannister and Felicity Hope of the search and rescue team were due to arrive. He read through the badger baiting case which was due to go to trial later in the week. The evidence was strong and Bob was hopeful of a change of plea. It really pissed him off that suspects left it to the last minute to change a not-guilty plea to one of guilty. It was their right, however, so there was nothing he could do about it.

At 10am Simon and Felicity arrived and the three set off for Loch Garr Estate. They made for the west end of the estate first to examine the peregrine site. At this stage of the investigation Bob wasn't bothered about being seen by the keepers and they managed to take the search and rescue Land Rover to within half a mile of the crags.

As they walked towards the top of the crags the signs were ominous. 'If this site is occupied we should be seeing at least one of the peregrines by this time,' explained Bob. 'I'd expect one to be circling us screaming in alarm but there's not a sound.'

'They wouldn't be likely to attack though Bob?' queried Felicity.

'No, very few raptors will attack, though some hen harriers come close to attacking and it's not unknown for a buzzard to attack someone running or cycling past if they're near a nest with young. You might expect a big fierce eagle to attack but they usually clear off and watch from a distance. You're much more likely to be attacked by a wee bird like an Arctic tern if you're near its nest.'

At the top of the crags Simon hammered a spike into the ground and attached a long nylon rope to it. Felicity said confidently, 'I drew the short straw and I'm going down the rope to the ledge the pigeon may be on. When I'm finished there I'll abseil to the bottom and you two can meet me there.'

Bob gave Felicity health and safety instructions about handling anything she found and looked on in amazement as she expertly lowered herself over the edge.

A few minutes later there was a radio message from Felicity. 'There's the remains of a pigeon on the ledge. It's partly eaten and there are three very small dead chicks near it.'

Bob responded with an instruction. 'Can you photograph them before you bag them up?'

'That's done. I'm heading down to the bottom now. I'll radio when I get there.'

'Thanks Felicity. Wait at the bottom and we'll join you for a search in case one of the adult peregrines might be lying about.'

Twenty minutes later the three police officers were conducting a line search back and forth among the heather below the crags. A little while later Simon shouted, 'A dead bird here. I think it's a peregrine but I'm not too sure.'

Bob confirmed the find as a female peregrine. 'The likelihood is that the bird ate some of the poisoned pigeon, which kills pretty quickly. It's less than a hundred yards from the crags. It probably took off and just glided down to crash-land here. The chicks might also have succumbed to whatever the pigeon was laced with but they could also have simply died of starvation. With his mate and chicks dead the male would just clear off. What a bloody waste of a lovely bird.'

Next on the list of jobs was the examination of the bench in the shed identified by Brock. The drive to Masterfield's house didn't take long and he was nowhere to be seen when the officers arrived there. Obtaining sweepings from the top of the bench was quickly completed, though there was no sign of a stick that was reported to have been used to mix the tub's contents. Job done, they headed back to Perth.

Bob's mobile rang as he was parking at the police station. 'Bob, this is PC Doug Guthrie at Pitlochry Police Station here. We've stopped a car that was heading south on the A9 near Blair Atholl. There is no insurance cover for the car so it's being seized. The driver had some personal cannabis in a tobacco tin in his pocket plus he tested positive for cannabis so he's being arrested for driving with cannabis in his system. There was another tobacco tin on the back seat. There were five birds' eggs in the tin, which was filled with cotton wool. The driver is a Walter Waghorn from Durham. He also had maps of parts of the northwest of Scotland and of Orkney on the back seat. Do you want to look up to Pitlochry and help us deal with him so far as the eggs are concerned?'

'I'll be there in thirty minutes Doug. I'm in my car now and ready to leave. Don't let him make a phone call, we'll probably have to get his home address searched.'

Bob enjoyed his drive up the A9. He loved the hills and crags around Dunkeld. He loved the variety of forestry, even the green of the bracken, though it was beginning to take over some parts of the countryside. The River Tay, the longest river in Scotland, ran parallel to the road for part of the distance and he could see one or two anglers trying their luck. Salmon were much scarcer than they had been a couple of decades earlier but this particular year was showing some promise. This could have been because of an intensive annual programme of re-stocking with salmon fry in the upper tributaries by the Tay District Salmon Fisheries Board. As he neared Pitlochry the hills in the distance had morphed into mountains and the last half mile of the road into the town ran almost beside the lovely River Tummel, which was dammed for electricity supply but had a famous salmon ladder where the public could watch the salmon through a glass screen as they made their way upstream. The journey had been made even more pleasurable by Calum Kennedy blasting out songs in Gaelic and in English. Bob fast forwarded to *The Road to the Isles* track and sang along with Calum, 'By Loch Tummel and Loch Rannoch and Lochaber I will go… '

Waghorn's Ford Mondeo was parked at the back of Pitlochry Police Station. Bob began a search along with PC Doug Guthrie. The main items of interest inside the car were a digital camera and a spare memory card, which Bob hoped might show where Waghorn had been and what he had been up to. On the floor behind the driver's seat lay a trowel, which Bob took possession of though he wasn't sure at that time if it was significant. 'Better to be safe than sorry.' From the boot he took possession of a tractor tyre tube and a gadget for inflating tyres. Hidden in the spare wheel compartment were three plastic ice cream tubs which were full of birds' eggs. They had been blown, each with a singular small circular hole in the centre and were protected by cotton wool. One of the tubs also contained a small drill which could have been used for making the holes in the eggs. Bob remarked loudly, 'Bastard. They could all have developed into rare and lovely birds.'

In the office, Doug Guthrie showed Bob the eggs in the tobacco tin. There were five and they were a glossy white colour. 'I'd guess these are kingfisher eggs Doug.'

He looked at the eggs in the tubs. There were two eggs that were long and narrow, fawn in colour with black spots. 'I think they're either black-throated diver or red-throated diver eggs,' Bob guessed. 'That explains the tube in the boot: for floating Waghorn out to a nest on a small islet on a loch.

'These four in this tub are probably whimbrel eggs. They're very like curlew eggs though I'd say that curlew eggs are a bit darker.' Bob continued his inspection. 'These five roundish white eggs appear to be hen harrier eggs.

One has a blueish tinge; it was probably just laid the day they were taken. These next four could well be greenshank eggs. All of these are rare birds that nest in the north of Scotland and on Orkney. The kingfisher eggs could be from anywhere. He's maybe collected them on the way south. Even though I've a reasonable knowledge of birds' eggs I'm no expert and we need now to get Ralph Murdoch of RSPB Investigations to identify them and give a statement so that there can be no dispute in court.'

Doug was like a dog with two tails. 'I was happy to take a driver off the road for driving under the influence of drugs and without insurance, but the recovery of these eggs has made it a much more interesting case.'

'We're not finished yet. I'll phone my wildlife crime officer colleague in Durham and get Waghorn's house searched. He'll have an egg collection somewhere, hopefully it's in his house.'

With the search of Waghorn's house in hand, Bob and Doug had a look at the photos on the camera. 'He's photographed the eggs before he's taken them from the nests Doug. That's not uncommon with egg thieves. Look at the two eggs in the diver's nest,' Bob remarked, pointing at the photo on the screen, 'it must have been tricky carrying a camera while floating over water in a tractor tube.'

The next image was of a loch with a small island about fifty yards out from the bank. 'It's quite a large loch, maybe more likely to be in the north of Scotland than on Orkney. Black-throated divers tend to nest on larger lochs but that's only a rough guide.'

In the next photo there was a nest of heather stems amongst tall heather. 'This is likely to be where the hen harrier eggs came from Doug. It's a pity none of the rest of the photos show background that might identify a locus.'

Waghorn had also photographed the whimbrel eggs and the greenshank eggs in their respective nests before he plundered them.

'Here's an interesting one,' said Bob. 'It's the bank of a river, seems quite sandy. There's a hole half-way up the bank which is probably the kingfisher's nest hole. It's a pity again that there's no identifying features that could show where this is. I bet this is what the trowel was for: to scrape into the nest chamber to collect the clutch of eggs.

'I'll photograph the eggs and email the photos to Ralph Murdoch at RSPB Investigations in Edinburgh for provisional confirmation of the species. We can get on and interview Waghorn after that. Ralph can see the eggs themselves in due course.'

Waghorn declined the services of the duty solicitor and his interview was unproductive, with a 'no comment' response throughout. 'I'm not overly concerned that he's saying nothing Doug. What we've recovered in the car is more than sufficient for a conviction.'

Ralph Murdoch had returned Bob's email by the time the interview was completed. The eggs were of black-throated diver right enough, whimbrel, greenshank, hen harrier and kingfisher. Ralph had added the reminder that all these species were on Schedule 1 of the Wildlife and Countryside Act as specially protected birds.

Bob was well aware of the rarity of the bird species and decided, 'I think because of that we should try to get Waghorn kept for the court in the morning. We'll rattle out the wildlife report now. Your traffic and drug case can go in separately.'

By the time the report was completed Bob had a call from PC Jacob Tomelty, the wildlife crime officer leading the search in Durham. 'We've had some success at Waghorn's address. I don't think we have his full collection, maybe just those eggs he's collected this year, but there's a total of seventy five eggs, many of which are Schedule 1 birds, the most interesting being two eggs of a golden eagle.'

'That's a good result nonetheless Jacob, I take it you'll be reporting the case to the CPS where you are?'

'Yes, we'll be doing that. If he gets jailed in Scotland, he can look forward to jail again in England when he comes out.'

Chapter 34

Walter Waghorn appeared at Perth Sheriff Court from custody. He pleaded guilty to all of the following charges:

1. From a place or places in Scotland unknown to the prosecutor, you did take 20 eggs of five species of bird included in Schedule 1 of the Wildlife and Countryside Act 1981
2. For the purposes of committing an offence under the Act, you did have in your possession 4 maps, a tractor tyre tube, a drill, a trowel, a camera and two memory cards, and a Ford Mondeo car all capable of being used for committing the offence
3. You did drive a motor car while above the prescribed limit of Delta-9-Tetrahydrocannabinol in your blood
4. You did possess of one sixteenth of gram of cannabis resin.

The fiscal, Meg Runciman, explained to the court the circumstances of the stop-check by the police and the finding of the various eggs and other items. She read out to the court some details on the report of the preparation done by Bob to make the court aware of the rarity of the birds.

'M'lord, as well as all five species of birds' eggs taken by the accused being included on Schedule 1 of the Wildlife and Countryside Act, in other words some of our rarest birds in Scotland, the hen harrier and whimbrel are red-listed species. The red list of birds is made up of species which are globally threatened, where there has been a historical population decline in UK during 1800–1995, where there has been at least a 50% decline in the UK breeding population over the last twenty five years or longer, or at least a 50% contraction of the UK breeding range of that bird over last twenty five years or longer.'

Meg turned the page and continued, 'The other eggs, those of the kingfisher, black-throated diver and the greenshank are birds that are amber-listed. These birds have a moderate (25–50%) decline in UK breeding population over the last twenty five years, a moderate (25–50%) contraction of UK breeding range over the last twenty five years, or moderate (25–50%) decline in UK non-breeding population over the last twenty five years.'

The fiscal thumbed back a couple of pages and went on to describe the purpose of the various items seized by the police. She added, 'The black-throated diver only lays two eggs, so the rate of the population increase is slow. The pair that lost their clutch of eggs to the accused have lost their chance to raise any young this year.

'In relation to the items seized by the police I would ask that the court order forfeiture of all of them. I include in this the accused's Ford Mondeo motor car. The vehicle was used in the commission of this crime and without a vehicle the accused would have had much more difficulty in accessing the various places in Scotland where, by his admission, he took those eggs.

'Moving on now to the charge of driving a vehicle on a public road. The level of cannabis in the accused's blood was above the prescribed level of 2 microgrammes per litre of blood set by the Drug Driving (Specified Limits) (Scotland) Regulations 2019. I'm sure M'lord is well aware of the risk to other motorists and pedestrians from anyone driving with their faculties impaired. Lastly, in relation to the charge of possessing cannabis resin, my intention is to no longer proceed with that charge.'

Waghorn's defence solicitor now got to his feet. He was the duty court defence solicitor and had little knowledge either of his client or of birds.

'M'Lord, my client would like to express his deep regret for taking these birds' eggs. The idea of starting a collection of birds' eggs came from a friend of his. The friend advised him how to find nests of birds and what equipment he might need to take with him to do so. This is his first outing to take eggs and he seems to have been extremely lucky with his finds.'

Meg jumped up and addressed the court, 'M'lord, my friend may wish to consult with his client before he goes any further with this line of mitigation.'

The defence solicitor leaned over to Waghorn in the dock and a whispered conversation took place. It was noticeable that the solicitor was becoming angry. He addressed the court again. 'Apologies M'Lord. I withdraw the last statement and have nothing further to say in mitigation in relation to my client's taking of eggs. In relation to driving over the limit of cannabis in his blood, he informs me he had smoked some cannabis the previous evening and he was of the opinion – the mistaken opinion – that any traces in his system would have cleared. He apologises for this error in judgement.'

The solicitor took a sip of water from his glass on the table and continued. 'My client admits his previous convictions, though none are analogous to the charges here today. He is in full-time employment as a van driver and is in a position to pay a fine. He is a family man with a wife and two children at secondary school. He is the breadwinner for the family and considerable hardship would be caused to the family if he receives a prison sentence.'

The sheriff had been taking copious notes as the prosecution and defence put forward their respective case. It was now his turn to speak.

'Mr Waghorn, would you stand please.'

Waghorn stood almost to attention in the court, dreading the outcome of his unscheduled visit to Perth Sheriff Court.'

'Mr Waghorn, you have pleaded guilty to three serious charges. The people of Scotland are entitled to have the protection of the court when wild bird egg thieves come from elsewhere to steal the eggs of extremely rare birds. As well as the interest of the people within this country, many visitors come to Scotland for the express reason of looking at or studying our wild birds. You have, at least in part, deprived them of that opportunity. You have lessened their enjoyment of the glorious sight of rare birds in their natural environment, whether that be on Scotland's lochs, moorland, rivers or in the air.

'In respect of charge 1, the taking of twenty Schedule 1 birds' eggs, you will go to prison for four months. That sentence is discounted by a third because of your early plea of guilty. The maximum period of imprisonment available to me in relation to this offence is six months. I can warn you that this maximum penalty is under review and that if you continue taking wild birds' eggs you may find yourself imprisoned for a substantially longer period.'

The sheriff paused for a minute to allow the accused to appreciate the pending increase in penalty. 'In respect of charge 2, the possession of equipment that could be used for the commission of the crime, you will go to prison for one month. The sentences will run concurrently.

'In respect of the third charge, that of driving with cannabis in your blood in excess of the permitted level, you will be fined £200. Again that fine is discounted by a third. You will be disqualified from driving for a period of twelve months. The camera and memory cards, the tractor tyre tube, the maps, the trowel and the drill will be forfeit by the court. In relation to the request by the prosecution for the court to forfeit your car, I have considered that carefully and can tell you that you have come within a whisker of losing your car. If you come before a court again where you have used your vehicle to commit crime the outcome may be much less favourable.'

Satisfied with the sentencing of Waghorn, Bob headed off to see Frank McArthur to have samples taken from the pigeon bait and the dead peregrine and her chicks. He then took the samples, together with the sweepings from Masterfield's bench, to SASA, where he left them with Dorothy Abernethy for analysis. Since he was at the west end of Edinburgh, he called in to the offices of RSPB Scotland to give Ralph Murdoch the good news about Waghorn's conviction and sentence.

'That's a decent sentence Bob,' agreed Ralph as he switched on the kettle and put two tea bags into a bright pink teapot. 'Had it been a few months later I think Waghorn might have had a bit longer than four months in jail. It looks like the maximum penalty is to be extended to five years.'

'That will clear the way for the use of surveillance on 'private' land of course Ralph. We've been unable to do that because up until now most wildlife crime didn't qualify as 'serious' crime. A court option of a five-year penalty changes everything. The police will be able to apply for authority under the Regulation of Investigatory Powers (Scotland) Act 2000. That will be a major step forward.'

'We've already had success in getting the evidence with our surveillance equipment, it's just that the Crown Office won't let it get to court. Let's drink to a new era in crime detection,' chuckled Ralph as he poured two mugs of tea.

After half an hour of useful chat Bob was ready to head back his office. As he was about to go out the door Ralph shouted, 'Hang on Bob, I've just remembered a bit of information that came in yesterday, wait till I find it on our intelligence system.' Ralph fiddled with the computer keys then said, 'Yes, here it is. An anonymous caller left a message that a Donald Turner of Invermay Place in Kirriemuir catches finches in his garden. He describes Turner as a 'older guy in his seventies.' I've looked at the map and Invermay Place is right on the edge of Kirriemuir next to woodland so his garden might indeed be suitable.'

'Finch trapping is usually a wintertime crime, isn't it, when birds are in flocks?'

'Yes it is, though he might well have some illegally taken birds from last winter.'

'We'd never get a search warrant on anonymous information but I'll look into Turner and see if I can find out any more. If not then I'll flag it up for action when we get a cold spell in the winter.'

Once he was back in the office Bob checked out Donald Turner on SID. He was only known as being a firearm certificate holder. A check with NWCU was negative. An open-source check on the internet brought up a Donald Turner as the treasurer of the Northeast Cage Bird Society and showed a photo of Turner holding a goldfinch. His photo fitted the age bracket. Bob next phoned the firearms licensing department.

'Yeh, Donald Sampson Turner, date of birth 230748, 3 Invermay Place, Kirriemuir, is the holder of a target rifle.'

'Is he due a visit any time soon?' Bob asked.

'He's due to renew his certificate by 31st October this year,' was the answer.

'Could you please mark down on his file that I be called in advance of this date to go with the firearms enquiry officer or police officer or whoever is going to visit him?'

A visit might be a good chance to gather more information, but Bob intended to look at the house and its setting the next time he was in the area.

Bob had a visitor a few minutes later. It was DC Hamish McColl, who had collated the items of interest elicited from the Loch Garr Estate gamekeepers during their interviews.

'Bob, DS Bill Reid and I are going to bring in Nigel Roberts tomorrow. We hope to be able to charge him with vicarious liability in relation to the events on Loch Garr Estate. Let's quickly review the evidence to support this.'

Bob thought for a minute, 'Okay, the main evidence comes from the killing of the birds we can definitely link in to poisoned baits, in other words those that are found near enough to the bait for us to be certain that the pesticide in the bait has killed it. Setting out poisoned, poisonous or stupefying baits is also relevant, as of course is the possession of pesticide. Even if the court doesn't think the traces of pesticide found in Masterfield's vehicle and on his clothing are sufficient then he had possession of the tub of pesticide he handed over to Albert Curtis. Other offences are likely to be added into vicarious liability later in the year but these are the ones at present, at least from this investigation.'

'Would you be available tomorrow when we bring in Roberts in case we need to clarify or ask anything during the interview? We'll bring him in to Perth police station.'

'I have a trial at Dundee Sheriff Court, badger diggers. I'll be in the office though until I get a shout from the fiscal that the trial is starting. If I'm at the court I'll have the phone on silent. I hope you manage to get enough evidence to charge the bastard. Albert and Mike Curtis and Jock Scott say he's singlehandedly wrecked the reputation of grouse shooting. I don't disagree with them.'

After a couple of long days Bob headed home early, much to Liz and Toby's delight. The three of them had a long walk round the perimeter of a nearby larch wood. A buzzard, probably with well-grown chicks in a nest near the edge of the wood, followed them at a distance.

By 6 o'clock an Indian carry out was on the cards for the evening meal and Liz nipped out in the car to collect it. Bob opened a bottle of red wine to let it breathe and read over the statements from the badger digging case in preparation for the next day's trial. Meantime Toby was tucking heartily into a dish of chicken, carrots and green beans.

Chapter 35

Meg Runciman phoned Bob at 10am. 'Two of the three charged with badger digging have submitted pleas of guilty that are acceptable Bob. I took out the charges that were under the Protection of Badgers Act, which might have been double jeopardy as they arise from the same set of circumstances as the charges relating to animal fights under the Animal Health and Welfare (Scotland) Act. I preferred the animal fighting charges as the penalty is twice as high: twelve months imprisonment as opposed to six months. I'm hoping that the court will impose imprisonment rather than a fine; they're three pretty horrible individuals.'

'Which one is pleading not guilty Meg?' queried Bob.

'Clint Mcleish, that's Clint Wayne McLeish, I can't get over that name. I wonder if he'll arrive at the court on a horse, all guns blazing?' Meg howled with laughter. 'We're the only trial in court 3 so we should be starting shortly. It's a lady sheriff, Sheriff Ross. Could you come to the court now as I'll take you quite early on.'

Bob had only to wait half an hour in the witness room when he was called to the court. The fiscal went through his evidence carefully, giving Bob time to explain to the court the ecology of badgers and typical injuries caused both to badgers and dogs by having to fight each other. More specific evidence would be led by the SSPCA officers and the vet who treated the dogs. Sheriff Ross had already viewed the video of the badger being pulled from the sett, running off, being shot then set upon by dogs before being hit with a spade.

When the fiscal finished leading Bob through his evidence Sheriff Ross had a question. 'Are you sure of the identification of the person who hit the badger with the spade Constable McKay?'

Bob had no doubt that the sheriff had recognised McLeish on the video but wanted on record that indeed it was him. 'Absolutely M'Lady. As soon as I saw him at the interview stage I recognised Mr McLeish,' Bob pointed towards him, 'the person in the dock, as one of the two men who ran after the badger and shouted encouragement to the dogs to attack it. Mr McLeish then hit the badger hard on the head with the side of the spade.' He noticed McLeish scowling at him and trying to stare him out.

'Did three men not run after the badger Mr McKay?'

'Indeed M'Lady, but one was carrying out the filming.'

'Thank you, Mr McKay.' The sheriff addressed the defence solicitor, 'Mr Green, would you carry on please.'

Bob looked at Mathew Green. He was one of the regular defence solicitors in Dundee and Bob had crossed swords with him in trials in the past. Not a pleasant individual, he frequently tried to bully witnesses. He had little success with this tactic on police witnesses, but it seemed to impress his clients. Green was regularly pulled up by sheriffs for trying to intimidate civilian witnesses, many of whom would be giving evidence in a court for the first time.

Bob was happy that Green would know bugger all about badgers. He was staggered when Green said, 'I have no questions for this witness M'Lady.' Even though Bob was not part of the search team at McLeish's house he was surprised that Green didn't ask at least one question to try to make a fool of him. And curry favour with McLeish.

Bob was excused by the sheriff and would have loved to sit and listen to the rest of the trial but he was aware that Nigel Roberts was likely to be in custody in Perth and that he might be required there.

Hamish McColl and Bill Reid were in the CID office when Bob looked in. 'We've got Roberts here but we're waiting on his bloody solicitor coming from Edinburgh,' Hamish snorted. 'Unlike his dogsbodies he's not satisfied with the duty solicitor, he wants the solicitor from Edinburgh who he deals with all the time. That'll no doubt cost him but I'm sure it'll just be pocket money to him.' A smile crept across Hamish's face. 'The longer the bloody solicitor takes to get here the longer Roberts gets to appreciate the splendour of our cells. Hopefully it will be a practice run for a shared cell with a junkie in Perth Prison someday soon. Cup of tea Bob?'

The three officers sat with their tea, going over anything that might trip Roberts up during the interview. 'He'll maybe say nothing at all of course,' said Bill Reid. 'He'll be well schooled by the solicitor, but it's a reverse burden of proof so if he can't show due diligence he'll be fucked. I'll be surprised though if he hasn't kept his hands clean and kept his distance from the illegal stuff.'

'The keepers have to get their instructions from somewhere though.' Bob interjected, 'With the illegal practices that have been taking place on Loch Garr Estate the orders must come from him somehow. There's no way that raptors and other protected wildlife are being killed if he, as the bloody estate owner, doesn't want them killed. He knows as well as we do that more predators of any sort means less grouse killed on a shooting day.

To hell with the law.'

Hamish's mobile rang. 'That's the solicitor here now. We'll make him wait a bit, I've not finished my tea.'

It was mid-afternoon by the time the solicitor had consulted with Roberts and the interview was concluded. Hamish and Bill looked into Bob's office. 'We've charged him with vicarious liability,' Hamish said. He started off the interview with 'no comment' responses but he's such an arrogant bastard he felt he had to get his tuppence worth in. He couldn't resist telling us he was in charge of all these gamekeepers on Loch Garr, had been in charge of the gamekeepers on the other estates in his past role, and that he's one of the best at bringing on grouse numbers to a huge shootable surplus.'

'That's a good start then Hamish,' Bob remarked, 'That's one element of vicarious liability established. He just needs to show now that he did not know Masterfield was using pesticide to poison wildlife and that he took all reasonable steps and exercised all due diligence to prevent this happening in the first place. If he wants to avoid court, he'll need to satisfy due diligence in advance of the trial. That's down to him now.'

Hamish nodded and carried on. 'Once he was in full flow, boasting that all the work he supervised was carried out within the law he said he had written to Masterfield instructing him not to do anything that broke the law and that if he did so he would be sacked. I've no doubt he'll produce a letter to that effect, which he'll have written just to cover his arse.'

Bob added, 'Yeh, the real situation is that the headkeepers know that they have to produce grouse by eliminating any threat to them, otherwise they won't keep their job.'

'We'll need to show that Roberts was very hands-on, at least in terms of dishing out instructions. That's in the statement from the keeper who left after a week, what's his name again?'

'Mark Mason,' Bob answered.

Hamish thought for a minute, 'I wonder if Brock can tell us any more about Robert's close supervision of Masterfield. I think we'll re-interview him. I'll phone him and see if he'll come in here. With what he's told us his days are numbered on that estate anyway.'

In the late afternoon as Bob was packing up for the day Meg Runciman gave him a call. 'Sheriff Ross found McLeish guilty of all the charges. I'm surprised he pleaded not guilty, when the evidence came out from all the witnesses it was very compelling. PC Maggie McPherson who searched McLeish's house was a particularly good witness and was able to bring out his violent character even from her short time with him in the house.

ALAN STEWART

Sentence is deferred till next week as the sheriff wants all three accused in court. Jail time methinks.'

'Hopefully the sheriff will ban them from keeping dogs Meg, that would really be the icing on the cake.'

162

Chapter 36

Later in the week Hamish McColl looked in to see Bob. 'We saw Brock in the police station yesterday. He's obviously keen now to be as helpful as possible so as not to be linked in any way with Susan McLaren's death. We asked him about how Roberts passes on his instruction to the keepers. He never deals with the under keepers, always Cyril Masterfield. Brock's heard him sometimes telling Masterfield what to do, and probably more often giving him a dressing down for doing something wrong or not doing something he should have but he can't say that he's heard Roberts telling him to do anything illegal. This interview didn't really add much to the pot of evidence.'

'That's a pity Hamish but it's good to know he's still on side, which must be quite difficult for him until he gets away from the estate. I know the result of the interview by NWCU of Mark Mason, the keeper who left Loch Garr Estate in disgust, but had Mason ever had any training in using or storing chemicals or a direction not to break the law?'

'He'd had no such training, yet he'd had it on the estate where he did his trainee gamekeeping. Mind you with him only having been on Loch Garr a week his statement will have less importance than that of the under keepers who had been there longer. I think we could get going on the reporting of this case now Bob and fill in the blanks as the various tests are completed.'

'I agree Hamish, it's all testing from SASA we're waiting on. Let's put tomorrow aside and get most of this case on to the system. I'll phone Meg Runciman shortly, go over the evidence and see if she thinks of anything we still need to do.'

Just before lunchtime Bob called Meg. He was pleased to hear her say that there was nothing else she could think of that had still to be done or anything else that could bolster the evidence already available. She would know better, however, once she had read the complete report.

Over a mug of tea Bob returned his thoughts to Roberts. He emailed a list of estates connected to Roberts to the firearms licensing section with a request that they give him details of keepers who had moved on from these estates and where they had moved to. He could take it from there and see if any of them might be worth interviewing.

The allegation about the Kirriemuir finch trapper was also preying on Bob's mind and he decided that with an afternoon of nothing needing immediate attention he would have a run to Kirriemuir, Kirrie as it was known locally, and see the lie of the land at Donald Turner's address.

From the A9 dual carriageway Bob turned off onto country roads. Through the villages of Luncarty and Stanley, he crossed over the River Tay at the lovely hump-backed bridge at Cargill, then on to the Beech Hedge near the village of Meikleour. For the umpteenth time Bob marvelled at this gigantic hedge along the road on his left. Recognised by the Guinness Book of Records as the highest hedge in the world, planted in 1745, it is one third of a mile long and 100 ft high. It had recently been pruned and was looking tidy, if a bit threadbare. He knew it would be back to its former glory in a couple of years.

Bob drove through the town of Blairgowrie, famous for its berryfields and the massive crop of raspberries picked every year by huge squads of pickers, many of them travelling folk. Bob knew that this seasonal work is now mainly carried out by Eastern Europeans, but the past is forever enshrined in the song *The Berryfields of Blair* sung by traveller Belle Stewart.

> There's travellers fae the Western Isles,
> Fae Arran, Mull and Skye;
> Fae Harris, Lewis and Kyles o' Bute,
> They come their luck to try,
> Fae Inverness and Aberdeen,
> Fae Stornoway and Wick
> Aa flock to Blair at the berry time,
> The straws and rasps to pick.

His route to took him past the town of Alyth, and shortly he was crossing the county boundary between Perthshire and Angus and then on to the town of Kirriemuir, which serves most of the Angus Glens.

It didn't take Bob long to find Donald Turner's address in Invermay Place. The large private houses were on both sides of the street, with Turner's side backing on to oak and birch woodland. Bob drove slowly past No. 3, the second house on his left. Looking through the gap between No. 1 and No. 3 he could see sheds in the back garden though it was impossible to make out what the sheds might be used for.

After driving back out of the street Bob turned right along the country road past the woodland. About fifty yards past the corner of the wood there was a gate and a ride running through the woodland that seemed to run parallel with Invermay Place. Bob parked his unmarked car in the wide gateway, having to share space with a load of conifer branches, old fence posts, rusty fence wire and half a bag of solidified cement that someone had obviously slid off a flatbed lorry, almost blocking the entrance through the gateway to the woodland. Fly tipping enraged and exasperated him with hardly anyone ever convicted of it. Bob wondered what investigation the local authority made into rubbish that was dumped. He made a mental note to visit the local authority environment services and see if he could offer some help in identifying a suspect and dealing with that suspect once identified.

Bob climbed the gate and walked along the ride till he thought he might be about opposite No. 3 then walked quietly through the woodland till he could see Turner's sheds. Edging gradually closer he could see that one of the sheds had a wire aviary attached. Several birds were on the perches, which he identified as mostly greenfinches. The birds seemed quite relaxed and content, and their feathers and tail seemed in pristine condition. Bob was more interested in any birds that may be on the ground, as wild-taken birds tend to flutter about on the ground in preference to being on perches. Only two greenfinches were on the ground and they were happily feeding in a dish of seed.

From what Bob had seen, Turner certainly kept cage birds but there was no evidence that those in the outside aviary at least, were wild-taken birds. He'd no doubt that more birds would be in cages inside the shed and hoped that when he visited later in the year with the firearms enquiry officer Turner might be willing to show them his birds. Meantime he'd have to give the cage bird enthusiast the benefit of the doubt.

When he returned to his car Bob heard a call on the radio for a unit from Kirriemuir to attend at a hare coursing incident. It was at a farm on the west side of Kirriemuir, which was on his way home. He made for the farm and met the officers, who had just arrived ahead of him.

The vehicle involved was a red Ford Transit, but the farmer had not managed to get the reg number. The farmer explained the circumstances to the officers. 'I was up at the farm and saw this van stopping at my road-end. A big chap with a black lurcher and smaller brindle lurcher got out, climbed the dyke into a field we hadn't long cut for silage. The silage was baled and the guy kept behind the big round bales and walked in on a hare that was feeding in the field. I shouted and he turned tail and ran back to the van with the dogs. He threw the dogs into the back of the van and it took off.'

The young uniformed constable noted details and when the farmer had finished giving a statement he thanked the officers for attending and went back to whatever farm work he had been doing beforehand. The young constable seemed keen to progress the investigation but wondered if any offence had been committed.

Bob gave him chapter and verse. 'Under the Protection of Wild Mammals (Scotland) Act 2002 and also under the Wildlife and Countryside Act 1981 it is an offence to *attempt* to hunt a wild mammal with a dog. In this case there is no corroboration so the case couldn't stand on its own, unless of course the person involved admitted what he was doing, which is unlikely. To get a case we'd first of all need identification of who was involved, and without a vehicle number we're struggling. It's a distinctive vehicle so it may crop up again somewhere, though these guys seldom keep a vehicle for any length of time before selling it on. Good that you're interested; if you have any other dealings with coursers make sure you give me a call for help or advice. Would you submit an intelligence entry to SID?'

Bob was pragmatic in that most hare coursing incidents remain unsolved because of lack of evidence but frustratingly many cases remained were unsolved due to the lack of knowledge on the part of officers or poor investigation.

Chapter 37

The pathologist's report into the death of Susan McLaren made grim reading. The analysis showed that she had died because of the pesticides carbofuran, isofenphos and bendiocarb being in her system. The technical cause of death used by the pathologist on the death certificate was that death had resulted from respiratory failure and hypoxia due to bronchoconstriction leading to tracheobronchial secretion and pulmonary edema. The report allowed Hamish and Bob to get the case reported to the fiscal. The SASA examination showed that the pigeon recovered from the peregrine nest site had been laced with the same mix of pesticides and ingestion of those chemicals had caused the death of the female peregrine.

The date for the sentencing of the three badger diggers had arrived and Bob drove to Dundee Sheriff Court to hear the verdicts.

Meg Runciman briefly reminded Sheriff Ross of the evidence against each of the three accused. The respective solicitors for Alastair Black and Peter Wilson gave a short spiel in their defence, but it was clear they were struggling to put forward anything that might lessen their sentence. Wilson had appeared from custody, flanked by two prison officers, as he had recently started serving a two-year sentence for the two kilos of cannabis and the fourteen deals of amphetamine found hidden in his garden. Each of the solicitors stated that their client admitted the previous convictions listed against them.

Andrew Green, defending Clint McLeish, began his defence. 'M'Lady, my client regrets his part in this incident and realises now that digging out badgers is an extremely cruel activity. He states that to an extent he was led by his co-accused, Peter Wilson. My client no longer keeps any dogs and does not intend to have any more.'

Meg Runciman stood to address the sheriff. 'M'Lady, the reason Mr McLeish has no dogs is that they were seized by the police, had to undergo considerable and expensive veterinary treatment, and are now in the care of the SSPCA awaiting the decision of this court on the matter of forfeiture.'

Andrew Green continued, 'M'lady, I was just about to add that.' He scowled at the fiscal and went on, 'It's understandable you may be considering a prison sentence. My client is fit and more than willing to carry out a community payback penalty. He would also be in the position to pay a fine in instalments. He is a family man and his family would suffer if he were to be imprisoned.'

Meg Runciman jumped up again, remembering a snippet of information passed to her by Bob. 'I'm sorry to interrupt again M'Lady. It is my understanding that Mr McLeish's partner left him, taking their young child with her, shortly after the police searched their house.'

'Is this the case Mr Green?' the sheriff asked.

Green quickly conferred with McLeish in the dock before replying. 'My client tells me this is true, though he is under the impression this is temporary and he hopes that she will move back in with him.' He quickly sat down and offered no further defence.

The sheriff addressed the three men in the dock. 'Would you please stand. Mr Black, you have pled guilty to wilfully killing a badger. In respect of that charge, you will go to prison for four months. You have also pled guilty to taking part in an animal fight. To set a dog against a badger, where both animals are at risk of sustaining substantial injury and where the outcome for the badger is bleak, irrespective of injuries inflicted by the dog, is a despicable and extremely cruel crime. In respect of that charge, you will go to prison for eight months. You possessed a shotgun, which appeared to have been the weapon used on the badger in the video. The shotgun had been stolen some time ago, though there is no evidence that you were involved in its theft, but you kept the weapon and indeed ammunition for the weapon, while not the holder of a shotgun certificate. In respect of that charge, you will go to prison for eight months. Your pleas of not guilty to other charges have been accepted by the prosecution, and though you have pled guilty to the possession of cannabis resin I will admonish you on that charge. The periods of imprisonment will run concurrently. There is no indication that you own any animals, but your conduct shows that you could not be trusted to care for them with any degree of humanity. You will be banned from keeping any animals for a period of five years.'

Sheriff Ross took a sip of water then addressed the second accused. 'Mr Wilson, you have pled guilty, along with your co-accused, to wilfully killing a badger. I sentence you to four months imprisonment in respect of that horrific charge. You have also pled guilty to keeping or training an animal, namely your dogs, for the purpose of an animal fight. It is absolutely horrendous to pit two innocent animals together so that one can injure or kill the other. In a modern, caring society this must receive a substantial punishment. It is a pity that the maximum sentence is twelve months, though take note that this is due be increased shortly. In respect of this charge, and taking account of your plea of guilty, you will serve eight months imprisonment. In respect of your plea of guilty to causing unnecessary suffering to a dog, a Lakeland terrier, by failing to provide it with veterinary treatment, you will be sentenced to four months imprisonment. The prosecution has accepted not guilty pleas to other charges and in respect of your possession of cannabis resin you will be admonished. The sentences of imprisonment will run concurrently but will begin at the end of your present sentence. It is clear you are not a fit person to be in charge of animals. I therefore ban you from keeping any type of animal for a period of ten years. I will also forfeit your two dogs.'

After another sip of water the sheriff addressed Wayne McLeish. 'Mr McLeish you were found guilty after trial of wilfully killing a badger. The maximum sentence is six months imprisonment, which is what I will impose. To facilitate this you kept or trained an animal, namely two dogs, for the purpose of an animal fight and indeed you took part in an animal fight. I find this cruelty despicable and is not something that should be taking place in a civilised society. You will be sentenced to the maximum of twelve months imprisonment on each of these two charges. As you would hear me tell Mr Wilson the penalty for someone found guilty of these charges is likely to be increased soon to a maximum of five years. Please bear that in mind. After trial you were found guilty of, along with others, trespassing on land with a firearm. In respect of that charge you will be sentenced to four months' imprisonment. The last two charges of which you were found guilty were causing unnecessary suffering to a bull lurcher dog and to a Patterdale terrier by failing to provide veterinary treatment. On each of those charges you will be sentenced to four months imprisonment. The periods of imprisonment will all run concurrently. As I do with your co-accused, I consider that you are not a fit person to be in charge of any animal. I therefore ban you from keeping any type of animal for a period of fifteen years and I will forfeit your two dogs.'

In the circumstances Bob considered the sentences appropriate but couldn't wait for the substantially increased penalties that would soon be made available to courts for animal welfare offences and many wildlife offences.

Chapter 38

The firearms licensing section came back with a list of gamekeepers whose work had formerly been directed by Roberts. There were thirteen gamekeepers listed with their new addresses. Some had simply moved between the estates listed. Most had originated in the north of England and some had moved back to grouse moors in that area. One had moved to an estate in the south of England. There were no grouse there so he must have got fed up with *Lagopus lagopus*. The keeper that was most interesting had moved from a grouse moor in England and was now living in a village in Cumbria. His firearm and shotgun certificates had been cancelled. So it seemed that thirty one-year-old Shane Fitzgerald was no longer a gamekeeper.

A wee bit more digging by NWCU for Bob revealed that Fitzgerald had been a headkeeper. 'Now why would a headkeeper give up his firearms and shotguns? I think that needs to be answered Dave,' Bob commented to Dave Kemp the Senior Intelligence Officer at NWCU.

'Would you like Dougie Williamson, our Investigative Support Officer covering the north of England, to visit Fitzgerald and find out Bob?' replied Dave. Bob explained the circumstances to Dave and asked that Dougie note a statement if relevant.

Bob was hardly off the phone when it rang again. 'Hello Bob, this is Neil Lister of Scottish Natural Heritage. We've been notified of a JCB in the upper River Tay near Aberfeldy moving gravel out of the river to repair a bund that was damaged in a storm over the winter. Where they're shifting the gravel is in an area quite rich in freshwater pearl mussels. I'm just heading up to see. Do you want to meet me there?'

'Yeh, that's a good idea. I know that Constable Stuart Roberts, the wildlife crime officer at Pitlochry is on duty just now so I'll see if he's free as well.'

The three met on the north side of Aberfeldy. With binoculars they could see the JCB operator still working in the river. They parked a bit closer and it was only a quarter mile walk to reach the river. The operator had removed tons of gravel from the Tay and had nearly finished replacing the thirty yard gap in the bund. He came out of the cab when the officers approached.

'I can see what you are doing but who are you working for?' Bob asked.

The JCB operator was a Kenny McNab, which fitted with the sign on the machine reading 'Kenneth McNab, Contractor, Aberfeldy.' 'Chris Craig, the owner of the land here, asked me to repair the bund. His field was flooded in the winter when it collapsed and he doesn't want that again. I'll be covering the gravel with earth and sowing grass seed on it. It will be as good as new.'

'Did Mr Craig mention anything about freshwater pearl mussels in this part of the river Kenny?'

McNab seemed genuinely concerned, 'No, nothing about mussels. Will this work have damaged them?'

'It will have wrecked any mussel beds where you've been working and the mussels downstream will likely have been suffocated by the silt you stirred up,' Bob replied. 'You'll need to stop now.'

'I'm really sorry about this. I never gave mussels a thought,' answered McNab quietly.

Stuart Roberts noted a statement from McNab while Bob took photos of the JCB, the devastation to the river and the partly completed bund.

Neil Lister took Bob aside. 'Now that I see which part of the river we're dealing with I know that Chris Craig is well aware of freshwater pearl mussels in this stretch of river. One of my colleagues and I were surveying the river for mussels a couple of years ago and Craig came down to ask what we were doing. He thought we were looking to take the mussels for the pearls some of them contain. I remember he was really aggressive to start with but cooled down pretty quickly.'

Bob had been thinking of how to prove that an offence had been committed. 'Any mussels will have either been flattened or removed from the river with the gravel where the JCB has been working. Can we survey the river downstream of where the work has been to see what has happened to the mussels there?'

'I can come up with one of my colleagues tomorrow. The water is low enough to wade quite a bit of it,' Neil answered helpfully. 'It's also worth looking upstream of the work as well to make a comparison.'

The arrangement for a survey was agreed and Neil headed back to his office. Bob and Stuart would eventually interview and charge the owner of the land, Chris Craig, but that would wait until a full survey had been completed.

Back at the office Bob thought back to Gordon Gregor, the budding taxidermist, and wondered if the case had been to court. He checked through lists for Dundee Sheriff Court and found that Gregor had been dealt with the previous week. Surprisingly, he had pled guilty to all of the charges. For the possession of the buzzard, the sparrowhawk and the tawny owl, all containing lead shot, he was fined £200 on each charge. For the possession of the two otters, mammals listed on Schedule 2 of the Habitats Regulations, he was fined £500. It was a decent result, especially as these fines would have been one third higher but for the guilty plea. It would have been an interesting case for whichever sheriff was in court; in a city court they wouldn't deal with too many cases involving raptors or otters.

'I wonder if he'll give up thoughts of stuffing birds now?' Bob said out loud. He was aware of Shirley Deans giving him a strange glance.

Chapter 39

Bob headed off early to meet Neil Lister and PC Stuart Robertson. Heavy rain was forecast for the afternoon and the upper reaches of the River Tay were likely to rise quickly. Rather than take the dual carriageway he headed out the A85 towards the lovely Strathearn town of Crieff, turned off just short of Crieff at the village of Gilmerton and drove north through the Sma' Glen. Part of this glen runs parallel to the River Almond, a tributary of the mighty Tay, and has a good run of salmon, though always most prolific at the back end of the year. The steep hills rose on either side of the road and at one point a golden eagle swept across the glen in front of Bob. He could see it was an immature bird by the patches of white on the underside of the wings as it glided majestically past.

The River Almond abandoned its juxtaposition to the road and it disappeared up another glen to Bob's left. Further along the road, near the hamlet of Amulree, a barn owl was still hunting above rough cover bordering the River Braan. It dived down as if on prey as Bob drove past, but he lost sight of it as he rounded a bend in the road.

Further still along the road Bob looked to his left hoping to see blackcock on a regular lekking site, but it was too late in the year; they had completed their flamboyant competition for the centre of the lek where they would attract the most females. The females, greyhens, would now be on eggs, or maybe even looking after a brood of chicks.

With the conical peak of the 3,500ft Munro, Schiehallion, in the distance ahead of him. Bob tried hard to remember the tune *Schiehallion* as sung by Gaberlunzie but it eluded him. He descended the steep hill to the town of Aberfeldy, where he met his three colleagues for the survey.

Neil and his SNH colleague, Roberta Small, donned thigh waders and life vests. They waded out into the River Tay a hundred yards downstream from where the JCB had been working. Each had a stick with a cleft end which they could use to pick up any dead mussels from the riverbed, and which also steadied them in the flow of water. Each also had a bucket with a glass bottom which gave them a clear view through the rippling water.

'There's a wee bit of silt on the bed of the river here Bob,' Neil shouted from his watery position. 'I've seen a couple of mussels so far that have some silt around them but they're still syphoning properly.'

'I'm the same,' shouted Roberta. 'There is a colony of at least half a dozen mussels that are still okay, even with some silt on the riverbed. A couple of them are pretty small. If they were much smaller they could be covered in silt but then of course I wouldn't have been able to see them.'

Neil and Roberta came out of the river and moved upstream about thirty yards. 'It's a bit different here,' shouted Neil. 'There's a couple of big mussels that are okay but there are one or two smaller ones that appear to be dead. They're closed and there's no sign of any syphoning movement. I can photograph them through the bucket rather than lift them so that they'll still have a chance if they're not dead.'

Roberta was searching in a backwater, where the water swirled round her legs. 'There's a couple of big mussels that seem to be dead here. The silt is much deeper and almost covering them. It's probably been swept in by the eddy.'

The next two moves up the river gave even more depressing results, with the only live mussels being on the far side of the river, saved by the fact that the JCB had gone just over halfway across the river to scrape gravel. All the other mussels in the first fifty yards downstream from where the JCB had been working were covered in silt and were dead. Smaller ones would be completely covered.

Upstream of the riverbed work the two SNH staff were pleased to report that any mussels they found were syphoning perfectly and had been unaffected by the JCB work.

Neil and Roberta looked to be frozen when they came out of the river, even though it was still late summer and not a cold day. Stuart gave them some sympathy, as their hands had been mostly under water for the best part of an hour. 'We've been busy too though,' he laughed. 'Bob's been taking photographs and I've been taking notes.'

The SNH staff were thanked for their considerable help in gathering evidence. They left to return to their office in Perth and Bob and Stuart set off to meet the owner of the land, Chris Craig.

Craig was expecting their visit, having been warned by the JCB operator. 'I'm really sorry about this,' he apologised, 'I was down to the river last night and never realised we'd need so much gravel. I thought a couple of scoops plus the rubble that had been washed into the field would have done the job.'

The landowner was charged with intentionally or recklessly killing or injuring freshwater pearl mussels, which are on Schedule 5 of the Wildlife and Countryside Act, and intentionally or recklessly damaging or destroying the mussels' place of shelter, approximately seventy yards of the riverbed of the Tay.

'Craig knew of the mussels in the river, he apologised for what was done, but why the hell did he do it,' pondered Stuart as the two officers walked to their cars.

'Maybe he's just sorry he was caught Stuart. There's an arrogance about him, as if he can do what he likes on his own land,' replied Bob unsympathetically. The first spots of rain began falling from a rapidly darkening sky. Typical of Scottish weather, the rain was coming down in sheets within five minutes.

'We just got finished in time Bob. It'll not be long before that river would have been too high for the SNH folks to wade.'

'And too peaty or muddy for them to have seen anything.'

During the afternoon Bob took a phone call in his office. 'Dougie Williamson here Bob. I saw Shane Fitzgerald this morning. He's a real decent chap. He had been a gamekeeper in Lincolnshire but he said that rearing thousands of pheasants was not his thing. He moved to Yorkshire to a grouse moor. He hadn't been there long when Roberts moved in to advise on grouse moor management. He enjoyed the new experience at first, especially when he was made head keeper.

'Roberts then began to deal with Fitzgerald a lot more, giving him orders directly. Fitzgerald didn't mind hard work but he was being asked to work extraordinary hours. He was seldom at home and his wife was getting seriously fed up with never seeing him. It seems the marriage almost broke up.

'He was out on the moor with Roberts one day when they saw a hen harrier. Roberts was apparently fuming and told Fitzgerald he wasn't doing his job properly.

'Did he tell Fitzgerald to get rid of the harrier, Dougie?'

'No, but Fitzgerald had no doubt that's what was expected of him.'

'Last year Roberts moved him to an estate in Inverness-shire to be head keeper there. He didn't want to go and had a feeling anyway that Roberts was trying to get rid of him. His wife flatly refused to go and went to stay with her parents.

'One day when Roberts was at the Inverness-shire estate he came looking for Fitzgerald. He was absolutely furious and said that the estate owner had been out on the moor and had seen a food pass between a male and female hen harrier. 'Do you know what that means Fitzgerald?' he roared at him. 'That means there's a fucking nest. We've got a nest of harriers on the moor.'

'It got worse, Bob. Roberts slapped Fitzgerald on the face and shouted,

'Sort it.'

'I've got all this in statement form. The assault had been the final straw for Fitzgerald. He left just days after that. He told me he'd had enough of gamekeeping, and of course he'd no longer any need for his rifles and shotguns. He and his wife now have a cottage in Cumbria and he's volunteering on an RSPB reserve.'

'That's just what I'm looking for Dougie. That should make a huge difference to the vicarious liability charge, but it won't get him convicted for his criminal practices that have killed a wee girl. It might bring us closer if we could get evidence of a conspiracy charge with Masterfield, the head keeper, but unfortunately we can't make that link.'

Dougie's phone call had made Bob's day but he still couldn't envisage Roberts behind bars with the evidence available.

Chapter 40

Several months passed before the date for Masterfield and Roberts' trial in the High Court in Edinburgh. In the interval Vince Jones had pled guilty in Forfar Sheriff Court to blocking out a swift and a house sparrow from their nests. He was fined £200 on each charge.

The result of DNA and fingerprint testing on the bottle thrown at the farmer and the bullet casing found during the subsequent investigation that proved that brown hares had been shot at night was unfortunately negative. That was a real disappointment to Bob.

Chris Craig had pled guilty to intentionally or reckless killing or injuring freshwater pearl mussels and intentionally or recklessly damaging or destroying the mussels' place of shelter, approximately seventy yards of the riverbed of the Tay. Stuart Robertson had sat in at Perth Sheriff Court when the case was called and he related details to Bob later that day.

'Meg Runciman read out almost word for word what I'd put in the report,' Stuart said, 'about the fact that rivers in Scotland host a high proportion of the world's freshwater mussels, that they are almost as endangered as the tiger, and that the River Tay is one of the strongholds for this important mollusc. She told the court that it would be years before this part of the river recovered its mussel population and that Craig had been well aware of the presence of mussels. She also said that crime committed against freshwater mussels is one of six wildlife policing priorities decided by the UK Tasking & Co-ordination Group based on advice from the UK Statutory Nature Conservation Organisations and other experts.' Stuart took a breath and continued, 'The sheriff asked for further explanation, which thankfully Meg managed as she's been to at least one of the Tasking and Co-ordinating Group meetings.'

'That's the value of including an impact statement in the report Stuart. Prosecutors and sheriffs can't be expected to know automatically what the environmental impact is of every wildlife crime. An impact statement should help the court deliver a verdict that reflects understanding of the ecology of the species and fairness to the public. Anyway, sorry for interrupting, what was the verdict.'

'Craig was fined £2,000 for killing the mussels and £4,000 for damaging their habitat. Not a bad sentence.'

On the morning of the trial and as he headed for Edinburgh High Court Bob reflected on how competent Meg had become at marking and prosecuting wildlife crime cases. She was the newest fiscal in the Wildlife and Environmental Crime Unit but had grasped the complexities of wildlife law remarkably quickly. Crown Office had dropped some of the charges so as not to make the trial overly complicated for the jury but had kept the charge of the possession of traces of pesticides to allow that evidence to be led and give a more detailed account of Masterfield's use of pesticide. When she had received the case, she'd had a meeting with Bob and DI Sneddon to discuss whether there was sufficient evidence either available or that might still be obtained against Roberts to justify charging him with culpable and reckless conduct. This was by far the more serious charge and that which had brought them to the High Court. Frustratingly they had to agree that there was just not enough evidence.

Meg had decided, because of his young age and the less serious offences committed by Brock, to use him as a witness. She had let Bob see the charges against Masterfield and Roberts in advance of the trial. They were:

Masterfield
Shooting red deer stags out of season
Shooting red deer stags at night without authority from SNH
Shooting a red deer stag without lawful authority or written permission
Unlawful possession of a red deer, firearm and ammunition
Unlawful possession of the pesticides carbofuran, isofenphos and bendiocarb
Set out a pigeon bait laced with carbofuran, isofenphos and bendiocarb to kill a wild bird
Kill a wild bird, namely a peregrine falcon
Kill a wild bird, namely a buzzard
Culpable and reckless conduct by contaminating a domestic water supply
Culpable and reckless conduct by setting out a woodpigeon bait laced with carbofuran, isofenphos and bendiocarb whereby Susan McLaren picked it up, was poisoned and died

Roberts
Vicarious liability, in respect of the charges relating to the pesticides and killing the wild birds

Bob took his seat in the police witness room. The trial was being heard by Lord Abercrombie. Keith Darrowby QC was the advocate depute prosecuting, ably assisted by Meg Runciman. Alex Moore QC was defending Masterfield while Jacob Brough QC was defending Roberts. Thirty prosecution witnesses had been cited to give evidence and the trial was likely to take a week.

Despite the court starting at 10 o'clock it was just after 11 before the jury of nine women and six men was picked and seated. The first witness was Albert Curtis.

Albert gave an account of his time as a gamekeeper on Loch Garr Estate before it was bought over by Roberts. He spoke of the inexperience of Brock and of Masterfield as the new head keeper, and made it clear that Roberts was really the head keeper. He related the discovery of a rabbit bait and a dead buzzard near his house and the fact that Masterfield had given him a tub of pesticide that looked like carbofuran to use on baits.

There were objections a couple of times from Jacob Brough QC when Albert strayed off-course and gave opinions that Roberts was behind some of the illegal activity. Albert apologised and was led carefully by the advocate depute through the evidence of the recovery of the rabbit, the buzzard and the tin of pesticide he stated he had been given by Masterfield and had buried.

Albert explained in detail the finding of the deer in his water supply and its subsequent recovery by Bob. The advocate depute ensured that the court was aware of the proximity of the dead deer to the house and that it was the only water supply for Albert and his wife. Lastly, he was asked to identify Masterfield and Roberts, and he pointed to the two men sitting in the dock. It would not be lost on the jury that Masterfield was dejected and sitting with his head hanging forward, while Roberts was sitting arrogantly upright, taking in everything that Albert said and shaking his head at much of the evidence.

Alex Moore QC asked Albert if he had ever seen Masterfield shooting any deer on the estate, which he answered in the negative. He put forward the suggestion that Masterfield had never given Albert any pesticide and that the tub and contents may well have been pesticide that Albert used or possessed before the change of estate ownership. Albert denied that angrily. The QC spoke at length about the water supply, the volume of water coming down the burn which he claimed would have considerably diluted any impurities and finally asked if Albert had in any way felt sick during the period the deer could have been in the burn. Albert's answer was that he had not felt sick but the QC was trying to make the point that the dead deer had been no risk to his health.

Jacob Brough QC asked Albert how often he had met Roberts and if at any time Roberts had said to Albert, or Albert had heard him tell anyone else, that illegal practices can or should be carried out. He answered that he had not.

In his re-examination by the advocate depute, to clarify the issue of illegal activity, Albert was asked if he had ever been given any instruction by Roberts about the use of storage of pesticides or that he should *not* break the law. Albert's answer to this negated any value to the defence of his earlier answer.

Albert's wife, Liz, was next and corroborated the fact that the burn was the couple's only supply of water that was piped to the house.

Jock Scott was the next witness and gave evidence about driving the Land Rover when Masterfield shot a red deer stag at night and out of season. Defence QC Alex Moore quizzed Jock about who shot the deer, making the allegation that it was him rather than Masterfield. He finished with the line, 'It's your word again that of my client. If my client gives evidence he may well strongly dispute your version.' Jock looked like he was ready to strangle the QC.

The former under keeper, Charles Brock, was next to take the stand. He had since left Loch Garr Estate. When asked by the advocate depute where he now worked he answered that he worked in a supermarket as a checkout operator. Well knowing his new situation the advocate depute asked him why he was no longer working as a gamekeeper. He replied, 'I applied for several jobs as an under keeper on grouse moors in England and Scotland. I got none of them so applied to two estates in Scotland that have pheasant and red-legged partridge shooting. I got neither of these either. I was later told I was rejected because I spoke up about what I witnessed on Loch Garr Estate.'

Brock went through his evidence clearly and concisely, without attracting any objections from either defence QC. His evidence was particularly strong in relation to the shooting of deer by Masterfield on Loch Garr Estate and the shooting of the stag over the boundary on Hillside Farm. The jury seemed shocked at his vivid description of Masterfield shooting and injuring, then shooting and killing the red deer that was thrown into Albert Curtis's water supply. He admitted that he wasn't aware the burn was Albert's water supply when the deer was thrown in but that Masterfield had told him and was laughing as they were driving away.

Masterfield's QC said very little in defence. That was probably a tribute to how well Brock gave his evidence.

Robert's QC asked if Roberts had ever told Brock to do anything that was illegal. Brock's truthful answer that he had not drew re-examination from the advocate depute to establish that Roberts had never told Brock *not* to break the law or had given him any instruction in the storage or use of pesticides.

Brock was the final witness of that particular day. Bob, of course, confined to the witness room, had heard none of the evidence and hoped it was going well. It is a long day sitting in a witness room and he hoped he didn't have too many more days to sit around before he could give his evidence.

Chapter 41

Mark Mason was the next witness. He described lowering Masterfield down to a peregrine nest site with a dead pigeon, and how he had been instructed to drive Masterfield in the Land Rover at night while Masterfield shot deer. He was appalled at deer being left lying where they had been shot and knew that this was not the place for him to work as a gamekeeper. The advocate depute led evidence of Mason's view of Masterfield's lack of experience and that it was clear to him that Roberts was issuing just about every instruction. This last comment made Roberts' QC jump up and object but Lord Abercrombie allowed the answer to the question.

In cross-examination Masterfield's QC asked Mason if he was able to state that the dead pigeon that had been placed on the peregrine's ledge had been interfered with in any way, for instance by being laced with poison. Mason truthfully responded that he had no evidence that the bird had been laced with poison but could think of no other reason for Masterfield going to all the trouble of putting it there.

The next witness was Shane Fitzgerald who told the court he had been a head keeper with Roberts on a grouse moor in the north of England. As head keeper he received orders directly from Roberts. He told the court how Roberts had become very angry when he and Fitzgerald had been out on the moor and Roberts had spotted a hen harrier.

He told of his move to a grouse moor in Scotland and that Roberts had come to him absolutely furious one day stating the owner of the moor had seen a food pass between a male and female hen harrier. For the jury's benefit the advocate depute asked him to explain the significance of a food pass. Fitzgerald was a confident witness and looked directly at the fifteen members of the jury while he described the nesting behaviour of hen harriers; that they nest on the ground in long heather, that the female incubates the eggs and remains covering the young chicks when they hatch, that the male does the hunting at this time and returns with his catch, which are mostly voles and meadow pipits but can also include young grouse. The female, when she is aware of the male returning, comes off the nest and flies to meet the male, who drops the prey item which is then neatly caught in mid-air by the female. The female usually lands away from the nest to eat the prey or to pluck it if she has chicks, then returns to the nest either to continue incubating eggs or to feed the chicks.

He was asked by the advocate depute, 'Would most people not be in awe at seeing such an amazing spectacle of nature as this?'

He responded, 'Most people would love to see this. I love to see it. It seems Mr Roberts isn't a fan.'

Taking advantage of having such an articulate witness the advocate depute continued, but had to avoid framing the question specifically around Robert's views on hen harriers. 'Why would some people not like to see hen harriers on a grouse moor Mr Fitzgerald?'

'Hen harriers do prey at times on grouse chicks,' Shane Fitzgerald replied, 'especially in years of low vole numbers. If they take grouse chicks that reduces the number of grouse available later in the year for shooting. They can at times spoil a grouse drive by either shifting the grouse from the area of the drive or making them sit tight in the heather and not fly towards the guns. They are absolutely beautiful birds. Unfortunately, they are the most hated birds on grouse moors.'

Avoiding specifically naming Roberts again, the advocate depute asked, 'So if a person was being paid to produce large numbers of grouse for shooting he would not be best pleased to have hen harriers nesting on the moor?'

Shane Fitzgerald had caught on to the method of questioning by the prosecutor, 'I'd put it stronger: some people would be furious.'

The advocate depute had been building up to the next question. 'Did Mr Roberts have any other reaction Mr Fitzgerald?'

'Yes, he did.'

'What was that?'

Fitzgerald paused, looked straight at the jury and replied quietly, 'He slapped me hard across the face and said, 'Sort it.'

'What did you understand from what Mr Roberts said?'

'It was a clear instruction to get rid of the harriers. To kill them.'

'Did you do that?'

'No. There was no way I was going to be breaking the law.'

Lastly the prosecutor elicited from Fitzgerald that in neither of his places of employment by Roberts had he received any training in the storage or use of pesticides, nor had he been told that he must always stay within the law.

There was no cross-examination by Masterfield's solicitor. Jacob Brough QC, defending Roberts, tried to elicit an admission that Fitzgerald was mistaken about Roberts complaining when he saw a hen harrier on the moor and that he was referring to a carrion crow. Fitzgerald had no problem batting off that line of defence, and similarly with a claim that he was lying about being slapped by Roberts.

Young Andrew McLaren was next into the witness box. He was gently led through the evidence by the prosecutor. He told of the finding of the almost-dead buzzard and his sister picking it up and cuddling it close to her chest to try to keep it warm. He recalled her briefly putting the buzzard down and blowing her nose several times. They both made for home, hoping that their parents could help the buzzard but Susan started to stagger. Andrew had asked her what was wrong and she'd said she didn't feel well and had difficulty breathing. She eventually collapsed, still holding the buzzard. Andrew told the court that when his sister couldn't speak, he realised something was seriously wrong with her and he ran home as fast as he could to get his father.

For a youngster he had done extremely well in giving evidence in the highest court in the land, a court that, given the serious and unusual nature of the charges, was packed with spectators and press. Two of the nine female jurors were in tears and the whole jury must have been affected by the boy having to recount in public his devastating experience.

Andrew's father, Willie, gave evidence next, and when he described running home with his unconscious daughter in his arms the two women jurors were again in tears. Several of the jurors glowered at Masterfield and Roberts as if they had already made up their minds that these two men in the dock were responsible for taking a young girl's life.

One of the most traumatic parts of any trial where someone has been killed is establishing the cause of death. This evidence was given professionally and sensitively by the two pathologists who carried out the post-mortem examination of Susan, with the samples that they took from her body being confirmed by analysis at SASA as containing traces of the pesticides carbofuran, isofenphos and bendiocarb.

Much of the rest of the trial was taken up by the recovery of various items and their subsequent examination by specialists: the chemistry and the DNA labs at SASA, ballistics experts, and the veterinary pathologist, who also gave evidence about the injurious pathogens that could be released into the water from the dead stag. The jury seemed enthralled by the forensics linking the stag taken from Albert's water supply to Masterfield's Land Rover, the bullet from the stag's head to Masterfield's rifle and the tyre tracks near to where Susan and her brother found the dying buzzard to Masterfield's Land Rover tyres.

Bob and other police witnesses also gave evidence, which included details of the interviews of the two accused. Having given evidence this freed the way for Bob to sit in on the remainder of the trial.

Chapter 42

At the end of prosecution evidence Jacob Brough QC put forward a motion of no case to answer in relation to his client, Nigel Roberts. He quoted the wording of Section 18A of the Wildlife and Countryside Act 1981 and continued, 'I accept that Mr Masterfield falls into the category of being an employee of my client. I also accept that my client manages and controls the exercise of the killing or taking a wild bird on Loch Garr Estate. However, for my client to be guilty of vicarious liability my client must know that raptors were being killed by Masterfield, if indeed the jury accept as fact that Masterfield had killed birds. I appreciate that this section of the 1981 Act is somewhat different in that to a degree there is a reverse burden of proof, but my client maintains that he has no knowledge of any illegal activity. Furthermore, there is no evidence from the Crown to suggest that he has such knowledge.'

The QC thumbed through his notepad and went on, 'The second requirement of this part of the legislation requires that my client took all reasonable steps and exercised all due diligence to prevent the offence being committed. As can be seen from a document taken from Mr Masterfield's house and already produced to the court my client wrote to him expressly forbidding him to break the law. I would submit to M'Lord that there is no case for my client to answer and that he should be dismissed from the court.'

Lord Abercrombie addressed Keith Darrowby QC and asked for his reply to the defence QC.

The advocate depute stood up. 'M'Lord, I contend that Mr Roberts is well aware of illegal activity in relation to raptors on Loch Garr Estate, indeed he directly ordered illegal activity towards nesting hen harriers when he ordered his head gamekeeper at the time, Mr Fitzgerald, to 'sort it.' That was no idle remark or comment in my view; that was a direct order from an employer to an employee. Again, in my view, it matters not whether the employee carried out the order, simply that the order, an illegal order, was given.'

It was now the advocate depute's turn to refer to his notepad, 'I accept that a note was found instructing Mr Masterfield to stay within the law on Loch Garr Estate. My view is that the note does not tell the whole story, or even the true story. I do not believe that a note is a safeguard against a charge of vicarious liability when no parallel oral order is given to stay within the law, coupled with the absence of any training in the storage or use of chemicals. I submit that Mr Roberts has failed the test of due diligence and that the court should reject the motion of no case to answer.'

Lord Abercromie had been making notes and took a few minutes to consider the arguments before repelling the motion of no case to answer.

The trial was to continue with defence evidence from two head keepers from other estates under the direction of Roberts. Each had produced letters that had been lodged as productions in the trial, instructing them to stay within the law at all times. The first head keeper to give evidence told the court that he received training in the use and storage of chemicals. He stated that he had passed this training on to his under keepers.

In cross examination the advocate depute asked how long he had been under Roberts' direct charge. 'I came as a head keeper from another estate into Mr Roberts' employment just over a year ago.'

'When did you receive this training on chemicals?'

'In July this year.'

'Is that not after the tragic death of Susan McLaren?'

'I don't really know when that was.'

The advocate depute read out the date on the charge of culpable and reckless conduct, which was six weeks before the training alleged by the witness. The second head keeper was not called to give evidence.

It was now the turn, if they wished, for the two accused to give evidence on their own behalf. Alex Moore QC rose and stated that his client would not be giving evidence.

Nigel Roberts, who thought himself above all this court nonsense, had been determined to give evidence, against the advice of Jacob Brough QC. His QC sensibly cut the evidence as short as possible, leading him through the written instruction to all head keepers for whom he had management responsibility to stay within the law, plus the regular visits to the head keepers to ensure that they were doing so.

The QC was well aware of the detriment to his client of the instruction to 'sort it' to former head keeper Shane Fitzgerald. 'What did you mean when you were aware of nesting hen harriers on the grouse moor where Shane Fitzgerald was head keeper and you said 'Sort it?'

Roberts drew himself to his full height in the witness box and answered, 'Hen harriers can reduce the numbers of grouse and I'll be perfectly honest in that we don't really want them on grouse moors. However, the law states that they are protected and my staff are well aware of this. Hen harriers nest in areas of old, long heather. What I wanted Fitzgerald to do – and he would know this perfectly well – was to burn out these areas of long heather during the winter when heather burning is allowed and long after the harriers were finished nesting. This would, in time, allow the heather to regenerate and provide feeding for grouse on the young heather shoots and it would prevent, in a legal manner, the harriers from nesting there again.'

When it came to the prosecutor's turn for cross-examination he made the most of the discrepancy in the date that the defence witness had received chemicals training, making the point that the training was simply a belated attempt by Roberts to rectify his failure to carry out due diligence. He had also to destroy Roberts' attempt to twist the term 'sort it' to his advantage.

'When you instructed Mr Fitzgerald to 'sort it' I put it to you that this was an instruction to either kill the hen harriers or to destroy the eggs or chicks in the nest and get the harriers to move on.'

'No, that's not true. Fitzgerald knew exactly what I wanted him to do.'

'Mr Fitzgerald, as you would hear, clearly gave evidence to the effect that your instruction meant to get rid of the harriers.'

'My keepers are well aware that I have no truck with them taking matters into their own hands and breaking the law. I would not defend them and it would mean instant dismissal.'

'Mr Roberts you not only instructed Mr Fitzgerald to get rid of the harriers but you did so while you were, in Mr Fitzgerald's words, 'absolutely furious', and you also slapped him on the face. These were not the actions of a responsible employer who wanted a patch of heather burned later in the year. I put it to you these were the actions of an angry employer who wanted an instant remedy to a situation that posed a threat to grouse numbers, less grouse to shoot on 12th August and less kudos to you for producing a successful shooting day.'

'That's not the case. I've said what I expected of him.'

The prosecuting QC sat down and there was no re-examination by the defence QC, who addressed the judge and stated that the defence case was concluded.

Lord Abercrombie addressed Keith Darrowby QC and invited him to begin his address to the jury. The summing up took over an hour and was followed by the address to the jury by the two defence QCs, which took a further hour.

Lord Abercrombie now addressed the jury on matters of law. He concluded by declaring that the case against Mr Masterfield was complex but that they should not feel rushed in their deliberations. He asked them to retire to consider their verdicts on the two accused and the nine women and six men filed out of the jury benches to the jury room.

Chapter 43

It was a two hour wait for Bob. He'd been asked by DI Sneddon to phone him when the summing up had started. He was now joined by the DI and the two waited patiently in an otherwise empty witness room with a drink and a sandwich. Meg Runciman looked in on them for a minute.

'What is your forecast on the verdict Meg?' asked Jonathan.

'It's always hard to guess what juries will think but all of the witnesses came across well in the court. The evidence is strong against Masterfield in most of the charges. With Roberts it will depend on who the jury believes in relation to these now famous words, 'sort it.' The slap across the face might tilt the verdict in the prosecution's favour. What Roberts said is uncorroborated but there is a degree of corroboration from the absence of any training in dealing with chemicals. At the end of the day it's up to the defence to show that Roberts carried out due diligence. The judge did explain the law well in relation to the reverse burden of proof.'

At last, the court officer looked into the witness room to say that the jury were ready to be called back into court. Bob and Jonathan took their seats on the public benches in what was already a courtroom packed with interested spectators. Bob noticed a couple of gamekeepers, though they were dressed in ordinary attire. He saw Ralph Murdoch from RSPB Investigations sitting a couple of rows in front. He also spotted Willie McLaren out of the corner of his eye sitting right at the back of the public benches. The press benches were completely full, every journalist with their notepads and pencils at the ready. He expected that outside the court he and the DI would be asked for a comment, whatever the verdict.

The jury trooped into their benches, took their seats, and the court officer went to collect Lord Abercrombie.

'Court,' he declared, and everyone stood as he led in the judge and pulled out his chair to seat him.

Lord Abercrombie thanked the jury and looked to the clerk of the court to establish verdicts from the jury.

The clerk addressed the foreman of the jury. 'Have you come to a decision on a verdict or verdicts?'

'We have,' the foreman replied.

'In relation the charges against Mr Masterfield, what is your verdict in charge 1?'

Bob had a copy of the indictment in front of him. 'That's shooting stags out of season,' he whispered to Jonathan.

'Guilty,' said the foreman.

'To charge 2?' said the foreman.

'That's shooting red deer stags at night without authority from SNH,' whispered Bob

'Guilty.'

'To charge 3?'

'Guilty'

That's shooting a red deer stag without lawful authority or written permission. That's the one over the boundary, whispered Bob'

'To charge 4?'

'Not guilty'

'That's the illegal possession of a red deer, firearm and ammunition. I'm not sure the jury would understand that charge,' said Bob.

'To charge 5?'

'Guilty.'

'That's unlawful possession of the pesticides,' said Bob. 'It doesn't look good for him now.'

'To charge 6?'

'Guilty.'

That's setting out the pigeon bait for the peregrine,' said Bob.

'To charge 7?'

'Guilty.'

'That's killing the peregrine. The next charge is crucial, killing the buzzard. If he killed the buzzard he killed Susan,' said Bob in a whisper.

'To charge 8?'

'Guilty.'

'Wow,' whispered Jonathan.

'To charge 9?'

'That's the first culpable and reckless conduct charge, the deer in the water supply,' said Bob.'

'Guilty.'

'Thank you,' said Bob quietly.

'Charge 10?'

'This is it, killing Susan,' said Bob

The court was hushed, awaiting this verdict more than any of the others.

'Guilty.'

A sigh of relief rippled through the court. Masterfield hung his head. He was ashen white.

'All the work has been well worth it Bob,' said the DI.

The foreman continued on to the verdict in the only charge against Roberts: vicarious liability.

'And the last charge, charge 11?'

'Guilty.'

Bob looked across at Roberts. Even side on he could see that he was furious. In contrast Bob could have jumped up and cheered the jury. He looked back at Willie McLaren and could see the strain on his ruddy face gradually lighten, evidence of some relief for the grieving father.

Lord Abercromie thanked the jury and adjourned the court to give him time to decide on sentence. He took twenty minutes and returned to take his seat.

The judge looked at the two accused in the dock and ordered them to stand. Bob looked over at the two accused. Masterfield looked as if he was barely able to stand. Roberts got up off the bench reluctantly, a man used to ordering other people about rather than taking orders.

The judge was stern. 'Mr Masterfield, you have undertaken a series of illegal acts, beginning with an attempt to exterminate deer on the estate where you are employed. Not only did you kill the deer illegally but failed to enter them into the food chain, a completely unnecessary and immoral waste of life. You continued your indulgence in killing wildlife by the illegal use of pesticides. This is a crime that features regularly in the media. The poisoning of birds of prey is reviled by the general public and discredits game shooting and the role of gamekeeper.

'I am limited by the statutory penalties under the Deer (Scotland) Act 1996, and in relation to the three charges under that Act you will go to prison on each of these charges for the maximum period, which is three months.

'Dealing now with the repulsive use of pesticides to kill wildlife, the public expects a court to impose a penalty that reflects the seriousness of the crime. Unfortunately changes that are in the pipeline to increase penalties have not yet been enacted and I am limited to the current maximum penalty of six months' imprisonment. This will be imposed on each of the four charges relating to the illegal possession or use of pesticides.'

Masterfield was shaking and must have known that within seconds he would be sentenced to a much longer spell in prison.

'I come now to the two most serious charges. The various bacteria that were released, or could have been released, into a domestic water supply from the gut of the dead deer had the potential to cause serious illness or even death. This was a despicable thing to do and I would hope that a sentence of two years' imprisonment will reflect how seriously this court considers this act.

'Coming to the last and most serious charge, you were setting out baits laced with a deadly pesticide where any creature that encountered them was at risk of serious illness or death. Birds of prey or foxes may have been your intended target but these deadly chemicals had the potential to kill much more. As it happened a young girl tried to rescue a buzzard that fell victim to your poison. In doing her good deed she lost her life by ingesting some of the pesticide. What you did was completely reckless, with deadly consequence, and you will go to prison for seven years. All of these periods of imprisonment will run concurrently. I hope this sentence causes others who set out poisons in the countryside to reflect on the possible consequences of their illegal acts.'

Masterfield clung on to the rail in front of him to keep him upright.

Lord Abercrombie now addressed Roberts. 'Mr Roberts, you have been found guilty of being liable vicariously for the illegal actions of one of your employees. The illegal acts have had terrible consequences. I am hamstrung by the totally unsuitable statutory penalties available to me. A financial penalty, even at the maximum range available of £5,000 would neither be suitable punishment nor a deterrent to others. Courts are discouraged from imposing a period of imprisonment less than one year. That leaves me only with a community payback penalty, which I will set at the maximum of three hundred hours.'

Masterfield's jaw dropped as he turned to look at Roberts. He was clearly shocked that he was going to jail for seven years and the man who had orchestrated the criminality was able to walk free. Roberts walked from the dock without a backward glance.

When Masterfield was put in the cells below the court to await transport to whisk him off to Saughton Prison in Edinburgh, he asked the escorting police officer if he would go back into the court and ask Constable McKay to come and see him.

Bob was given the message and entered Masterfield's cell. He found him sitting on the bench within the cell shaking uncontrollably. 'Constable McKay, I want to tell you everything about Roberts,' he said in a whisper.

Acknowledgements

I would like to thank the following for their generous help with legal issues and other expert advice: Peter Brownless, Royal Botanic Garden Edinburgh; Catherine Erskine, Cambo Estate, Kingsbarns, Fife; Fiona Howie BVMS MVM MRCVS FRCPath, SRUC Veterinary Services; Charles Everitt, Investigative Support Officer (Retired), NWCU; Elizabeth Sharp, Senior Analyst, SASA; and Christine Danbolt, Wildlife and Environment Crime Unit, Crown Office.

Special thanks go to editor and publisher Sean Bradley of Thirsty Books for his patience and thoroughness in dealing with work on the book that I always needed done yesterday, and to my daughters Janet and Andrea for reading the unfinished book and making some invaluable suggestions.